ELEANOR RUSHING

ELEANOR
RUSHING

by

Patty Friedmann

COUNTERPOINT
WASHINGTON, D.C.

LIBRARY OF CONGRESS CATALOGING-IN-PUBLICATION DATA
Friedmann, Patty.
Eleanor Rushing / by Patty Friedmann.
p.   cm.
ISBN 1-58243-003-9
I. Title.
PS3556.R5647E58   1999
813'.54—dc21   99-12665
CIP

Printed in the United States of America on acid-free paper that
meets the American National Standards Institute Z39–48 Standard.

COUNTERPOINT
P.O. Box 65793
Washington, D.C. 20035-5793

Counterpoint is a member of the Perseus Books Group.

9 7 5 3 1 2 4 6 8 10

FIRST PRINTING

For Lynda

ONE

I think it is impossible to change the world unless you are truly evil and so mad for control you never sleep. And it's ridiculous to try to change *yourself* at all. Scientists have studied identical twins who feel pain in the gut at the same time, as if everything were laid out from the moment they were conceived. Sometimes I figure all you can do is watch yourself, as if you're viewing a simple, dull film; eventually you find out what was going to happen. Unless death catches you by surprise.

So I go to City Council meetings. I haven't missed one in four years, not even for a case of B-type influenza, which I probably picked up from a crowd in the City Council chambers. Sitting in those meetings is the only way I can pretend to feel any breezes of serendipity. Somewhere between the global and the personal, they play out the grandest battles of silliness, and I like to guess at them. When I was twenty-three I lived in Washington, D.C., and sat in regularly on the proceedings of the U.S. House of Representatives. But they mumbled and shuffled a lot, and you couldn't see their eyes unless they passed close by. It was good to learn about carcinogens in the Iowa corn after the drought and how the turnips in western Montana swelled like giant melons for years after Mount Saint Helens blew, and I believed money should be set aside to study such matters, but I couldn't see the congressmen's eyes. So I came home to New Orleans.

Maxim denies it, but we saw each other for the first time at a New Orleans City Council meeting. It had been going on for four hours, a Thursday, last October, with no break, and the chamber was full of angry people, all brimming with piss and hunger. It was shaping up to be one of the best, with a chance of violence. Whenever you pit selfless green people against hard men and harder women, someone is going to break out and charge across the room with fists flying. The ones who usually broke were the ones who saw themselves as selfless, who were thinking about a fine earth or a lovely city that would be here after they were dead; that meant a lot more to them than the merchant worries of the businessmen. The businessmen could cut their losses, start over, enjoy the process of proving something again.

This time they were fighting over gambling, and I knew what point they were all missing. I felt the way I'd felt in fourth grade, when I'd answered so many questions correctly that the teacher had refused to call on me, and so I'd sat shimmering in my place, waiting to hear someone else figure out what I already knew.

The City Council was willing to line up gambling boats all along the riverfront docks, so each night men in suits could unload sacks of money the way longshoremen unload coffee. The green people wanted clean parks alongside the filthy river, and the short, oily Greek and Indian businessmen wanted gamblers everywhere in the French Quarter, spilling dollars into their shops. They were equally selfish, the green people and the men who sold T-shirts in the front and hookahs in the back of their stores. They all wanted something to show off.

I was considering running over to the public library to do some fast reading so I could get up with popular quotes and tell them all why they were wrong, when he came forward to take the microphone. "Dr. Maximilian Walters, pastor of Uptown United Methodist Church," he said.

He was the whitest man I'd ever seen. I was in the first row of the left section, so I could see his eyes. His hair was silver, his skin as pale as a sunless child's, his eyes white-gray. He could have gone to any dark continent two hundred years ago and startled the aborigines.

He smiled in Mrs. Legendre's direction, having taken the microphone after her, and his teeth were straight and white, too. Mrs. Legendre was a tiny Junior League–haircut woman with the power only tiny women and men can have to come up fierce and unassailable. Mrs. Legendre wanted no gambling boats along the entire stretch of the river where the public School of Music and Dance sat. "Before I begin," he said, "I'd just like to remind Mrs. Legendre that everyone in the arts is a gambler." She gave him a closed-lipped smile, more seductive than appreciative. I sat up taller in my seat. Mrs. Legendre had rich, streaky hair like mine, but I was striking where she was merely serious.

He threw a single phrase at the City Council, and I was undone, though half of them were swiveled around in their chairs talking on telephones. They made me furious doing that, though sometimes they do it when a speaker deserves rudeness. The process of government isn't clean if every word isn't heard. "You are all mired in details that make no difference," he said.

He said nothing then, and the noise level dropped. He waited. "You are all mired in details that make no difference." His voice was low and almost sad, and the room became a more polite place. He repeated himself once more, then stepped back from the microphone as if he were going to return to his seat.

"Go on, sir," the councilwoman from my district said. I hadn't voted for her in the last election; she was too condescending.

"John Wesley," he said, as if anyone in the room other than me knew who John Wesley was. "John Wesley abhorred gambling, and so people in our church are supposed to abhor gambling, too. But John Wesley didn't pass any particular judgments on gambling; he hated gambling because right then, a couple of hundred years ago, all the poor coal miners blew their pay on it. Now I've sorted out the difference between gambling as sin and gambling as good social policy. But you haven't. Don't tell me you have; you haven't. I hear it. Some of you have been downright *shrill* up here." I looked toward Mrs. Legendre, but she was listening as if in a thrall that only let through what made her want him. "If it's sin, don't have it at all. If it's good social policy, have it on every street corner. A church on one corner, a bar on another, a sweetshop on a third, a casino on the fourth. Line the river with docks for gambling boats. All the way to Baton Rouge. Make every risk-taker in the entire United States feel he has to come down here, right now. With all his money, of course. You want bright, empty parks? How about thousands of trumpet players and tap dancers who can't earn a living? You want the streets filled with fools who'll buy whatever you feel like selling them? It's all one and the same.

"You're mired down in details. And details don't make a difference. Thank you," he said softly and walked slowly away.

I began to applaud, and there was no other sound in the chambers. Perhaps he sat next to me because of the clapping. But I think all along he knew I was there, waiting for the right answer, knew it was time to come to me. He settled gently into his seat, and I continued to clap, my hands in front of his face, for a few seconds. Then the din and rudeness started up again in the room. "You were magnificent," I whispered, a thrill running down me.

He patted my hand, then with one swift movement pushed himself out of his seat from the armrests. "See you later," he said, not looking back. He slipped out the side exit.

I knew then how much he was going to want me. How much he was going to battle with his holy behavior until he gave in. He probably has told everyone—his wife and that damn Ellis Ryan and the police and anyone who'd listen—that he has no recollection of that day he went before the City Council—or was it the City Planning Commission? Or the Zoning Board? Or the Ecumenical Council? They all run together in his mind after a while—he goes before whomever so frequently, on so many matters, that no details stand out. He is lying. I sat in that same seat, front row, third from the aisle on the left side, and I delicately stroked my hand where he'd touched it until the City Council adjourned for the day, at 9:46 that evening. I remember everything.

Two

When I was ten, my mother and father died in the crash of Eastern Flight 66, and for reasons I've never understood my grandfather sent Naomi to tell me. I suppose he had a lot of business to take care of right away. My family will end with me on both sides, a daughter of only children whose parents themselves were only children. That's a great deal of money and genetic potential to filter down to a single individual.

Naomi had told my grandfather she could drive, and he told her to take my father's Mercedes and go get me in Tennessee. Naomi was twenty-three years old, and she could keep a car on the road all right, even at high speeds, but she couldn't read anything that hadn't appeared in the Scott-Foresman primer, so it took her three days to get within a hundred miles of my sleepaway camp. No one had told Mrs. Carlton, the director, she was coming, and when Naomi called collect from the side of the highway, Mrs. Carlton refused to accept the charges. Naomi tried again, this time person-to-person to me. Mrs. Carlton told the operator to hold and waddled on her stocky, unfit legs all the way up to my cabin. "Do you have a friend named

Naomi? Who likes to talk like a Negro?" she said to me. It was rest period, and the seven other girls in the cabin strained to listen from their bunks. It was the first time rest period had been interrupted.

"We have a housekeeper named Naomi. And she's *black*."

"Ah," she said, wisdom in her voice. "Girls generally don't try tricks like that until they're thirteen." I shrugged. Mrs. Carlton put her finger to her lips, as if no one had noticed her terrible presence, and motioned me to follow her.

"This had better be good," she said when we were in her office, her hand covering the phone receiver as she held it out in front of her. It was a heavy black desk model, the paint rubbed off at the edges. She put the phone to her ear, then pulled it away and looked at it, as if some tiny demon had slipped a slender feather out of the earpiece and tickled her eardrum. "Hung up," she said, slamming it into the cradle. It rang again, and I sprang for it. I'd had time, going down the hill behind her, to have decided that my parents, one or both, or my grandfather, or all three were dead. I was sure it was my parents, because they went to New York too often for no reason. My heart was racing so fast that it sent every drop of blood in my body up to my head, and I was heavy-brained and trembling with a funny sort of excitement. "Where are you, Naomi?" I said into the phone.

"Damn if I know. Tennessee, but that's about it." I could hear truck traffic in the background.

"Do you accept the charges?" the operator said.

"Yeh, yeh, yeh," I said, an adult in that split second, without trying. "What happened?"

"Not supposed to tell you until I get there. Tell me how I get there."

I lost logic. I was in Tennessee, and Naomi was in Tennessee, and I had to see her right then, but I was ten years old and knew nothing more about the roadways up there in the mountains than the landmarks I'd passed coming in. A child's landmarks—a Dairy Queen, a billboard for Ruby Falls. Naomi was never going to find me. "I don't know where I am, for God's sake," I said. "Tell me what happened, because you're *never* going to get here." I was close to screaming.

Mrs. Carlton took the phone away from me. "What is this all about?" she said, the way rich women were supposed to talk to maids. She nodded, impatient. "Beg pardon?" she said, nodding again. "So give me your location." Her eyes rolled toward the ceiling. "I have to know more than that." After a minute she covered the receiver with her hand. "This is all very unfortunate," she said.

"Somebody's dead," I said.

"Shh, shh. She's getting the man at the gas station. Of all things."

It took her ten minutes to put Naomi onto the road that would bring her within a couple of miles of the camp, but that was as far as she could get without having to say, "Now stop the fussing, or you're never going to get here." I had time to race forward mentally, to push my parents into a distant haze from which something new and better might emerge. Joys and attentions could come instead. Going to camp already had taught me how to push people away through geography. With camp it had been simple: to tamp down the ache of not being tended, I asked a girl from home to mail me dozens of sticks of chewing gum wrapped in the Sunday *Times-Picayune*. With terror at the

death of my parents, I could shift a grim fantasy to a splendid one, go from sadness that my mother would never see
the tray I was painting for her in the crafts hut to a rush of
joy, knowing I would become a treasure at school. Friends
would be fascinated with me for having no parents, and I
would get party invitations and valentines from everyone.
They'd walk in a protective circle around me at school,
stroking my hair. And the pretty teachers would hug me,
give me extra chances. My mother would have taken the
tray and shoved it into the back of the butler's pantry. She
preferred the finest things; that's why she was always drag-
ging my father onto a plane to Dallas or New York.

Mrs. Carlton was going to wait two hours, then go up to
the junction in the camp van and wait for Naomi. I almost
said that I wanted to go, but I'd have had to spend two hours
with Mrs. Carlton, waiting, then untold amounts of time
sitting in the van at the side of a two-lane undivided highway, straining, looking for a familiar car, answering polite
questions from Mrs. Carlton, who knew how to run a business but didn't know what to say to young girls. She'd jump
out and shush Naomi, and I wouldn't get to ride in with her,
wouldn't find out why she was there until she was inside the
camp property. I told Mrs. Carlton I had campcraft after
rest period. "And horseback riding after that. And I forget
what after that. Oh, swimming." That schedule required a
lot of clothes changing, a lot of jogging from one end of the
camp to the other, and I sniffled.

"Look, you have a good afternoon," Mrs. Carlton said,
and I heard her sigh heavily as she gently prodded me out
of her office. Annoyance that comes of missing a nap was
in that sigh.

I didn't worry that afternoon. I told my campcraft counselor I thought my parents were dead, and she looked at me queerly; she was nineteen, not yet reverent about parents, either. "You're weird, Eleanor," she said, then showed me how to hack a vee into a fat log.

"I might chop off all my toes," I said after a while of swinging the hatchet over one shoulder and then the other. I didn't like the idea of being weird, but I did like the idea of keeping her guessing. "I might chop off *your* toes."

"You're a little shit," she said pleasantly.

"No, I'm not," I said. She left me alone, maybe to get through the entire log before the hour was up, maybe to swing wrong and hit a major blood vessel. Sweating and furious, I quickly reached that satisfying final chop through the bark and into the dirt while another girl was still missing her log on half her swings.

Naomi came to me at the riding ring. A skinny black woman with the funk of the road all over her, standing at the rail and wondering what the hell white folks were going to do next with their money: I saw her as I rounded the far side of the ring, the saddle slapping my narrow buttocks while the horse trotted along and I paid no attention. I screamed her name, and the rest of the class, spine-straight and posting for all they were worth, stopped and turned to look at me. I jumped down, my foot catching in the stirrup so I landed on my back, and I left the horse standing there, curious about the first rule-breaking girl he'd ever carried.

I set out at a bowlegged run, jodhpurs chafing, ready to throw myself against Naomi so what she told me would be muffled and safe. But Mrs. Carlton was with her, and she

held an arm out straight, palm forward, to bring me up
short in front of Naomi. "Get that horse," she said to the
riding instructor, then motioned me away from the ring,
off toward a thicket alongside the path from the stable. I
always associate the sour straw smell of horse pee and the
acrid odor of preadolescence with the moment when I
learned about my parents. "They gone, baby," Naomi said,
and I flung my arms around her waist; Mrs. Carlton
couldn't make up any more rules for me. I didn't cry, didn't
sob, just nuzzled against Naomi's bony chest, squeezing
my eyes shut so I wouldn't have to know anything. The
smell of me and the horses mixed with Naomi's baby powder that had been sweated through so she had little balls of
white paste on her brown skin. We stood there, my hold
not letting anything happen, until Mrs. Carlton began
shifting from one foot to the other, brushing ever so lightly
against branches that overhung the path. Naomi was quick
to pick up the signals of irritable, busy southern white
women. "Where you want me to bring her?" Naomi said.

"We'll take her to her cabin," Mrs. Carlton said, as if
Naomi were suddenly going to break loose in the camp
and steal all the girls' radios.

"Where you cabin is?" Naomi said, leading me back
downhill toward the main camp, filling the path with herself and me so Mrs. Carlton had no choice but to trail behind. I pointed ahead, my other arm around Naomi's
waist, pulling her gently in this direction or that as we
walked to my cabin. "You know how planes going to crash
when they taking off and when they landing but not in between?" she said. "They plane get all the way to New York;
then it crash. I figure they *knowed* they was going to die.

You *know* you maybe going to die when the plane coming in for a landing." I shrugged a shoulder, steered Naomi up a path away from the lake, and I heard Mrs. Carlton leave from behind us, satisfied Naomi was silly enough to be harmless; she could go rest up before supper. She could take a small gamble with me since I had no parents who were going to wrangle with her about bad decisions.

When darkness wasn't far off, Mrs. Carlton made a decision that had little to do with me and much to do with good business. Every girl in that camp came from somewhere south of Maryland, and Mrs. Carlton had to be cautious about tales that'd go out in letters home. She saw Naomi as a contaminant. "I'll be frank. You wouldn't want me to be less than frank, right?" she said. Naomi and I were sitting together on the bunk below mine, and Mrs. Carlton was sitting across from us on another lower, her thick knees crossed so I could see the tops of her white socks under her slacks. Naomi nodded, tired and resigned. "All our colored help goes home at night. In fact, the only colored person I think's ever been here at night's the little nurse we had last summer up in the infirmary. And I'm here to tell you she was on her feet *all* night. You understand?"

"Sure," Naomi said.

"No," I said, and Naomi told me to hush.

"Anyway," Mrs. Carlton said, tight-lipped, "if you'd like, I'll put Eleanor in the infirmary overnight, and you can stay up there with her. The chairs are quite comfortable. I've sat up in one more nights than I like to think." She gave us a hopeful little smile.

"You think maybe you could find me a hotel? I could use me a bath. And probably I been asleep maybe five hours since I been in New Orleans. Total. I could use me a *bed*, too." Naomi was using the voice she saved for answering the phone at our house. "Rushing residence," she'd say, practically crooning. And when it was someone calling for her, she'd break out of it. "Shoot, man, I told you don't be calling me a hundred time a day."

Mrs. Carlton said she could certainly come into the office and phone around. People can know things even when they haven't been told them outright, and Mrs. Carlton knew Naomi had no way of going through the Yellow Pages of the half-inch phone book. "Never mind. I can just drive around. Probably I passed a million hotels coming up here," Naomi said, patting my knee to reassure Mrs. Carlton. With a promise that my counselors would pack and ship my things, that Naomi could leave with me whenever she was up tomorrow, Mrs. Carlton rose to leave, bumping her head on the upper bunk, her eyes tearing. "Maybe she coming back," Naomi said, offering no sympathy.

"No, I'm absolutely not," I said, looking Mrs. Carlton straight in the watery eye.

No one spoke to me that evening, and I quietly packed my most private things into a duffel. I'd sneaked to the drugstore before I'd left home, spent a month's allowance on sanitary napkins, a pack of razors, and a can of deodorant. Those supplies were to cover all the shames of puberty, things no one would offer to tell me about. I'd only been at camp a few weeks, and I hadn't had the nerve to take them out, though the other girls displayed theirs with zest, shaving their bald underarms in the shower so everyone else could see. I wasn't ready to need those things, and they were still in the paper drugstore sack, under a pile of flannel shirts on my shelf. I packed only my panties and an extra pair of sandals. Clothes that little rich girls bought in bulk to spend two months in the Tennessee mountains were of no use in New Orleans. Any time of year, much less summer. I hoped my camp clothes, all from the list, would disappear. My mother had given the list to Naomi, sending her downtown to D. H. Holmes on the streetcar. Naomi in turn had handed the list to the salesclerk, who wanted to make no decisions on matters of taste. Everything was red, white, navy, or military green. Naomi had sewn a name tape in each item, embarrassing me mightily; I had wanted someone to write my name with an indelible laundry pen in the necks and waists of all my clothes. With neat, slanted, capital letters.

Naomi was going to sleep in the Mercedes a piece of a mile up the road from the camp gate. "You need me, you sneak out, I be to the right, down a little ways, just enough," she told me, and took my sleeping bag with her. I couldn't imagine needing her badly enough to travel that far in the dark. I was lying on top of my stripped bunk, wrapped in a navy wool blanket, so new it had no pills on it, and I shook with cold. I felt it most in my feet, and I could make no contortion that would put my feet into a warm fold where they would not be so icy. The cold became too much, and I felt the way I had once with a hundred-five-degree fever, panicked for warmth, sobbing for warmth. I sat up and curled myself into a ball, rubbing my upper arms with my hands, rocking back and forth. The girl who slept below me did nothing about the motion for a while and then, with a sleepy huff, rolled herself up in all her covers and slid down onto the floor. I knew I was going to be chilled for the rest of my life, and with that notion I sloughed off a thick layer of terrors. I wrapped the blanket around me, slid down to the floor on the side opposite the one on which my bunkmate was lying, scuffed into my sandals, and went looking for the Mercedes. In the dark, I was to be feared, hooded in almost-black, and I could run, making my own heat, until I found the car. I remembered from last winter that the car could warm up in three minutes, even idling. I ran fast, blanket trailing, picking up dust and pine needles, and nothing caught me.

Naomi wasn't in the car. All the doors were locked, and as I ran around from one door to another, struggling with the handles and banging on the windows, I knew only that I wasn't going back to my cabin, that if I didn't find Naomi I was going to throw the blanket off myself and die right there. I screamed her name, and I heard her say "Eleanor?" from a clearing about five yards from the road.

She was sitting huddled on top of my sleeping bag, which was unrolled but not unzipped, one corner folded back over her feet. "Baby, you *scare* me," she said.

"I'm not exactly *un*scared," I said. Naomi patted the spot next to herself, and when I sat beside her she began tugging the blanket away so that she could drape it over both of us. She let in pockets of cold air, but I could feel her musky warmth right away, and I wiggled up close to her. "Jesus, girl, I been freezing," she said. I suggested we get into the car, turn the heater on. "You ain't never heard of carbon monoxide? You sit in a running car, you could teetotally die. And I don't trust no car that's *off*, neither." She slipped her arm under mine, finding my pockets of warmth. Her arm was as cold as a dead person's, and

I pushed it out. "We could leave. We could just go home," I said.

Naomi shook her head no. "The way I been figuring, you take a black girl, a white child, and a Mercedes-Benz, and you already got what look like a kidnapping. Going all the way through Mississippi ain't going to be no breeze anyhow, and I don't want that old cow calling up the state police after me." I giggled. "No, I got to get me some rest. And *you* got to kiss all those little friends goodbye. Tomorrow plenty enough time." At that she lay down her head on her big vinyl purse, holding me in spoons, as if I were a hot water bottle, and I wriggled around until my head lay on her arm, so I took in sour baby powder and ripeness with each breath.

I fell asleep, warm and sure, down into dreams. Naomi touched me, stroked my hair—she always had told me I had good hair, the kind of hair she'd always wanted when she was small, but the kind she'd never have, even with relaxers; I slid back down into my dream, I felt her fingers in my panties, I sat up, she didn't pull away, "What're you doing?" She didn't move her hand, slipped one of her dry, ashy fingers into my pink little crack and I mashed my knees together, and she licked the finger, over and over, as if it were dipped in sugar, getting it as wet as she could, she pressed my knees apart, easily, having more strength than I did, "You going to like this, you watch"; the wet finger slid back in, found my special bump. "Stop it."

She took my hand, pushed it down between us, into the nappiness in her drawers.

"No."

Naomi sat up, eyes round in a frown, as if I'd awakened her. Before she could speak, I ran, without the blanket, until I was back in my cabin. I washed my hands until morning, letting the water run, disturbing no one. The warm water took off the chill as each pulse of blood traveled through my hands. But at morning bells, I was still sure that my fingers stank, and I touched no one with my hands, said not a word, the rest of the hours that I was there.

THREE

I didn't utter a word for four years.

Silence was easy that morning at camp, because I was so queer no one came near me. My bunk was already stripped, and I was close to forgotten, so I slipped into hot city cottons, my hands smelling of Camay, the rest of me smelling of embarrassment and, clutching my duffel, I sat on the cabin steps. The girls in my cabin went off for breakfast, each saying "bye" as she passed, and it was fine with them that I gave back only a hapless sort of wave.

Naomi walked up to me with her arms folded across her chest, though the sun already had burned off the night cool, and I rose to go with her. "Oooo, thank the Lord, I thought for sure you was going to be gone," she said. I shrugged, walked a step behind her, as quickly or as slowly as she felt like moving. There were no processes, no send-offs; as far as Mrs. Carlton was concerned I wasn't going off with a stranger, and I wasn't coming back to her camp, and that was enough. Once in the car, Naomi turned to me. "Baby, where you gone last night? This a bad time, yeah, but you go running around in the pitch dark, I want to know what I'm supposed to tell you grandpa, you fall in some ditch and break you neck." I had no answer.

She placed a brand-new map of the southeastern United States in my lap and told me I was going to be her co-captain. I dropped it delicately onto the floor mat, not breaking a single fold, and crawled between the seats into the back. If Naomi noticed I wasn't speaking, she probably figured whatever I was doing was temporary, and fully deserved. I lay on the seat, determined not to fall asleep, to feel the silence for Naomi, but I had no watch, no sense of time; I'd been living by bells at the camp, days broken into small enough pieces that only the bored counselors needed to know the hour, each in her specialty, teaching the J-stroke or the half hitch six times a day. When it seemed like lunchtime, I sat up quietly, peeked between the bucket seats, saw it was nine-forty, flounced back down; Naomi said nothing. From where I lay, all I could see was the unchanging sky, a repeating scape of treetops running past me the way backdrops do in low-budget cartoons. I fell asleep full of annoyance.

I was starving, but I wouldn't get out of the car when we stopped, and Naomi came back to her bossy old self, leaving me in the car. I wanted to scream at her that you weren't even supposed to do that to a dog, for God's sake, but it felt better to keep the anger perfect inside me. She came out with a hamburger and a Coke, and I hiccupped for about ten miles. "Well, you saying something," Naomi said, looking at me slyly in the rearview mirror. I shrugged. I wanted to pee, and then I wanted to pee very badly, and then I could almost feel the pee backing up in my throat, and a little leaked into my pants, but still I said nothing.

"Bet you got to pee," Naomi said finally, pulling into a filling station. "Least I got to pee." I shrugged, letting her get the key for herself first, and bounced in my seat, then walked like a cripple when it was my turn. "Well, lucky thing I ask," Naomi called behind me.

We'd crossed the Alabama line when Naomi threw herself into what she saw as a game. She was doing well, backtracking, not needing a co-captain, not needing company, either, and so she sang as loudly and as badly as she could. She was picking up white people's radio stations. "Only women bleeeeeed," she sang, and I covered my head with my arms. "Well, nothing wrong with you hearing," she said.

By late afternoon I had heard about what her brother didn't do to get sent up to Angola anyway and how she quit Derham Junior High in eighth grade and how the man who made two babies for her was a light-skinned man who, with her, could make practically yellow babies, but he liked the poolroom too much. Up until then Naomi'd been someone who existed only during the hours when she was at my house; she stepped down from the St. Charles streetcar from absolutely nowhere in the morning, like magic, and stepped back up on it again after dusk. I listened to every word, making pictures in my head: a bald-headed Naomi-man up at the State Penitentiary at Angola; a Naomi not much bigger than me, getting to quit school forever and never again have to be judged; little Naomis with skin and eyes so jaundiced they couldn't live. For all she knew, I heard nothing, and she kept on talking to fill the air. It was possible that she'd talked to herself all the way up to Tennessee, too, though I imagined a lot of cursing and praying and making deals with God during the parts of those three days when she was lost.

When radio stations faded, Naomi stopped talking for a few minutes so she could concentrate on moving the dial along, halting for only seconds at country music—one twangy note and she was back into the static. Without Naomi's stories to fill my imaginings, pictures of my mother came, her face always in full creamy makeup, the rest of her in cinders and tatters. Except her shoes, pale yellow flats of the softest leather, encasing feet that were now hocks of burned meat. I wanted to ask Naomi what I would see of my mother, but along the road I'd decided that Naomi would enjoy my sadness, and I said nothing, grateful to fill my mind up with people undamaged on the outside.

When we pulled into a motel, she finally realized that I meant business. She told me to stay in the car; she'd be right back. She'd only been in the office five minutes when she returned to the car. "For Lord's sake, you better come inside, tell these people who we is." I shook my head no. She opened the door, took my arm and tugged gently. I knew she could get arrested if I wasn't careful, and I trudged alongside her. "Tell the man who you is," she said to me. I shrugged.

"Her mama *and* daddy just died," Naomi told the desk clerk. He was no older than Naomi, and we were in the middle of Mississippi, so maybe he wasn't much more worldly, either.

"Isn't that a little far-fetched?" he said.

"You read about that plane crash?" Naomi said.

"You name me somebody who *hasn't* read about that plane crash."

Naomi began fumbling for nickels in her purse. A newspaper box in the lobby showed a photograph of the plane wreckage on the front page. "They bound to have a list of the dead people by now. You watch. I tell you, this child Eleanor Rushing. Her mama got the same name. You watch." Naomi pulled out the newspaper triumphantly, handed it over to him.

"Anyone could of read that," he said.

"Jesus," Naomi said, looking at me. There was a huge fish tank along one wall of the lobby, and I was transfixed by the tiny tetras that caught rainbows of light when they moved exactly the right way. "Tell the man you damn name," she said. I looked at her wide-eyed.

"Look, lady, I think you better get moving down the road, how about it? I don't want a big to-do here."

"Tell you what," Naomi said. "I sit in the lobby, you give the child a room, let her sleep a while, take a bath, I be here right under you *nose*. I got to take this girl back to her grandpa, and she a mess."

I could see him playing quick television scenes in his mind, full of window escapes and stolen money. Nothing fit, of course, because Naomi's offer addressed all the fears he might think up. But he didn't see that, saw only that he was missing something and just hadn't figured it out yet. "You got about two minutes to have that car out of here, or I'm calling the cops," he said. "Come to think of it, maybe I'll call the cops anyway. You got a two-minute head start."

Naomi shuffled out of the lobby, slowly, and I shuffled behind her. "You got to do that way with them," she said once we were out. "One time I catch a man in my backyard, he taking my girl's bike, I swear ain't worth a dollar, and you know, with a shotgun house, you got nowhere to turn around in the alley, so I come up on him, noisy big dude, and he's coming behind me with a two-by-four. So I just *walk*. Remember that, somebody coming up behind you, just *walk*. Nobody going to come up behind you and hit you on the head for nothing."

I didn't look at her. We were still sitting in the curved drive outside the motel office. Through the glass I could see the clerk, out from behind the desk now, feet planted like a cowboy's in the middle of the room, hands on hips, waiting to see us go. I flipped open the glove compartment, pulled out the car registration with my father's name on it, handed it to Naomi. Naomi could read names with the same nosiness that makes kindergarten children able to decipher one another's names before they know the alphabet. "I don't know what you doing, but you getting on my damn nerves," Naomi said, then pulled off, leaving half the treads of my father's tires on the smooth pavement.

FOUR

I wanted Naomi to be half out of her mind by the time she got me to my grandfather's house. She talked and drove, pulled over and snoozed, her mouth open, her breath stinking of bad teeth and old coffee. I watched her, waking and sleeping; I stayed on the right side of the back-seat, out of line of the rearview mirror, perspiring onto the leather, rivulets starting at my hairline. "Four and eighty," Naomi said and looked over her shoulder to see whether I was interested. "You want air conditioning, you put four windows down, go eighty mile a hour." She wanted me to smile, or plead. We crossed into Louisiana, and she was hoarse from hollering into the hot air. "You better say something, you grandpa going to think you a lot of trouble, and then you watch, you going to be a fucking orphan, with no place to live." I flounced in my seat, watched the unchanging sky, arms folded, though she couldn't see me. When we came into the city from the east, she calmed down now that she wasn't going to spend the rest of her life lost on a highway. "I guess my mama *and* my daddy die, I go crazy, too. You crazy, just like that, don't take much. You grandpa got money, he send you to the doctor, you back to regular in no time." I snuffled with self-pity, and Naomi said, "You cry, you going to be all right. You do what you need to, you hear?" I stopped crying right away. I'd say something when I saw my grandfather and make her sorry. She put up all the windows, turned on the air conditioning.

We walked into my grandfather's house, a stone mansion full of echoes and finery, and Naomi cried to the emptiness, "What I'm supposed to do with a crazy child?" I had a room where I slept some weekends, a room of whorled-plaster walls painted the wrong pink for a girl, and I trudged up there to wait. Naomi went to sleep on the sofa in the television room, and I came down and found saltines and milk for myself three times before she woke up again. I left my glass in the sink unrinsed, took a new one each time, so that Naomi could keep track, not need to offer me anything. I didn't see my grandfather for three days. He came in to sleep a few of the nights, but he didn't come to my door, and I held my breath when he was in the hall.

When he came in to see me on the evening of the fourth day, I was so accustomed to my own silence that to break it would have been unholy. He walked into the room, where I'd been lying on the bed with my arms folded across my chest for days, moving only to pad downstairs into the kitchen for food or to slip into the bathroom quickly to pee. My belly ached from the curds and sugars, and I lay there, considering what might happen if I never moved my bowels again. I was imagining that everything was mostly water anyway, that anything I ate would eventually turn into tiny freeze-dried pellets deep in my guts, heavy as plutonium, so I'd walk around, this normal-looking girl, weighing three thousand pounds. Poppy stood in the doorway, and I sat up slowly, reaching my arms out to him. He came over to the bed and planted a dry little kiss on my cheek, ruffled my oily hair, nervous, not looking me in the eye, as if he were a child who might also lose his parents.

"Everything is going to be fine, Eleanor," he said, and I nodded vigorously. "You want something to eat?" I shook my head no. "You need anything?" No again. He stood over me, trying to figure. "Anything you want, you tell Naomi, you hear? I've got Naomi here full-time now, she'll take you wherever you need to go. You hear?" I nodded, not looking up. "This is a bad time, girlie, I know this is a bad time," he said, tilting my chin up toward him. "Okay?"

I nodded, my chin riding in his big hand. I wanted to know where my mother was, charred flesh and unsinged linen and leather; I couldn't picture my father. I gave my grandfather a questioning look, but he smiled and walked out.

He sent me to a psychiatrist when I'd been back in school six weeks and the teachers noticed I wasn't saying a word. My friends, of course, had noticed right away. They'd quickly made a complete circle, from sweet curiosity to peevishness to fury, and then back to the kind of sweetness that makes philanthropic clubs in rich children's schools possible. "We had a meeting," Patti Ann McCloskey said, as the rest stood behind her, not so bold. At that point, none of the rest had spoken to me for more than two weeks, except to shrill out in the bathroom, "You're just acting like a freak to get attention, Eleanor."

"We decided you have a right to be weird," Patti Ann said, and the rest nodded solemnly. I gave her a wide-eyed look. "Hey, you're going to drive the teachers nuts," she said, full of excitement at the prospect. They closed ranks around me, and when the teachers began to see I wasn't talking, my friends behaved as if I spoke a language only they, in their wisdom, could fully understand. "Eleanor needs to go to the bathroom," they sang out in chorus, as I stood at the classroom door with no other possible need. By then I was passing tiny loads of radioactive waste into the toilet once a week, otherwise walking around with a belly secretly filled with three thousand pounds of pain.

The doctor's name was Vigilante. He had a dollhouse and a backgammon board and a million foolish tricks. And questions. For me, life already had turned into something like a Wonderland of Twenty Questions. Everything became yes-or-no, and people had to build in their own nuances, their own shades of gray. Dr. Vigilante had a list in his mind, making no deductions, asking questions without narrowing his possibilities. He asked me if I ever had crazy thoughts, and I shook my head no, and for him that ruled out nothing. He still popped in questions to see if I knew what was real—has your picture appeared on the cover of several magazines this month? A ten-year-old could figure out what he was doing. He filled my first hour that way, and I smiled when he asked me whether something terrible had happened to me that I couldn't stop thinking about. I gave him a knowing nod, because that was what he expected. In truth I hadn't thought about anything but the exact moment I was living in for weeks. He talked to Poppy in the hall afterward, hiding behind whispers and long words, and

I could see Poppy was relieved that there was a name for what bothered me; all he had to do was have Naomi drop me off twice a week and I'd be fixed.

I began sleeping in cave darkness. If even a dot or sliver of light came into my room, I would search for as long as it took to block it out. After a few days, I saw the same leaks kept coming from the same places, and with daylight I fixed them well, with opaque rags and duct tape. At night, someone came into my room, Naomi or Poppy, and pushed into my bed, slipping one thick finger into my panties, lying alongside me with a rocking rhythm, speeding and slowing, until one long, choking sob came out, leaving a patch of dry, scentless cream in my underwear I found when I awoke. Naomi or Poppy, I didn't know, in full darkness, my eyes squeezed tight shut, my arms crossed in front of my face so my elbows bumped each other, and my nose was pinched to keep out any musk, my ears strained closed so any sound was muffled and anonymous. I made no noise in the night and couldn't figure out the words I might write in the day. I sometimes hoped it was Poppy, because I never saw him and wouldn't mind hating him. I saw Naomi early mornings, late afternoons, suppertime, all evening, and I didn't want to hate her. Taking in nothing through my senses, I pretended the person in the bed beside me was my physical education teacher, a woman who liked to make the punishment fit the crime, so if you forgot your sneakers you'd have to run laps around the field in party pumps until they were caked with mud and your feet felt as if no two bones were connected by anything. I took a secret pleasure in physical education for months, having found out quickly that it was a class in which mute obedience was all that was required; the teacher didn't learn I'd quit speaking until almost Halloween, when she asked us to count off for teams and one of my friends crowed with joy, "Hey, Eleanor doesn't talk, and you didn't even know it!" After that, the teacher figured she'd torment me straight into speech, and she pushed me past endurance at every task, letting the other girls go while I did knee bends until I fell onto the floor sobbing. "Nothing wrong with your vocal cords," she said happily. A number of people enjoyed pressing me to make a sound, any sound; the easiest, of course, was a cry of pain. Sometimes in the bed I pretended the person with me was Dr. Vigilante, because he knew so little, and he deserved to be so bad.

At first he was smug, waiting for me to break a little, and three times he let me sit for the full hour while he said nothing. I figured he was daydreaming, thinking about easy money, and I daydreamed, too. My senses were so keen, giving nothing out and taking everything in. I knew with a few years more silence I could probably know everything there was to know. I would put it all together so I had a very tiny key to all the problems in the world, cancer and craziness. It seemed to me a lot of people were thinking the key was God, but that was only because they talked so much they saw and heard nothing. I could see myself on the front pages of all the papers, smiling, saving the world. After three sessions in full silence, Dr. Vigilante must have felt guilty, and he worked at me in earnest, setting games out in front of me. I played, board games where I pulled a card that told me to suck my thumb, rounds and rounds of backgammon in which I didn't get any meaner than I'd been at the start. I was a good girl, a learning girl. In school I was turning into something of a mathematical genius, silently trudging up to the chalkboard and doing fraction problems with alarming speed and accuracy.

He put the dollhouse on the low table between his chair and mine, then he lay a fistful of tiny dolls down next to it. I gave him a queer look, because dollhouses were for small girls, and I'd quit imagining long ago. At school I listened to my friends set out their dreams for one another, but we were ten, and now we used words and obsessions for play. At best the imaginings were two-dimensional, made up of full-lipped boys with pale eyes on Thursday-night television. I cocked my head at Dr. Vigilante, folded my arms across my chest, and sat back in my chair. "I just want to see what your family looks like in its house; just show me that," he said.

I studied the house for a long time, knowing he wanted a message from me. I moved a little of the furniture around, not to make Poppy's house or my old house but rather to please myself. I liked the idea of absolutely terrific order, and for a while I worked at fixing the furniture in each room around its edges so there was a lot of space in the center of each floor. A good house for roller-skating. No dolls had roller skates. It didn't matter. I collected all the furniture and piled it into a single room, packing rectangle against rectangle, so neat, with no dead air, even toilets and bathtubs, until the room was as geometrically full as a moving van. Now the house was a perfect house for roller-skating, upstairs and downstairs. Except in that one room.

I picked through Dr. Vigilante's ragtag pile of dolls. Probably when he went into business they'd all been shiny-haired and neatly dressed, but he'd no doubt had a great number of angry children in his office over the years, banging them up in equal measure, the mamas and the daddies and especially the 'born babies. I wasn't looking for anything but newness, the way most children won't eat anything that's had a bite taken out of it. White, yellow, orange, black hair, thick-shouldered men and lithe women, children with painted-on shoes and socks. No black people. Black people probably thought life was generally too funny to go to psychiatrists. There were so many nicks in the paint, so many half-dressed figures, I thought about leaving my house empty, but then, at the bottom of the pile, as if she always sank there to protect herself, I saw a woman doll. She had a cap of shiny dark hair, the way mine had been before I went to live with Poppy and quit getting haircuts. I examined her for perfection, found no scrapes, and I sat her in the chimney. Solid, tiny buttocks on the rim, feet planted on the floor of the chimney that wouldn't have existed in a real house. Her limbs were soft rubber I could bend as I wanted, and I gave her excellent balance, blew on her to make sure she wouldn't move, then sat back triumphant. "Very good," Dr. Vigilante said. "Time's up. I'll see you next week."

Naomi came in to collect me each time, in case the doctor had some message for my grandfather. I stood to the side, still in the office, while Dr. Vigilante was telling Naomi in tones that talked down to both her and me that I was doing quite well. Naomi took his way of talking to mean she, too, was supposed to talk down to me, she was part of the team, and she picked up the doll I'd placed so carefully in the chimney. "What you doing with this, big girl like you?" she said.

I began to scream. I screamed in the office, I screamed in the waiting room, I screamed in the corridor, the elevator, the taxi. Through traffic, filling the tight-sealed vehicle and maybe being heard by no one on the outside. I screamed until I was inside Poppy's house and up in my room with the door closed behind me. My throat hurt for three days after that, but no one knew it.

FIVE

I walked into the church service in the middle of his sermon. I opened the door at the back slowly, stepped through, and for a fraction of a moment he stopped speaking. I was dressed in a white wool suit, and the church was so full of dark cherry wood, and I must have been an exquisite apparition to him, so much so that people turned around to look at me. He looked down at his notes, began speaking again, and I walked down the right aisle toward the front. Uptown United Methodist Church has two aisles, and brides go down the left and come up the right. But eyes naturally go to the right; that's why newspapers put all the lead stories there. I didn't quicken my pace or move apologetically out of his line of vision, and I took a seat in the empty front pew. In the center. He stood at the center of the altar, in a light suit, silver hair razor-neat, pale hands gesturing, a man of perfect symmetry, and everyone else in the church was dark and helpless.

He was talking of good trees bearing good fruit, saying that figs don't come from thorns, grapes don't come from brambles. Jesus talk, Luke talk, but I wasn't in the mood to be taught, and instead I pictured figs, ripped by thorns, open and ripe, juice and tiny seeds spilling in sunlight, as if a sweet clitoris lay deep inside. Put in your thumb and pull out a plum, and say what a good boy am I. I began to smile, so close to him that he had to be getting my images faster than God's, and he stumbled on his words, imagining himself plunging his cock inside those sugary juices. I uncrossed my legs slowly, and I thought for a moment he might stop speaking, might come right down to the front of the church and fuck me gently. There was high color in his cheeks, pure white light in his eyes, and for the sake of the good men and women who'd come to the church that morning, I lowered my gaze so that he could continue. You can know a good person by the good that he does, he was saying, and I considered right away the arguments against him. "And what about the man on death row whose mother beat him until he had no brains left?" he said. Precisely, I thought, so pleased. "Do you think this is what Jesus was talking about? Matthew says that you cut down every tree that does not bear good fruit. Throw it on the fire." Matthew? "Luke," I whispered. "Matthew 7:19," he said, as if he were going to say it anyway. In the front pew, the bulkhead, there were no Bibles, no hymnals, no emergency aircraft exit guides to reach for. I would check it at home. I minored in religion and philosophy in college, and I had an RSV full of highlighter marks, notations in the margins that were cold and smart. I would drop by with the citation, and he would have gotten what he wanted. He was challenging me from the pulpit, because he knew only I was listening. He could tell me things that no one else would notice; really, it was only he and I in the church that morning.

I didn't put in any money when they passed the collection plate. I waited until everyone else had filed out, and then I took my place, last in line. When I was close enough to see him, his wife saw me, and our eyes met for less than a second, and she edged away from him, disappearing down the steps to the church basement. She was a sorry sort of woman, the kind of fat woman whose jowls fill between her cheeks and her ears so she looks front-on as if someone has flattened the back of her head, pushing all the pulp to her face. Her hair was a mix of errant gray strands and shocks of bleached orange, all poofed into a helmet for her pumpkin face. What killed me was that she was as cheery as could be, as if she were a woman in the right place, smiling and laughing out loud so her thick pink tongue slopped happily in her mouth.

I pressed a check into his hand. It was for a hundred dollars, but I'd folded it so he'd have to find out later, think about it until he was alone and could take a look. He unfolded the check and read it. "Eleanor," he said, holding my left hand with his right, "people love you for what's inside. Will you remember that?" I nodded and smiled at him. "I hope you'll come back next Sunday," he said, and I nodded again.

Six

Dr. Maximilian Walters had been in the *Times-Picayune* twenty-seven times since 1978, when he arrived in New Orleans. That included three letters to the editor, three photographs in Nell Nolan's column, and four feature stories. I called up the library at the newspaper and told the man I was working at the church, getting scrapbooks ready for a hundredth-anniversary celebration; could I have all the citations since Dr. Walters came? "The man is so terribly charismatic, but you know how those types are, completely disinterested in order. Or perhaps in self-aggrandizement," I said, knowing that librarians are tuned in to order, averse to limelight, and so are willing to help bring both down on other people. The man on the phone had one of those voices that goes with ponytails and earrings and pallid complexions, and he laughed knowingly with me, then gave me a list of dates and page numbers as fast as I could write them down. "He's on the obituary page another hundred-forty-two times," the librarian said when I was finished. "Seriously?" I said. "Probably," he said. "They do a lot of presiding, you know. But people pay for the listings, and we don't put ads in the database." He was laughing with the joy of playing with another person while he was alone in a room with just facts.

"Maybe you should." I was thinking about rich possibilities to be found in little items full of names of people who'd known him at intense times. Charities, morticians, and cemeteries, the same ones used over and over.

"Then *everybody*'d get a turn. Eventually. What's the point of that?" he said. I laughed. I was feeling like telling him how my parents had made the front page, not just of the *Times-Picayune,* but also of every other paper that sold copies off of mutilation stories. But maybe he'd want to know me, and then he'd track me, look for couples killed in the Eastern crash, get names of survivors, call the church and ask for Eleanor Rushing. I thanked him in a most final way and hung up.

I considered not photocopying any of the articles about Maxim I found on microfilm down at the public library. I read each word, looking for meaning, until I knew entire passages by heart. "'I've been called Maxim since I was a child. Maxim as in adage, not as in the French restaurant,' the genial young pastor joked. 'I suppose my parents expected me to be a homiletical type even when I was small.'" September of 1978. Religion page treacle, probably edited by a Jew trying to suspend all disbelief. In the photograph, Dr. Walters had black hair, a slender wife, and two small children dressed for church. The little girl had on too many petticoats, but that was the mother's fault. Yale Divinity School. I figured that. One post before this one. So he was no older than fifty now. Nineteen eighty-two, a social scene photo, celebrating the hundredth an-

niversary of the church. Oh, dear. Telling untruths to librarians was never a good idea. Especially idle ones, who
didn't move forward from question to question but fretted
instead about old details. I sidetracked, found that the
congregation held its first meeting in 1882 in a storefront
on Dryades Street, where there was now a dry cleaners.
Hundred-year anniversaries could come every few years
now, for cornerstones and stained-glass windows and
births of early pastors.

His hair was silver and his wife was fat by 1987. They
weren't in photographs together in the social column.
With time he'd become more beautiful, and her plainness
had swelled out where everyone could see it. In a line of
dressed up, posing churchpeople, she was laughing, her
arm around a man's waist; I could see her short fingers, her
unpainted nails, peeping through the folds of his coat.
Nothing sexual about it, but again I saw her comfort, her
sureness of place, and I felt sad for her. Dr. Walters was
photographed alone, arm resting on the mantel of his
host's fireplace. A portrait, with light bounced from a high
ceiling. A Darlene Olivo credit, naturally. I'd get a print,
once I'd let the *Times-Picayune* rest for a while. I photo-
copied everything.

When I finally left the downtown public library, it was
dark outside, and I was full of understanding. He was a
man who'd behaved perfectly all his life; people do not get
into Yale unless they live up to every expectation that's
thrown in front of them. Even in the seventies. "The
streets are on fire? I'll stay in my room and do my studies,
thank you." "People are dying out there for no reason?
Well, I have prepared a powerful text on that subject. I'll

have it on your desk Monday morning, and if you approve, I'll deliver it in Chapel Thursday." A good young man. Who married young and sensible, needing a stolid wife at his side as soon as he arrived in town. So she produces babies with her poor black eyes in his pale face, babies that look as if they play in wormy dirt and get no iron in their diets? He loves them because he is a good man; he teaches them to ride bicycles because people can see him out on the sidewalk, being good-natured. He laughs with his wife in public. And he becomes so inured to middling goodness and blandness that it takes a jolt of loveliness for him to notice he doesn't have what he deserves after all. It fell to me now to please him, to give him tiny sips of me until he was comfortable being so happy. With me, he'd become so powerful that churches and city chambers couldn't hold him. He was a man brimming with truths only he could make look remarkably easy; it was time for him to quit wasting them on deaf and silly people. I would let him be gentle and slow, knowing what scandal could do.

Their house was on the same square as the church, so the church faced St. Charles Avenue, and their house sat behind it, facing Prytania Street. Probably there was a path or a gate between the two properties, somewhere in the thick of the block. Burglars loved those blocks, where the shrubbery was so old that freezes rarely killed it, and often as not the back fence was nothing more than rotted wood held up by foot-deep vines. I drove past the church, and it was dark except for two small lamps on either side of the doors. It was on my way home. Poppy's house was three blocks farther uptown. I cut over to Prytania Street. Traffic was heavy on Prytania, because it was only five-thirty, and I couldn't drive slowly. Passing, I took in a few clues. Curtains open on a broad picture window, lots of light inside. Mirrors, incandescent bulbs? No one moving at the front of the house. A Chevy van parked in a small curved drive at the front. A drive that had to make its turn within a sixty-foot property line. I circled the block again. Traffic was faster, more impatient. A cat on the porch, mottles of black and white with no symmetry. A decal on the Chevy van, University of Georgia. Poor man. I turned toward St. Charles, pulled over next to the side entrance to the church. He needed me. I could feel his spirituality, sent up in the form of prayer in case anyone was judging him; it reached me as a wish, floating over the block, then settling down, so I'd excite him. I circled the block again. Getting into the flow of cars on Prytania was still not easy, and I noticed that now the stream passing was late-models, each with driver and no passenger, equal numbers of men and women, all haughty with having done bits of cheating all day, now talking on car phones in case anyone was watching. This time I concentrated on the window, and as I passed the house I saw shadows cast on walls, moving. If something happened on Prytania Street, someone would come out, if only from curiosity. I took the block one more time, waited at Prytania until the headlights coming toward me on that street were spaced far enough to belong to a car with a V-6 engine, then pulled in ahead of it. In the rearview mirror, I saw the silhouette of a white man, narrow-headed with a fine haircut, crisp white shirt collar visible in half light. I hit the accelerator and then, in front of the house, I hit the brakes. Hard and flat out, and he smashed right into the back of me.

The collision happened more quickly than a true accident, where every motion is slow, every fraction of a second is remembered. Impact, and it was over; I supposed it had something to do with the lack of surprise. I didn't get out of the car. The man in the car behind me slammed out of his and stomped toward me, inches from the yellow line, not noticing that traffic was building up behind him; I could see it all in my side mirror. "What the hell do you think you're doing?" he said.

"I could've killed their cat," I said.

"What cat?"

I pointed toward the Walterses' porch, where a pipe-thin young boy stood. "It ran out in front of me, I saw it." The boy was watching, alone. "Where's your cat?" I screamed at him. He shrugged. "I probably killed your cat, God, I'm sorry, I thought I stopped."

"My cat doesn't go out in the street," the boy said.

"What?" Cars were backed up for two blocks now, motors idling, radios closed in by tight windows, a wellspring of dull sound.

"My cat doesn't go out in the *street*."

The man who had hit me was walking toward the Walterses' porch now. "Forget the goddamn cat. Go phone the police."

"You hit me, you know," I said softly, walking up next to him.

"What's that supposed to mean?"

"It means you'll get a ticket if you call the police."

"It was your fault." He was so loud and close I could smell his breath, sour with shock. He began looking around, panicky, hoping some witness had stayed to tell his side of the story, but by now traffic was moving around the two cars, flowing as soon as the red light at Napoleon Avenue stopped cars coming the other way. With Carnival blockades and no money for police, New Orleans traffic could heal itself as fast as a scratch on a healthy child.

"Hey, where's my cat?" the boy said.

The man perked up. "Your cat's sitting in the doorway of your house," he said. I looked, and there it was, silhouetted, a circle atop a circle, two triangles for ears, its little knees all that broke the cartoon lines. "Your cat was probably in your house the whole goddamn time. Right?" The boy just stared at him. "This woman stopped for jackshit nothing."

"A person doesn't stop for nothing," I said.

"You stopped for goddamn nothing." He looked pleadingly at the boy, as if he were going to settle the matter, once all the evidence was in. But the boy was just watching, now holding the cat in his arms. The cat wriggled free, and the boy scooped him up again, held on, and seated himself on the top step, settling the cat on his lap. "I swear, she comes out of absolutely nowhere, then she stops for nothing."

"I think he's okay," the boy said, looking the cat over.

"Of course he's okay. Get me a phone," the man said.

"No matter what, you should've been able to stop in time, you know," I said. "*I'll* go call the police. May I use your phone?" The boy nodded, glad not to have to get up and dump the cat. "I'd have settled this nicely, if you hadn't been so mean," I said to the man before I turned and walked into the house.

The house was full of photographs, so the eye saw nothing else, no design, no harmony; instead it was drawn to detail, to antique portraits in silver filigree frames, to bright, flat school pictures of children at so many stages that it was impossible to count the actual children. There was at least one boy and one girl, photographed at least once a year, so thirty pictures could have meant two children or fifteen children, all from the same gene pool. Montages were framed on walls, family shots, full of generations, and in the tiny office where I found the phone there was a color photograph of Maximilian Walters shaking hands with Jimmy Carter. I had never lived in a house with photographs, except for one tiny Bachrach black-and-white of my grandmother that Poppy kept on his dresser. She'd had it done before she underwent chemotherapy and lost all her hair, then all her adipose tissue, and then her ability to breathe without screaming for help. "If you're going to have a picture of yourself in your house, have it painted by an artist," my mother once told me. "Photographs aren't art, they're *news*. And you don't hang up the news in your living room." When my mother died, Naomi pulled out an old newspaper society shot of her and my father from a Rex ball in about 1965. She was in a formal, so naked, and he was in a tux, and I'd wondered, looking at the dry old clipping, what on earth they'd done with me that night. I liked to believe that I'd been only a few months old, that I shouldn't have been left at all.

When the police dispatcher found out there were no injuries, she lost interest, and only the recording beeps gave me any sense my call was being logged at all. I asked her how long it might be, told her that traffic was backing up. Pressure them, and they'll never come. "Never knew an accident when that *didn't* happen," she said. I laughed.

"Well, I'll be here until they get here," I said. "Though the man who hit me might kill me."

"A Chrysler New Yorker going uptown at five-thirty? Not the type," she said deadpan, and I laughed again.

If I learned the man's name that night, I forgot it within a month or two. He stayed away from me, a busy man who was letting countless people down with this delay, though he had no cell phone. "You finished with the phone?" he said when I walked out of the office, then he disappeared inside, emerging only to ask every half hour whether the police were there. I shambled back toward the front porch, where the Walters boy stood waiting, watching, because there was a real possibility someone could come along and steal one of the cars. In a scene like that, a man could have slipped into the driver's seat, looking knowledgeable, hotwired my car, and driven off.

I studied the montages of photographs in the side hall, figuring family trees, figuring what the child he'd have with me would look like. I computed that he had a boy and a girl when he came to New Orleans, the ones in the newspaper article, and the boy on the porch had been born since. Three children. No wonder his wife was so fat. She came to town slim and full of self-control, and here she had her third baby, and people expected her to get right up, still thick and sloppy, and serve at the church supper, tasting small platefuls of spaghetti and sauce for hours on end. Good-naturedly. The sort of woman who'd say, "Oh,

I still haven't lost the weight from when I had a baby." And how old is your baby? "Eight." Good laugh, a mouthful of food, and there she was.

"You don't live here by yourself?" I said to the boy on the porch.

"My dad's Dr. Walters."

"Oh?"

"From our church. You came to our church."

"The church around the corner? That's your church? That's your dad's church?" He nodded vigorously. "Hey, I really like your church, I think I might join your church."

"I saw you there. You had on white."

I had on white again. A white silk blouse, a palest cream skirt. "Probably you think I always wear white," I said.

He shrugged. "I don't know."

"I'm honored you remembered me."

"You sat in the front row."

"Yeh, I sat in the front row," I said and laughed.

He sat with me in silence for a while, staring at the cars, as if the drama were going to continue. The cat was on his lap, and sometimes I'd reach over and pat it, but the boy never took his eyes off the street. A companionable silence; I could stare out at the street, too, and imagine him with me on the weekends when his father would have him. Maxim would be busy; the boy and I would go fishing. I hated everything about fishing, but I was prepared to make sacrifices.

"Do you like fishing?" I said. He shrugged, said he had homework, would I watch the cat, please. "And would you call me if the police come?" I said yes, dragged the boneless cat onto my own lap. "What's your name?" I said to him as he stood up over me. Max, he said. "I saw pictures in there. You've got an older brother." He gave me a puzzled look. "Don't you have an older brother?" He nodded. "So why's his name not Max?"

"I don't know. I guess because it's a crummy name."

"It's a fabulous name."

"Okay," he said, having had enough.

"I'm Eleanor."

"Okay," he said and went inside.

When all there is to see is traffic, you can notice a great deal. For instance, every two minutes, a magical fifteen-second lull falls. The light at Napoleon and the four-way at Jefferson stop cars coming from both directions, and unless someone pulls in from a side street, no cars pass on Prytania at all. Blind people already know this, I'm sure. Engineers plan those sorts of breaks, but only for big intersections. They probably don't know precisely what goes on in the middles of off-blocks, except in front of their own houses. Computers will refine their science one day, so everyone will have lulls, and there won't be any more guesswork for those of us who have all our senses.

The Chrysler man came out onto the porch, looked around, moving with the stiffness of the very peeved. "My attorney says we can move the cars," he said. "All I need is to get rear-ended. Not that it matters. I'm sure everything under the hood's shot to hell."

"We can leave?"

"No, we can't leave, for Chrissakes. We can *move* the cars. They can *look* at the cars and see what happened."

I pulled my car over in front of the house next door to the Walterses'. The man got into his Chrysler. "You're probably going to have to push," he said, but the motor turned right over, smooth, no clunks, and the car slid in right behind mine. "Well, a piece of goddamn luck after all," he said, then stomped back into the Walterses' house.

I was alone on the porch with the cat when Dr. Walters came walking around the corner from the church. "Hi," he said, low, expectantly, as if we had an appointment.

"We meet again," I said.

"Are you waiting for me?" he said.

"No, the police." I pointed toward the two cars. "I thought you knew."

"I didn't hear a thing." He wasn't looking at me but straight ahead, and I could stare at him in profile. He knew that. People take on a certain sensuousness, a slackening of the jaw, tongue resting loosely inside the lower lip, when they know they are being watched by someone else very sensuous. Streetlights behind him made every line of his profile stark and fine. A perfect man, brow just so, nose as narrow and straight as a young girl's. Oh, his mouth, I could see the smallest glint of wetness on his tongue, I wanted to see him full-face, I wanted to touch tongues, just a flick, I slid down to the next step, cat on my lap, a liquid movement, so I looked up at him, and he had to look down at me.

"Maybe you didn't hear, but you knew," I said, low.

"Maybe," he said and smiled. We were looking directly into each other's eyes, and he looked away quickly. "Which one's yours?"

"Guess."

"No, thanks."

"Come on, guess."

"Why?"

"I'm just curious, what you think of me."

"I don't know you."

"You know some things about me."

"I know you like to sit in the front row."

I laughed. "Only when you're speaking," I said. He was silent for a while. "Oh, come on, guess."

"What's this all about?"

"I'm bored."

"You don't seem like the type who's ever bored."

"Okay, I'm *not* bored. I'm keeping from *being* bored. See, you know a lot about me."

"That's your car in front. Only people who have no worries spend all their time avoiding boredom." It was a year-old Mercedes. I'd figured it meant something when I bought it, but I wasn't sure that was it.

I didn't say anything for a moment. "I really love listening to you," I said.

"I have a lot to say every Sunday morning."

I gave him a conspiratorial sniff, as if I were already on the church board. "No, really, you understand everything, don't you?"

"Sometimes that's my job. But sometimes it's *not*."

I laughed. "You get paid to defy understanding."

"You understand everything, don't you?" he said and laughed back.

We sat in silence, and I knew he was thinking about me, figuring the best thing to say next, taking his time. It was a cool, wet evening, but I felt absolutely nothing, as if I were nothing more than a warm, embracing spirit there on the steps next to him; I couldn't feel the weight of the cat, could see my hand stroking the cat, could feel nothing.

"What happened?" he said.

"What do you mean?" I wasn't breathing. The words came from somewhere else.

He gave me a queer look. "You don't have to say if you don't want. But it looks like the other person's fault."

"Oh, the accident."

"Are you all right?"

"Probably not," I said, smiling at him. He looked at me, making his decisions, and I said, "Your cat ran out in front of my car."

"He never goes out in the street."

"I think he does."

"I've never seen him do it."

"Of course not. Cats have secret lives."

"Well, he'd be dead by now if he went into Prytania Street."

"No, he wouldn't."

I stood up suddenly. It was the fifteen-second traffic lull, and the cat, surprised, bolted down the steps and across the street. "See?" I said. "Now you don't have to worry about him."

"I never worried about him *before*," he said, then he dodged his way across the street to retrieve the cat.

SEVEN

When I woke up the morning after the accident, supine in my bed, I couldn't raise my head. The necks of women and small children are such slender stalks that it is a wonder they carry around heavy skulls covered with hair and full of humors with such control. If I tried to lift myself with my elbows, the pain frightened me, but I tried going beyond the pain, and I didn't have the strength to sit straight up, no matter what. It was after nine o'clock, and Poppy already would be gone. Naomi shambled in between ten and ten-thirty every morning, and I lay waiting to hear the alarm beep that signaled someone had opened the kitchen door. I dozed, and when I woke again, it was after eleven. "Naomi!"

"What you want?" Her voice was muffled by distance.

"Come here."

"Shit, baby, you *wait*. You think I got nothing else to do but come running up them stairs?"

"It's an emergency."

She came into my doorway five minutes later, holding a broom upside down. "You don't look like you got no emergency."

"I can't fucking move."

"Oh, Jesus," she said, disgusted.

"I'm not lying, I had an accident. Last night. My car's almost totaled."

"Not that new car."

"Christ, I don't care about the car. I can't lift my head."

She said she'd be right back, and she propped the broom up against my doorjamb, holding her place. "What the hell you done?" she said when she came back finally. "That brand-new car never going to be right again, you know."

"I have to pee, Naomi."

"Then roll over. You think I'm walking in here with a bedpan, you got another thing coming."

I rolled to the side, holding my head as if it were a huge hat that would fall off, worked my way into a prone position, and when I stood up I felt perfectly fine, as long as I didn't jostle. I asked Naomi how she knew to do that. "I don't know. I guess after a while you know just about everything."

She was still in my room when I came out of the bathroom. She was leaning on the broom, judging. "I guess you plan on suing," she said.

"Who'm I going to sue?" I hadn't considered the possibility.

"Looks to me like you been rear-ended. And you got whiplash, too, if you telling the truth. You got beaucoup lawyers would want that case."

"I'm not into that stuff," I said. I was planning to learn about loving and forgiving; I wanted to see if Maxim Walters believed in ideas that made sense. I had two tests to give; one, to find out whether they made sense, and two, to find out whether he believed them. "I have more money than I know what to do with as it is." I lay down on my bed, on my stomach, then rolled over. My neck hurt every time I moved.

"That's your trouble. What you need's a *job*. You grandpa's eighty-some years old, and he still go to work."

"He's pitiful, Naomi."

Being a distant man, a machine of a man, my grandfather thought less and less about the reasons for doing things as he got older. He had routines that he couldn't break: dry, white Bunny Bread toast and Luzianne black at seven-thirty, downtown on the streetcar at nine, lunch at his club after the market closed at three, home to stare at the front page of the *Times-Picayune* until it was time to eat whatever Naomi felt like cooking. Never mind that over the years the papers reported the dangers of low fiber, high caffeine, social irresponsibility, and thugs at the streetcar stops; Poppy wanted everyone, including himself, to know where he was at any given time. I doubt that thought or knowledge passed through his head at all anymore. Certainly he did nothing at his desk all day. I could phone or walk in, and he'd ignore me for an hour, say, "Enough, Eleanor," continue doing nothing. His mind was all there, and he was fully in the present, but he'd seen enough cycles to figure there were no more surprises, so he'd given up.

"You want to see pitiful, *you* pitiful." She said it with such affection that I kicked at her playfully, the weight of my foot's motion carried in my neck. I winced. "I ain't playing. You practically thirty years old, you ain't never had no job. No babies, no husband. That what you think you going to do the next thirty years? You might as well never been born."

"I'm an interesting person," I said. "I've been to school, I've read everything there is to read, I've lived other places."

"And who's going to take care of a interesting person when she get old?"

"You."

"Shoot, baby, I ain't going to be studying about you when you get old. You seventy, I be past eighty. You think I walk around here, toting you a tray, all bent over with arthritis, you crazy. I ain't got children for no reason. I'm eighty, I be setting up in my daughter's living room, collecting social security; somebody be bringing *me* a tray. *You* be setting in this big old house, with no sense, eating out the garbage can, pooing in you bed."

I began to laugh, rocking in the bed with pain. "Christ, you're mean to me," I said.

"You mean to me, too."

"You deserve it."

She knew what was coming. "I don't deserve nothing you been handing out for almost twenty years. It's one thing, being sorry for a child with no mama and no daddy, it's something altogether different when that child a grown woman."

"You ruined my life."

"I *save* that sorry life of yours. Who you think going to move in this haunted old house, leave her own children ninety percent of the time, take care of you? If you been left with nothing but a grandpa, you'd of starved to death when you was ten."

"You know what I'm talking about."

Every year or so, I'd try to get Naomi to admit what she'd done to me. But after a while, she'd take one fragment after another of what happened and tell me it was a lie, so there was no room for what she'd done. She'd never been in Tennessee, she'd say. Never been out of Louisiana, in fact. My parents didn't die in a plane crash, she'd say. My mother, in fact, was so afraid of airplanes that my parents took cars, trains, and boats everywhere they went, she'd say. It's documented in the *Times-Picayune*, I'd tell her, and she'd give me a look that said, Well, it might as well be in Sanskrit in the Calcutta Daily News.

"I know what you talking about, and you making me damn tired with that shit. You done told that stuff to you grandpa, and I still be working here, what that tell you?"

"That tells me that my grandfather doesn't give a damn."

"Get out that bed," Naomi said, annoyed.

"Hey, I really got hurt."

"Okay, okay," she said, believing me. "You want some coffee or something?"

"With a straw?"

Naomi laughed. "You something else," she said.

I went back to sleep, coasting down into dreams of Maxim Walters, imagining the cat into him and him into the cat, so they traded places on the porch, the cat seated next to me, aloof with wanting me, while Maxim draped himself loosely over me, his gentle body conforming to all my contours, his throat giving off a hum of simple pleasure. I stroked him, and I looked at the cat, and the cat's eyes were a seafoam green, full of longing, full, too, of wariness, of listening for danger.

Naomi wakened me gently. But I was so deep in still-
ness her whisper jolted me, and I tried to sit up. I let out a
cry of pain. My eyes were closed, and I didn't know what
time it was, and I was winded by the terror that pain is all
about. If we were guaranteed pain would lead to nothing
worse, we could ignore it. But all I knew then was my head
was going to snap off my neck like an overripe apple on a
thin stem, and then where would I be?

"I whisper," Naomi said defensively.

"I know," I said, and I let out a little whimper.

Naomi lifted my head as if it were a crystal punch bowl
and slipped a heating pad under my neck. "I knew you
wasn't in here calling no doctor, so I call one. He say put
this under you, three days you feel a lot better. I ask him
about neck braces. Neck braces for *court,* he say." I asked
her what doctor she called. Naomi herself went to storefront doctors who had offices in halves of duplexes and
took live chickens and Medicaid in payment, patient's
choice. Dr. Farraday, she told me.

"Are you crazy? He's a neurosurgeon, for God's sake." Dr.
Farraday lived next door on St. Charles Avenue, and we
used the same landscape service, so our grass was always the
same length as his, but that was as far as anyone went with
neighbors on St. Charles Avenue. "How'd you get Dr. Farraday?" I knew better than to think that a neurosurgeon was
sitting out in his yard midmorning, midweek, waiting for
Naomi to saunter over and ask for free advice.

"I ask his housekeeper. She got the number, you know."

I began to giggle, imagining a conversation between
Naomi and Dr. Farraday. "He ask you if I was going
to sue?"

"Naw, the way he put it, he say, 'I *assume* she not going to sue.' I tell him, 'You *assume* right.'" Ass-yume. Naomi chortled with delight. "He say, 'I come take a look at her, but you got to tell me absolutely there ain't no lawsuit in this.' So I tell him, 'look, that girl got more money than she know what to do with. And she too damn lazy to go sitting in some courtroom. That's too much like *work*.'"

I moaned and rolled onto my side, facing away from her, but my head flopped into the shoulder space, and I quickly rolled back to a supine position. "God, Naomi, you really talked to a doctor like that?"

"Shoot, he mess his drawers just like anybody else. You talk to enough of these maids on this street, you know there ain't nobody better than nobody else."

I'd forgotten that the most powerful information network in New Orleans runs along the public transportation lines. Housekeepers board the Leonidas bus or the Freret bus, transfers in hand, all on schedule, and tell one another stories about the same people every day. A lot of talk is their own news, of course, because their houses and their neighborhoods are full of psychosis and unexpected death, but their true stock in trade is the dirty secrets of the people they work for. Housekeepers know the truths about suicides, bankruptcies, homosexual affairs, and multimillion-dollar frauds when no one else does. A story can travel up and down the St. Charles streetcar line and over back fences without ever making the *Times-Picayune*. Rich white women know that if they want the truth, it is in the soiled sheets and the dusty desktops; all they have to do is sit in the kitchen acting friendly long enough, and they'll find out.

"You know anything about the church up the street?" I said.

"There's about a hundred churches up the street."

"The Methodist church. Three blocks up. I'm thinking about joining the Methodist church. The minister's sort of interested in me. As a woman, I mean. I was kind of wondering if you knew about him."

Naomi brightened. She belonged to St. Paul's African Methodist Episcopal Church, and over the years since I was grown I'd been to funerals and weddings there. I'd show up for any occasion, liking to see Naomi in makeup and perfume, foundation on her face a shade too light so she looked like an undertaker's model. Her shoes always matched her dress, and she tottered in heels ever so slightly, so I could believe the Sunday Naomi wasn't the real Naomi. Wobbling in the receiving line, grasping the hand of whatever woman stood next to her, she'd hug me and cry and whisper "This what you need" in my ear, hot chalky perfume filling my senses so I had a long moment of complete well-being.

"You want to go to church?"

"I want to go to *that* church. What do you know about *that* church?"

Naomi took a step back and folded her arms across her chest. "I know you up to no good."

"The man really likes me. I spent most of last night talking to him." I wanted to sit up.

"I thought you spent most of last night getting yourself half killed."

"He was with me after the accident. He waited with me for the police."

"You probably ran him over. Probably he was lying in the street, bleeding, waiting for the police. Probably he was lying there saying to you, 'Why you try to kill me, girl?'" Naomi was having a wonderful time, her eyes big as if she were on stage, and I began to laugh.

"Get out," I said pleasantly.

"That's a married man, I know that's a married man. If it's the same one I'm thinking about, he got a nice portly wife. You go after a minister like that, that's *low.* Especially if you go joining the church for that kind of foolishness. That's downright evil."

"This man's in love with me. I can tell he knows I'm what's been supposed to happen to him all his life. I'm what he needs. He'll be perfect with me."

"Baby, this *Naomi* you talking to," she said, and she walked out.

EIGHT

D r. Farraday came that night with his cool X-ray fingers and told me I'd be better in two or three days.
He was a dark man, with the sort of black hair that does-
n't gray until a person is about seventy. He wasn't much
older than I was, but he had hands that made him wealthy,
and he knew he was a God-player. The lights were dim in
my bedroom, and I was lying on top of the covers, warmed
enough from the heating pad that from time to time in the
afternoon I had called Naomi to open or shut the window.
"You got to think of a better way," she'd said the second
time. "I mean it," she'd said the third time.

"Would you like a drink? Naomi can fix you a drink," I
said to Dr. Farraday, his fine hands sliding over the back of
my neck, feeling all the little chicken bones. I was trembling at the touch. "Just stay put for a couple of days, and
you'll be fine," he said, smiling. I told him I had to go to
the City Council meeting tomorrow, and he gave me a curious look. "You can hear that on the radio," Naomi said.
Naomi was in the doorway watching, protecting the doctor. "Do you have to speak?" he asked me. "Lord, no,"
Naomi said.

"But I need to see what's happening," I said, figuring that all the whiny voices would sound identical on the radio, that the degrees of rudeness would be hidden. "It's on cable Channel Eight," Dr. Farraday said. He wrote "Channel 8" on his prescription pad, tore off the page, handed it to me. "What about the pain?" I said. "Just turn off the set," he said, and he and Naomi laughed. "Don't do this to me anymore," I hissed to Naomi as she followed him out of the room.

Watching the City Council on television was not a lot better than listening to it on radio. With two lazy cameras, I could view only one councilman at a time, often for a full fifteen-minute stretch. Seeing the red light, each behaved in turn. I lay on the divan in the solarium, and I composed phone calls to Maxim Walters in my mind. The City Council was talking about gambling again; I could phone with urgency, get him to run over there for me so he could write down everything they did, nothing they said. He'd have to come to my house and fill me in because his notes were too scribbly. There could be passion in issues; that's why people fucked and screamed so much in 1970. No, we'd have too little stolen time, and I didn't want to care about issues. I could say that I wanted to join the church, and he'd come over, and I'd be in my bedroom, soft with pain, and he would caress my body so gently, as if I'd break if I moved. Naomi. She'd know, and she'd take me straight to hell. I dialed, wondering what I would say when he came to the phone. "Uptown United," a woman said. I smiled. "I guess that's what you have to say," I said. "May I help you?" she said. I asked for Dr. Walters, and she asked who was calling. I gave her my full name, and she asked what I was calling in reference to. "What if it's personal?" I said, and she put me on hold. "Maximilian Walters, may I help you?" he said, coming on the line a full minute later.

"It's me," I said. He said nothing. "Eleanor. Eleanor Rushing." Still he said nothing. He couldn't talk; women were all around him, listening. "I really need to talk with you," I whispered.

"I'll be out of town through the weekend; could you make an appointment for early next week?" I slammed my fist down on the sofa cushion. I told him I was hurting right now. "The accident. You had the accident night before last." I'm sure someone was standing right over his desk. "And I'm really in pain," I said, low. He told me his flight was at 1:47, and I asked him where he was going. Nashville. I asked if I could phone him in Nashville. That wouldn't be a good idea, he said. Talking face-to-face is usually more helpful, he said. I told him I understood, hung up the phone, called the airlines.

When a man says that he has a 1:47 flight, he is not saying, Oh, I have an early afternoon flight, or Oh, I have a flight in three hours, and I can't manage to fit you into my schedule between now and then. Churchwomen would think otherwise, but he was saying that he wanted me on that flight. I had to phone only three airlines before I found which one had a 1:47 to Nashville. I made a reservation for first class. Last on, first off, in case someone was traveling with him. I packed a carry-on with only white clothes, shades of white, cream lingerie, ivory silks, pearls. I had no time for making choices. I put the heating pad in my bag, and it was still warm, pressing out creases; I folded a hot water bottle and stuffed it into my purse. "I'm leaving," I told Naomi as I walked through the kitchen to the back entrance. I cradled the bag in front of me, using the correct muscles. Sunglasses were cocked on top of my head, and I was dressed in dark slacks and dark shirt, with no makeup, a dark scarf draped around my neck, like a movie star.

"You leaving where?" Naomi said. She was sitting at the foot of the chipped enamel table that had been in the house since before I was born, watching the black-and-white portable TV Poppy had bought her for Christmas when I was eleven; he had said, "Oh, that wasn't what I meant" when she walked out the back door with it that Christmas Eve. Naomi had a dozen steaming halved mirlitons lined up in front of her, and she was scraping the pulp from each, her fingers dancing on the hot skin. Naomi stuffed mirlitons in volume, served Poppy two, froze the rest, pulled out a couple that stank of freezer burn every so often, fed him those, too.

"Leaving town. Just for a few days." She asked me if I was driving. I told her just to the airport. "You crazy? The airport halfway to Baton Rouge. What if the axle broken, you going to be sitting on the I-10 watching the planes take off. If you alive by that time." This is a Mercedes, I said. "And about as bad-looking right now as a twenty-year-old Chevrolet." Chevalett. She had a point. Night before last, on the street, the car looked almost tragic; in the garage it simply looked neglected. I asked her to call me a cab.

"You a grown woman. Not a grown woman with no kind of sense, but a grown woman. *You* call you a cab."

"They'll come faster for a black person."

"Where you get that idea?" she said.

"You ever buy Popeye's fried chicken? They always give the big pieces to the black people."

"They don't give big pieces to *nobody*. What that got to do with a cab?"

I told her never mind, and I called the cab company myself. "Tell them you an airport fare," Naomi whispered, and I waved her away.

I paced on the front porch, and every five minutes Naomi came out and said, "I told you say you going to the airport. They come for cash." At one o'clock, I filled the hot water bottle, ran for my car, and with the hot water bottle tucked behind my neck, I made it to the airport in fifteen minutes, left the car in short-term parking, got my ticket, and began running toward the gate ten minutes before departure. The flight was leaving from the far end of the concourse, and as I jogged along, I held the water bottle tight to my neck. The water sloshed and leaked the tiniest bit, and I was dripping with perspiration, but every one of my senses was keen, and I saw him twenty yards ahead of me. Alone. Suddenly I had time. I slowed down, drifted behind him. He walked at a smooth clip, a man with faith that small things did not go wrong for him. He was carrying a briefcase, so I knew he had checked his luggage: good information. I waited until he'd handed over his boarding pass before I entered the gate area. The flight attendant looked at my boarding pass, then back at me, then at the boarding pass, as if she were trying to figure out whether Eleanor Rushing was someone terribly famous. I put my finger to my lips, and she nodded conspiratorially, and I tiptoed onto the plane, giving her a wink.

My father'd always said when I was small that I was going to be famous for my beauty with a name like that. My mother always said back, Like Eleanor Roosevelt? My father said, You could do worse. And when I was about five, a song came on the radio once about Eleanor Rigby, and my mother said, Beautiful and famous? and my father laughed and sang the song, sticking my name in, until I screamed at him to stop, knowing he wasn't funny. I made the flight attendant refill the hot water bottle once by waving and pointing at it, and otherwise I stared out the window, acting renowned and thoroughly sated, tipping down my dark glasses only when we came in for a landing and I could watch the ground come up, smoothly with no scares, no sense that I was going to die. I was the first off, and I moved as neatly as I could past the baggage claim area, found a taxi, tossed in my bag, and told the driver to turn on the meter, and then to wait. "I can't do that, lady, I got twenty guys in line behind me, they'll kill me." I offered him twenty dollars tip, and he said, "Suit yourself," now my ally, willing to take on airport security and anyone else who scowled at him. "Christ, after a while, those bastards think they own the place," he said when an officer told him to get moving. I was on the backseat, kneeling to face backward because I couldn't turn my head, and though the meter clicked up only three times, it seemed like hours before Maxim Walters came out of the terminal and hailed a taxi. I told the driver to follow that cab. "You seen too many movies," he said.

"No, you have," I said hotly, but he laughed.

He drove crazily, keeping up with the other taxi, weaving even when he didn't have to. "Another hour, and you couldn't do this." I asked him why not. I wasn't looking at him, and he wasn't looking at me; we both were willing the other taxi not to do anything strange. "Rush hour." I said I thought we were going *into* the city. I don't know why I knew that, because I'd certainly never been in Nashville, but something about the texture of the roadside, even on interstates, gives a subliminal message. It may be nothing more complex than higher gasoline prices closer to the center of a town, but I can always tell if I am city-bound. "Hey, everybody goes nuts at rush hour," he said. "If you're going out, you're stuck, if you're going in, you see everybody else stuck going the other way, and it does something to you."

"You lost him," I screamed, no longer able to track the other vehicle.

"That's why the driver sits *here*," he said. "I can see him fine."

"This guy your husband?" he said after a while.

"My minister."

He laughed. "Figures."

"Why?" I said, dying to know.

"You got more religion per square mile in Nashville than any other city on earth, probably. Everybody comes here's got a Bible in his briefcase. Don't even have to put them in the hotels, probably."

"I'm from New Orleans," I said, and I remembered Maxim Walters had stood before the City Council and told them they should have a church, a bar, a gambling parlor, and a sweetshop on every corner. It seemed true to the numbers when he said it, because that was the way it was in New Orleans, venal and mortal sins three-quarters of the time, with pleas for forgiveness the rest.

"What you got in New Orleans's quiet religion. We're talking here about *noisy* religion," he said. "You Baptist?"

"No," I said, beginning to be annoyed. "My minister's Methodist, and he's very *quiet*."

"Sounds like you're not Methodist, either."

We edged into downtown and onto Union Street, and when I saw the other taxi pull to the curb in front of a hotel I told my driver to pass him up. "Suit yourself," he said. "Circle the block," I said, and when we got back the taxi was gone. "Okay, just sit here a minute," I said.

"You can't sit in front of a hotel. At least not with a fare in the cab."

I didn't see a doorman, but then I didn't expect one. The hotel was midprice and plastic, a dreadful combination. I don't mind absolutely pure squalor that costs next to nothing, and I don't mind glitz that's so gold and red and blinding I have to smile when I walk through the lobby, but I feel just too sad in these hotels with aqua-and-purple-paned lobby partitions that you can scrape with a fingernail and leave a dull line on.

"You saw him, right?" I said. The cab driver nodded. "Okay, you go in, and when he's checked in, you come out and tell me, then I'll go in." Slow, emphatic, careful: I had plenty of time.

"Jesus, lady."

"I thought you'd be used to this sort of thing."

"I don't *want* to be used to this sort of thing," he said.

I opened the cab door a crack and emptied the hot water bottle into the street, holding it low, making no noise or splashes, folded it up into my purse, slung my bag over my arm, as ready as a child approaching the school gate and not wanting to be seen arriving in a car. The driver came out five minutes later and said the man had checked in. I told the cabbie that was awfully fast. "When everything's slow, you can be *real* fast," he said, holding his hand out. I gave him forty dollars, and he looked at me with what might have been compassion. "I'm pretty sure that was him," he called after me.

Maxim Walters was waiting for me at the reception desk when I strode in. I had no time to think; he came toward me, as if he were going to the elevators. "Hi," I said.

"Hi," he said as neutrally as possible, in case someone was watching. Then he went into the elevator.

NINE

I spoke again when I was fourteen. I was beginning to be pretty, having passed that stage when a girl's nose is too bulbous for her face. Boys tagged behind, still greasy and round-featured: they enjoyed standing in front of me and trying to see if they could make me talk. All the girls but one had become tired of me. It was from envy, because the others chattered away at boys and drew silly attentions, but they didn't have what it took to drive boys insane. I stared back in the boys' eyes, and they never asked me anywhere, but I could sit in the school library at lunchtime and hear them talking about me. "She's in here, you know," one would whisper, and another would say in a normal voice, "Eleanor-r-r, I'm cal-l-ling you," as if I were a deaf-mute. I'd spent three years with the pure meanness of the middle-school teachers, composing notes of complaint to Poppy but never giving them; he wasn't the type to call the school on my behalf. Now I'd come into the kindness of the high-school teachers—poor, smart men and women whose job was to be trifled with by rich children, fine stuffed mousies for pampered cats. For my freshman year, the office gave me the same schedule as Patti Ann

McCloskey. Patti Ann was now my inseparable friend, even though in middle school the principal had seen to it that Patti Ann and I were never together because she made things too easy for me.

Patti Ann was my opposite. I already was pushing my full adult height of five-eight, and she was stalled below five feet even; that could have been her full adult height, too, but she was hopeful. Her mother was a happy little puff pigeon of a woman, with great boom-boom breasts, but her father was tall, and her older brother had grown six inches last year. Patti Ann had pale, clean, thin blond hair that she had bowl-cut since kindergarten, and her eyes were an unambiguous dark blue. Patti Ann was wonderfully fat. In every classroom, we now sat next to each other, and I was never in trouble anymore. I had known for years that no schoolteacher ever expects more than twenty syllables in response from a child; more than that, and the child is difficult. I could have given answers all along, writing them down fast, passing them up to the teacher to read aloud, with any inflection she wanted, but middle-school teachers enjoyed scaring me into greater and greater sadness, and they marked me down, never called on me, let it go at that. Now I was able to write down what I wanted to say, and Patti Ann would read it off, as if she were a war correspondent reporting directly from the front. "I could get away with never having a single idea, and they'd never know the difference," Patti Ann said to me one day after history class. It was true: by December of that year, Patti Ann gave no answers of her own, but the teachers said, "Good, good!" to her and remembered little more than that. We giggled in the hallway, until I noticed a number of girls had slowed down near us, waiting to see if I would finally do something freakish. Maybe I'd break into song.

At Christmas there was nothing but chocolate at school. Fistful of silver bells, half-ounce bags of nonpareils, tiny Whitman Sampler boxes: it was a measure of popularity if you had dozens of little gifts of chocolate from people who didn't know you well. I had none, of course, and I sat through my classes the day before vacation began and watched the others sneaking candy from their hands and getting bolder and bolder from the sugar. Patti Ann had a one-pound sack of M&M's a boy had given her. I sat in the row behind this boy in music class, moving my mouth, satisfying the teacher; I heard the boy screaming, "Do you hear what I hear?" as he cut his eyes at Patti Ann, listened to him make up lyrics that mocked Patti Ann, who stood next to me and sang through her nose loudly enough for both of us. I'd been with her when he'd given her the candy, and I'd folded my arms across my chest and shaken my head no vigorously, but Patti Ann clearly had been flattered as hell by the attention, and she'd eaten all the brown-shelled candies by the end of third period. "I hate the brown ones; I think I'll get rid of the orange ones next," she whispered confidentially to me, as she dumped the remaining hundreds of M&M's softly, noiselessly into the lap of her velveteen skirt. We were in assembly, and she crossed an ankle over a knee, chunky thigh and round calf meeting like a pair of buttocks, making a small triangle around a nice deep trough from which to pluck candies while the senior chorus sang the Carol of the Bells. Looking at Patti Ann's body in any state of undress was fun, because I marveled at how all the extra food moved so well to fill the thick contours; I knew what lay under the costly folds of her dress. The boy who gave her the candy came into the auditorium, strolled up the aisle to our homeroom row, and proceeded to step over six girls to get to a vacant seat. As he slipped in front of Patti Ann, he bumped her knee. Hard. The chorus was hitting the softest lilting sounds, Patti Ann's skirt gave way, and her lapful of candies clattered to the clean-swept cement floor. "Jesus, what a pig!" the boy crowed, and ripples of laughter spread out concentrically from where he stood. Patti Ann pressed her round little knees together, looked up toward the stage as if nothing had happened. And I began to cry. Noiselessly, I could cry noiselessly, but my body was so sad, so full of wracking pain, that a teacher had to lead me out of the auditorium, candy shells cracking under my feet.

"God, I'm glad you *don't* talk," Patti Ann said to me as we walked to the streetcar after school that day. We were both carrying totes full of books and sweaters, having emptied out our lockers for the holidays; I also had an overnight bag, and we were moving slowly. "Anybody else, they'd tell my mother what that shit did to me." She looked at me, ready to read my face; she almost tripped over an oak root bulging out of the sidewalk. I scowled at her. "You crazy?" I shook my head no. "Well, I'm *not* telling her. Bad enough that *I* know it happened. Christ, I'm going to remember that for the rest of my goddamn life. I'd give anything not to go back to that school." I shrugged, raising my eyebrows. "No, my mother *wouldn't*."

Her brother was home for the holidays. Not that he had far to come. He was a freshman at Tulane, and he was living in the dorms until he could live in his fraternity house the next year. "If John Paul can get into a fraternity, any-body can get into a fraternity," Patti Ann said aloud at the dinner table that evening, and I gave her a look of disap-proval. John Paul had been mean and smelly when he was twelve, but I'd watched him steadily improving over time, especially since he'd become reasonably tall and didn't have to act like a short boy anymore. He'd been going into ninth grade when I stopped talking, and he had said, right in front of me, the first time I'd walked into his house mute, "Hey, she's going to hear a lot more than you ever will," to Patti Ann, who was apologetic and nervous about me. Their mother, whom I continued to call Mrs. McCloskey in my mind, even though she told her children's friends to call her Barbara when they turned into teenagers, took every tack she could think of with me for the longest time. "She figures you'll talk if you just get someone to listen to your secrets," Patti Ann said, conveying a message, when I was freshly mute. "Your vocal cords will shrivel," Mrs. Mc-Closkey said to me a few months later. "But she can scream or cry or anything," Patti Ann said. "Hush," her mother said. Eventually she'd given up; when Mr. Mc-Closkey, who was still Mr. McCloskey to almost everyone, would say at the table, "I wish you had more friends like Eleanor; the silence is exquisite," Mrs. McCloskey would agree, with a light, self-conscious little laugh.

"Anybody can get into a fraternity, but I got into the best," John Paul said. He wasn't a narrowed fraternity boy yet; he sounded more like a six-year-old who had surprised even himself. The maid was passing a silver dish full of French-style green beans seasoned with fatback, the food of the ignorant rich, served by the sincere poor. I held up my hand to pass on the beans, and the maid slipped silently to Patti Ann. Serving people never knew if I talked or not; for all any housekeeper or waiter knew, I was arrogant, my smiles condescending. I ached to explain.

"Well, I know half the people in the 1400 block of Henry Clay Avenue, and you boys aren't the best when it comes to behavior." Mr. McCloskey was popping with pride.

"Yeh, Dekes rape and pillage," Patti Ann said, proud now, too.

"You don't even know what that means," John Paul said, looking at me as if I were suddenly older than his sister. I gave him a neutral stare, waited.

"We're doing world history," she said, and everyone at the table laughed.

I couldn't fall asleep that night, and I could see Patti Ann in the moonlight lying on her back in the other twin bed, a marvelous round mound, snoring. A Tomie dePaola girl, full of bread, and living in the north of Italy three hundred years ago. I tried to take on the rhythm of her breathing, to go to sleep with her, but she was breathing too fast, and I became annoyed with her, wishing her to slow down, then trying to speed up myself. I couldn't stop listening to her, and I became more and more wakeful, and when it was close to two in the morning I tiptoed out of her room and down to the television room.

One wall of the television room was glass. When I walked in, there was more light in the yard, nature's light, urban light, dirty light, than in the room. I found safety in darkness, in rooms where filtered light made unreadable shadows, and I turned on only the television set. Middle-of-the-night foolishness, too much color, everything garish for comedy. I switched channels, searching for black and white, and when I found "Christmas in Connecticut" on a UHF station I wanted to laugh. I despised that movie. It wasn't the cheap anxiety that comes from people swinging through doors to hide silly secrets in other rooms. It was that Barbara Stanwyck's dilemma was stupid, and I didn't forgive her despite the passage of thirty-odd years. Not at all. I lay back on the huge leather cushions on the sofa and folded my arms across my chest, wanting to see how long I could stand watching the movie, knowing I wouldn't be able to sleep afterward, giddy and angry.

The door in the glass wall slid open from the outside, and John Paul stepped in. He moved slowly, gently, so I startled him more than he startled me. He didn't speak, sidled over to see what was on television. "That is the worst movie ever made," he said softly, and I was impressed, because boys his age knew nothing about the funny, fumbling airiness that filled most people's minds between 1890 and 1970. Before that, diversion was only books, books boys like John Paul were forced to read and denigrate; after that came the popular culture of their lifetime, which they thought was so new it had to be the first truly creative spurt in modern history, filled as it was with clashes of color, sound, texture. I nodded vigorously in agreement. He stood in front of the set, out of my line of vision, rocking from one foot to the other, impatient, waiting, as most people probably do, for the plot to be different this time. Barbara Stanwyck flipped a pancake with her eyes closed, it came down perfectly, and John Paul kicked the OFF button with his foot. "Jesus!" he said, and I began to laugh with the punchiness that comes at that hour of the night.

"You want to see something?" he said, and I nodded. He led me out into the yard. The McCloskeys' house was as huge as Poppy's, with a separate room for the piano, another for the books; their life was full of compartments, with no overlap. But the yard was small, typical New Orleans, where peripheries were water, and land was mostly paved, so each year brought a good chance of a killing flood. When Patti Ann and I were little, other girls felt sorry for her, because her yard was given over to dark slate, with a dark slate pool in the middle. "I have fair children; I'll see them quickly if they drown," Mrs. McCloskey said to my mother one day when she dropped me off. "Well, I can't stay, Eleanor," my mother said, a warning, I thought, that if I drowned I wouldn't be noticed.

John Paul had a telescope set up on a blanket at the end of the yard. He beckoned me to follow, put his finger to his lips. "My parents' room is right up there," he said, then he muffled a laugh. "Never mind," he said. I sat down next to him on the blanket. It was a cold, dry night, with a cloudless sky, a sliver of a moon.

"How many stars can you see?" he said. I looked up, willing to count, or at least to partition the sky, count a patch, multiply out, as if I were guessing the number of jelly beans in a jar. "I'm kidding," he said. "My teacher says you can see three thousand, without a telescope." I began counting silently with my finger, and he gave me a quick hug. "You're probably very funny," he said.

The telescope wasn't powerful, it seemed to me, though squinting and attention can make up for a great deal, and

I didn't work hard enough, wanting to challenge him. John Paul showed me globular clusters and nebulas, constellations I'd never heard of. "See that star?" he said, pulling me away from the telescope. I tried to trace the vector of his finger, with so many stars, with parallax views, and I thought where he was pointing was a brighter star than the rest. "Okay, now look at it through the telescope." It took me a moment to find it, and then I saw the one star was two. I held up two fingers, appreciatively. "Binary stars," he said, looking straight at me. "Binary stars, they're so close together the gravitational pull of each pulls on the other. They usually look like one star. To the naked eye." I gave him a you-tell-this-to-many-girls? look, and he smiled, leaned over, and kissed me.

Of all my sad moments, that was the most delicious. I closed my eyes, and all I sensed was his mouth, barely touching mine, not rebuffed, now bolder, filling me up with softness, and I began to cry. Not so he'd notice, just a stream of happy tears, and then he began kissing my face, lips brushing my skin, taking me in; he thought the wetness was his own, and he kissed my mouth again, and I giggled at myself, still crying. "You're a complicated girl," he said quietly, and I smiled, kissed him back. I let his hands touch me, my face, my breasts, and then he was sliding one hand up under my skirt, along the places that never had been in the sun, and I wanted his fingers to move up to the vacuum, to be sucked in. He slipped aside the crotch of my panties, tried to push one finger inside me, into the tightest, most frightened place, and I began to scream. "No, no, no, no, no!"

"What?" he said, pulling back, looking at me as if he'd discovered a new corner of the universe. "Get your fucking hands off me," I said, so loud the lights came on in his parents' bedroom.

"I did it," he shrilled, and by now the entire family was coming downstairs, lights turning on ahead of them. "I made you talk." I slapped him across the face, but it was the last time I relied on gesture.

TEN

We fall in love with the familiar. Sometimes what's familiar is the appearance of someone we've already loved with passion—mother, father, a fullness of upper lip, a tendency to self-destruct. Sometimes we seek nothing more than comfort, having stared at one person's face long enough to enjoy his or her features when they show up on someone else. If a woman goes from one husband to another, at some point she'll say, Well, I certainly haven't learned my lesson, because the callow raised eyebrow of husband number four is exactly the same as the callow raised eyebrow of number three; she'll have gravitated toward the face, thinking she knows it well, learning too late that physiognomy tells a lot.

John Paul looked like Patti Ann, molded into different form by testosterone and a few extra years in the sun. Buttercup hair, unchanging slate eyes, a roundness of cheek that once would have laid nicely against their mother's boom-boom breasts, if she'd been the sort to hold her children. I'd talked through Patti Ann for so long, studying her face for understanding, that I was like a stringy baby duck, following the clarity of her expression everywhere. We had no sexuality between us, of course, and not even affection, because she subscribed to the ethos of the rich, of kissing air and touching only fingertips. John Paul was a fine, logical vessel for every bit of longing I'd ever had, and I hated him for trying to trick me. "You weren't trying to make me talk, you were just being selfish," I whispered to him in the kitchen the next morning, when he and Patti Ann and I were flinging open cabinets, looking for something to eat. Patti Ann heard nothing, still expecting silence from me, and she pulled out a box of cereal made of pink-star and aqua-moon kibbles and marshmallows. "Do you have any idea what kind of havoc that'll wreak with your triglyceride level?" I said, rolling out *triglyceride* like a gymnast who's choreographed a routine with all her best moves. Patti Ann frowned at me, having lost something.

The night before, when I'd become as eloquent as Molly Bloom for a fast moment, I ran for Patti Ann's room, flailing past her parents as they stumbled down the steps in a sherry haze. They let me by, of course, from habit, as I wasn't one for explanations, and I found Patti Ann in the upstairs hall, dry-mouthed and farty and mostly asleep. "Well, I've done it," I said, sobbing, and she stayed in her dream state a while longer, having imagined my voice in sleep often enough before. She followed along behind me, the cool air of the hallway blowing off some of the under-sheets funk. "I think you're really talking," she said finally, sitting on the side of her bed, opening her eyes wide just for a second. Then, while she sat there, smiling with half-closed eyes, I skip-talked my way through four years of thought level. Jokes about men that girls tell at ten, full of made-up names for penises that spit. "Don't put my brother and cocks in the same sentence," Patti Ann whispered like a drunk, and I tried out eleven, when romance makes a brief, end-of-latency appearance, so boys write "I love you" on scraps of looseleaf and pass them to girls who are different from me. "Oh, God, it was so beautiful out there in the dark, all alone," I said, and Patti Ann covered her ears. "You weren't all alone, you were with that goddamn John Paul," she said. Twelve, thirteen, when every teacher practically has an orgasm over the smallest slight. "I think I could've had an orgasm," I said, and Patti Ann was fully awake by then, throwing herself across her bed in disgust, her thick backside in the air. Fourteen. "Think he'll ask me out?" I said.

"Why do you even care?" She was talking to the space between the beds.

"He likes me. And I like him back. He may even be in love with me."

"Right. You woke up the whole fucking neighborhood when he came within five feet of you. He can probably tell you're thrilled."

"He went too far," I said softly.

"I don't want to *hear* about it. I don't want to *hear* about it. I don't want to *hear* about it." Each time she was louder, so finally she was screaming, and her mother opened the door, without knocking. "Enough is enough," Mrs. McCloskey said, pretending she said this to us often, and I laughed at having used up my airtime so speedily.

The McCloskeys housed John Paul in the dorm for the rest of the holiday. Mrs. McCloskey saw me as someone to be pitied, a victim who had to stay where she could see me while I healed. "I'm calling Naomi; we can't send Eleanor back to that big empty house *now*," she said, standing in the doorway of the television room that morning with her husband, delighted they'd found all three of us in one place. The leather sofa had four huge sections, enough space for a dozen people, and all three of us were sprawled, supine, watching Underdog cartoons; I felt truly sophisticated. John Paul was talking in Underdog's fruity voice at all the wrong times, and while Patti Ann giggled in spite of herself, I watched him in profile, watched his mobile mouth pushing out the funny sounds, remembering how soft his mouth was, forgetting how thick and rough his fingers were. "You can spend the days here, son, but you'll have to sleep in the dorm," Mr. McCloskey said, pleased as he could be.

"No problem," John Paul said, picking up the remote control to the television set and raising the volume. I looked at Patti Ann, who punched the air with a loose fist in triumph.

"What're you so happy about?" I said, wanting instead to give her a questioning scowl. She put her finger to her lips. "Hey, you people ought to try language sometime," I said. "Aw, fuck off," Patti Ann said good-naturedly to me, then flounced out of the room. "Be careful what you ask for," John Paul said as I was halfway out of the room behind her. "Very funny," I said, and he shrugged, his eyes still on the television.

"You think he likes me?" I said to Patti Ann as soon as we were in her bedroom behind a closed door.

"Oh, Jesus, I wish you couldn't talk. Or at least *wouldn't*."

"Thanks."

"You were a lot more interesting when you didn't say anything."

"I'm still interesting. Just easier."

"Liking a boy with pus for brains is not interesting. Liking a boy with pus for brains who also happens to be my goddamn brother is even *less* interesting."

"If I weren't talking, I'd still be thinking. And you'd know what I was thinking, so what difference's it make?"

"Plenty." She burrowed headfirst into her unmade bed until her rump was in the air again and her head was protected from unclean thoughts about her brother.

I sat there a while, sure I still had the talent of playing out accurate dialogues in my head. I could make sense of what people were not saying, familiar as I was with the nuances of silence. But Patti Ann had made a world-class change; no longer charged with putting every thought, hers and mine, right out there for the ease of everyone else, she was muted, into quiet, into curse words, into pure anger. "I'm still your friend," I said.

"Oh, don't flatter yourself," she said through the bedclothes. I could see her wiggling underneath, moving around until she was sitting up under the sheet and blanket, forming a round-topped tent over herself. She was probably cross-legged, with her arms folded, lower lip out.

"I'm sure a boy'll love you one day. I'm sure if I had a brother he'd have been in love with you for *years*," I said. She said nothing, didn't squirm. "He probably only likes me because I'm convenient," I said, not meaning it.

"Shut up, Eleanor." Her voice was muffled and distorted, and I laughed. "Shut up, Eleanor," I said in a Lenny Small voice. She flung the covers off herself, and her face was pig-pink with annoyance and carbon dioxide. "You're really an asshole," she said evenly. "No, I'm not," I said. She lay down, her face turned away from me, said she was going back to sleep. She worked her way under the covers, feet-first this time. I sat on the other bed, watching her, trying to think of nothing. Impossible, so I closed my eyes, and I could clear my head so far, but the vestigial colors on my retina played, asked to be defined; the demand of language was back. I asked Patti Ann if she was asleep. She nodded her head vigorously, yes, and I tiptoed out of her room with my day clothes in my hand. Patti Ann was the only one whose bathroom wasn't connected to her bedroom, and I slipped across the hall into the bathroom, got dressed, stood at the top of the back steps for the longest time, trying to imagine what I'd say if I saw anyone downstairs. I pictured each person, John Paul, his mother, his father; they might speak first, but I had no idea what any of them might say, so I went down to the kitchen, curious as to how I'd answer with nothing planned.

No one was in the kitchen. I padded into the television room, and no one was there, either. Now I was entitled to go from room to room, looking for company, and I slipped into the library, then the piano room. The McCloskeys' house was different from mine because so much of it was for showing off, so all the downstairs doors were always open. Patti Ann had taken piano lessons when we were about eight, but otherwise there was no reason for a piano, except to impress visitors with a costly piece of furniture that was always free of dust. Neither my parents nor Poppy had ever had a piano, or a library full of books for that matter, just rooms full of places to sit with the doors closed. Naomi went into those rooms twice a year with a dry dustcloth, and Poppy didn't care.

I found no one downstairs, so I went outside to look for cars. All three cars were gone; I knew John Paul's was in the shop. I checked the yard, the garage, for John Paul's yellow bicycle. No bicycle; I had the house to myself, as long as Patti Ann slept. I tiptoed up the front staircase and let myself into John Paul's room.

I hadn't been in his room since I was ten and repelled by the things a boy would fill his private spaces with. Once Patti Ann showed me the magazines full of squirrel shots that he kept between his mattress and box spring. I thumbed through them, silent and wide-eyed, never having seen a naked woman myself, stunned by the coarse black hairs and the open wound of the female calyx. "He plays with himself, probably all night," Patti Ann whispered, and I understood why a boy would find pleasure in looking at the shiny ripped place on a woman's body, already having a room full of guns and knives and other implements for tearing up flesh.

His room was different now. No color, white walls, one cot with rumpled white sheets, and, on sills and shelves, graveyard robbings. A stone cross, a marble vase with MOTHER engraved on it, a broken slab with AT REST in three-inch letters, a thick iron easel that held up a wreath of branches and sun-bleached blue ribbon. Everything hard to steal. John Paul's telescope stood in one corner of the room, almost hidden, as if he were embarrassed by science. The room was cold, with none of the old ripeness of frantic sexuality, and I sniffed the air for some scent of him; I breathed only clean southern winter air, which gave me a splendid sense of safety.

I tiptoed over to the closet, and all I found were four plaid flannel shirts, but I smelled them, too, and they held some of the musk of deodorant and earnestness. I memorized the scent, took it in as thickly as I could. The door to the bathroom was open, and I walked in softly, searching for more smells. The mirrored door to the medicine cabinet creaked as I tugged it open, and I looked around, expecting Patti Ann to come in. The cabinet was empty, except for a boxed tube of Colgate toothpaste. I shrugged in the silence, then peeked inside the laundry hamper, not sure I wanted to actually find shit stains in his underwear or spatters of come on his towels. The hamper, too, was empty, but the scent inside of it was the same as I'd found on the shirts in the closet, and I went back and took one of the shirts, folded it up under my sweater, and slipped back into Patti Ann's room, where I stuffed it into my overnight bag, hoping my clothes would now smell of John Paul, creating a contagion of scent, so eventually everything I owned would carry the sweet mustiness of him. Patti Ann awakened as I sat on the floor of her room, filled up with my secret. "What time is it?" she said, her voice thick with too much sleep. I told her it was almost noon, for Chrissakes. "What've you been doing?" she said.

"Waiting," I said.

When John Paul didn't come home that night, I decided to go looking for him. Patti Ann took forever to want to go to sleep, after hiding in a doze most of the morning, and all that kept me awake was the wildness of frustration. For fun, or maybe to punish herself, Patti Ann decided near midnight to interview me, as if I'd been a hostage for four years and now could tell my story of torture and loneliness. "What'd you really think when people talked about you like you couldn't hear them?" she said.

"Nothing," I said.

"Well, I thought they were extremely stupid."

"I know. *They* knew. You *told* them they were extremely stupid."

"You remember that?" she said, pleased with herself.

"I wasn't *deaf,* you know." I felt peevishly superior, the way I am when another person is wasting my time, but Patti Ann laughed. "I'm serious," I said.

She shrugged. "It feels strange, you know. I mean you talking. It's sort of like seeing Snow White at the movies and wondering what the lady looks like who does her voice. Only the opposite."

"You heard my voice. I talked until I was ten, for God's sake. If you know somebody when they're ten, you'll recognize them when they're twenty. Or fifty, probably. Voice and all." Naomi had told me that, and for all I knew it was true only for black people. Black don't crack, Naomi said at other times.

"What's your problem?" Patti Ann said.

"I'm tired of talking."

"Really? Literally?" Another scientist in the McCloskey family. I shook my head no. She thought for a minute. "Hey, maybe I'll stop talking. See how you like that." I said nothing, imagined how it would be at school, Patti Ann taking over my role, me taking over hers. It was enough that I had to go back after Christmas and make everyone so curious. We'd had a boy in our class one year from London, and people came up to him all the time and said, "Say *purple*," then went off giggling, as if they'd been so terribly precious. "You couldn't stay quiet for five minutes," I said, and Patti Ann laughed, liking herself.

After she went to sleep, I filled my pockets with all the cash and change I'd brought, disarmed the burglar alarm with the key in the front hallway, let myself out the door, and realized that finding John Paul on the Tulane University campus was not going to be easy. I enjoyed that idea, even enjoyed the possibility that someone might grab me and try to take my money. Christmas isn't like Mardi Gras, when crime drops because everyone's too busy chasing trinkets; at Christmas everyone's loose with drink and greed, and the worst robberies always happen then, sometimes pushing the murder record to new heights in those crazed last days of the year. I'd give the man my money, and he'd scoot off happy, and I'd go running to John Paul, who'd hold me and kiss me and feel sorry for me.

I took the streetcar up to Tulane, cut through the abandoned campus to the back, through shadow and the sound of moisture sizzling on power wires. I knew where the freshman dormitories were, because girls who lived uptown did most of their bike-riding practice on the Tulane pathways as soon as they were allowed off the block. It was a rite of passage, wheeling along, giggling and beautiful, imagining that college boys couldn't wait for us to get older. The distances on the campus were much greater on foot: a space that took seconds to fly across on a bicycle took big fractions of hours to cross by walking, but I didn't mind wasting steps; I had forever to find him.

With almost everyone home for the vacation, few cars and bicycles were on campus, and I found John Paul's candy-shell yellow Schwinn outside of Sharp Hall. Parked in a bike rack, no mistaking where he was. This was easy, and I wanted it to be hard. Maybe the door would be locked. But it opened with a nothing-to-lose, well-greased swing. A high-rise, now it would take hours of tiptoeing through the halls, looking for names on doors, distracted by the cryptic notes and public secrets of boys forced into reading nineteenth-century thought for the first time. I'd be caught by Security, have to scurry around to other entranceways. The elevator opened, and a brown-skinned girl stepped out. She wore jeans and a T-shirt with a sleeveless parka, but her black hair hung in a loose braid down her back, and I figured she'd be of no use, a girl who spoke no English, a scholarship girl from the Middle East who couldn't afford to go home for the holidays. "You looking for somebody?" she said, with flat Chicago vowels, and I told her John Paul McCloskey, and she said, "Yeah, his mother threw him out or something, fourth floor, last door on the right." I shrugged, not grateful.

I stepped off the elevator into an empty hallway, and the cool air was so full of loneliness that I didn't want to be there. Few places have made me feel so unutterably sad. Cemeteries aren't like that; motels along bypassed highways are. It's the shame in the hopefulness that I can't bear. On a number of the doors in the corridor were montages supposed to be full of personality, with four-color John Dempsey cartoons and cannabis decals, Bourbon Street signs and postcard-sized pictures of John Belushi. The boys who lived in those rooms during schooltime were skinny and oily and rich, impervious to original thought. What saddened me were their expectations, their full belief that girls wanted them and, more important, that other boys thought they knew everything there was to know. I expected better of John Paul, and as I tiptoed down the hall I was certain I'd find nothing on his door, the best statement of personality. Yet as I came closer I saw sheaves of color at odd angles, and only when I was in front of his door did I see that, while one side of the corkboard was covered with magazine photographs of naked women, their pubic hair and groin muscles all visible, the other side was indeed blank, save a slip of paper with JOHN PAUL in small print, half covered by a thumbtack. Consensus in other rooms, none in this one.

I thought about leaving; I had enough to carry me a few days, but it is the nature of doors to remind people that something is on the other side, if only they'd consider the possibilities. I saw no light under the door, so he was asleep. Maybe other girls dream about men who come storming across their screens, stirring up dust and blood and longing, but every dream I've had of men has put them to me in a state of sweet sleep. With skin warm and dry, a slowness to recognize me, pleasure that comes from absolute quiet.

Maybe the door was unlocked and I could slip in without waking him; I tried the knob. It made the smallest click. Locked. The sound was magnified, resonated through his room; that is the greatest fear of the very sneaky. He said, "What?" in a voice soupy with annoyance; I pulled my hand back, as if I could take away the fact of having touched the doorknob.

I stood still, took in a deep breath and held it until I thought I might cough, then expelled it in a rush. I decided to leave, walked back toward the elevator, free; he opened the door and called after me, a dark anonymous girl, "Hey!" I thought I might run, have him chase me, have a little of the Technicolor of other girls' dreams, but instead I stopped where I was, let him come up behind me. I didn't turn, and he came around in front of me; he was wearing only faded jeans, and his nipples were hard with the cold of the hallway. "Christ, Eleanor?" he said, and I nodded.

"I can't have you here in the middle of the night," he said as he pulled me into his room. With light from a curtained window, I could see that the room was like the corkboard on the door, divided down the middle, a room designed for the sureness of symmetry, but now as unbalanced as equal spaces can be, one side spare and neat, the other festering with unwashed clothes and half-eaten food and bits of anything taped to the wall. He turned on the overhead light.

"I saw girls here," I said.

He broke into a crooked grin. "It's weird hearing you talk," he said. I shrugged. "For Chrissakes, I got thrown out of the house because of you; they'll *kill* me if they find you over here."

"Your parents don't know what's going on unless somebody absolutely screams," I said.

"Yeh, and you'll probably scream," he said and laughed.

"Not if you're nice."

He looked at me, his arms folded across his chest. "You have to go back to the house," he said finally, and he sounded terribly sad. I nodded. He squinted at a clock radio across the room. I could see it easily: 1:11. Not the time I'd have guessed, but early enough. Time to weave through the streets for hours, bumping into each other and guffawing, not caring who heard us, moving on. I waited. "Really," he said after we'd stood there for a long time.

"You're not coming?" I said.

"You know I can't."

"I hope I get killed," I said quietly and walked out the door.

I was almost to the elevator. "You're not the type," he called after me, and when I was out of the building, I ran all the way back to the McCloskeys' house, happy as a thoroughly safe girl can be.

ELEVEN

When I was living in Washington, D.C., I sent Poppy a card because he was in the hospital for a duodenal ulcer that gave every impression of being a heart attack. The doctors administered nitroglycerin in the emergency room at Touro, and his heart stopped beating for a full minute. Eventually they figured out that his heart was fine; the doctor said his arteries were as free as midnight on a country highway. "Take care of that vessel you use to cart your mind around," I said in the card. "The man like to of died; the least you could of done was come home," Naomi phoned to tell me after I sent the card.

A body can empty out the mind so quickly; from Poppy's near-death I knew what's important is only to maintain the Lucite box on wheels that rolls the brain around. In spite of that belief, I could hardly resist the desire to quit thinking and let myself concentrate on sensation, good or bad. After I arrived in my hotel room in Nashville, I spent the first thirty-two hours in bed with a heating pad and room service. Pudding and pillows. Like a baby with a puddle of milk in her cheek, I lay about and dozed, shooed away the maids, told the kitchen to have my food brought in with the master key. I'd have been happy with cotton diapers. But I dreamed dreams that can only be constructed after years of living outside the cradle, following passage through all of Freud's stages that come after awareness of the mouth as the pleasure hole. I could carry a daydream just so far down into sleep, then I couldn't control it anymore; people who had no business in my dream would pop in, drag me to places I didn't want to go, so if I lay around imagining myself with Maxim Walters in a hotel room, then Patti Ann McCloskey Who-knows-what-now would come into the room, an inflated version of her childhood self, and she'd tell him what I really meant, and before I knew it I'd be with her in the house where all my dreams took place eventually, a house of unfinished walls and broken crockery with gables and dormers and scaffolding and rich women dressed in Fellini feathers who were damn angry to be there. I'd awaken with a start, sickened by being in that house again, put myself back into the hotel room, this time in one of the fine dresses I'd seen in the deep dream, and I'd be off again. After thirty hours I found I couldn't tug myself down even into a daydream, and I began planning what I was going to do. Maxim Walters was a good man who went to bed alone in strange cities and called his wife every night. I liked predictability in men, though I hated it in Poppy. It gave me control.

Midnight on Friday, I climbed out of the bed as if I'd never been hurt, washed every corner of myself, used each item in my cosmetic bag for what it was intended; nothing was optional, not tweezers, not perfume, except the contact lenses. I didn't put them in—myopia is romantic, like

Vaseline on a camera lens—I dressed in white silks, took only my room key, went down the back stairs to his room.

I rapped gently on the door, nothing happened, I thought he'd expect me, but I'd been in Nashville a while, maybe he'd given up; I knocked a little more boldly, he opened the door without asking who was there—even very religious people are not that foolhardy, he knew I was waiting—I said nothing, did nothing, relying not on word or gesture, but telling him everything; he was dressed only in boxer shorts, I looked down, he wasn't excited yet, I looked up; backlit with moonglow, his skin was pale and innocent as sweet death, as new and hairless as clean birth, surely he had never made love with purity before, any erotic moments up until now had been somewhere outside of him, his wife touching him for her own using reasons; I reached out to touch him, he backed into the room, watching me, he stopped moving, I closed the door behind me, I ran one finger from pulse point to pulse point, from his wrist, more pale than the rest of him, to his soft gentleman's bicep, to his throat, each time feeling more speed, then I placed my hand on his chest, and his heart was pounding now, sending all the blood down to a single light shaft; I ran my fingers along his cock, and he let out the purr of a safe cat, and I heard no more sound after that.

I did not want to steal his key, so instead I slipped down to the empty lobby, where I told the fuzzy clerk that I'd gone up the hall for ice and lost my key under the soft drink machine; I gave him Maxim's room number authoritatively, remembering Naomi had protected herself at that Alabama motel when I was ten by doing nothing more than holding her spine straight. The clerk gave me a duplicate, and I skittered back to the elevator, as if I were embarrassed by my clumsiness. I pushed the button for Maxim's floor instead of my own, but didn't notice until I read the numeral painted in the open elevator well. Pushing the wrong button was what I was supposed to do. I let myself into Maxim's room, grateful for the burnished aluminum door hardware that made no sound.

He was still asleep, and I looked through his things on the dresser, all neat, following the right angles of the surface like pictures on a wall, easy to put back in place, and I learned the most from his driver's license, the colors he considered his eyes and hair to be, gray and gray, so modest, his weight, 173, precise, no pride, his height, 6'1", his date of birth, July 11, 1943. I wanted to know the month and day, I didn't want to know the year; some people aren't supposed to have exact years of birth. I found a little book of addresses and phone numbers, flipped to the R page, didn't find my name, but then I went through the rest of the pages, looking for familiar names, found none; no one in New Orleans was listed at all. A date book. Monday, "phone Mrs. Rushing" with my phone number, along with "Normand Cleaners pick up" and "pay storage fee." Good, good, his wife and secretary probably thumbed through the date book, too. A clever man; "Mrs." was an excellent touch. He stirred in his sleep, but he didn't waken, and I went back through the address book, checking for numbers in Nashville. Seventeen people were listed with zip codes that started with 372. He hadn't written "Nashville, TN" on any of them, hadn't put area code 615 next to any phone numbers, as if he wanted snoops to know how easily familiar he was with the city. I found a hotel writing pad and pen on the desk, and I slowly, silently tore off the blank top sheet to take back to my room, then tore off another sheet. I didn't want to leave pen impressions on the tablet. I copied down all seventeen phone numbers, placing an asterisk next to the three names of women, check marks next to the five names of men; the rest were churches or offices. I took the two pieces of paper, left everything in his chosen order, and in my room's poor light I studied and pencil-shaded and compared with my list until I could make out the imprint of two telephone numbers on Maxim's blank piece of hotel paper. Both were on the list; neither had an asterisk or a check mark. Under one phone number was written "Sun. 10:30—lunch?" I looked in the Yellow Pages under "Churches—Methodist," found one that matched the number, jotted down the address, then lay back and waited for him to come.

Time passes slowly with wakefulness. In a doze, I can look at the clock once, then check it again soon after and find that two hours have passed. Now I could pace for a long time and see that the minute hand hadn't flicked at all. My clothes were damp with perspiration. I couldn't leave the room. I considered ordering food, filling time with food, but I looked at the room service menu and each possibility left me queasy. Oil was in everything, eggs, meats, cream for coffee, even. Dry toast, I had no spit. A Coke was a good idea. But I couldn't leave the room. I called room service, asked for a Coke. There's a soft drink machine, the woman said, helpful more than anything else. "I can't leave the room," I said. It would cost me five dollars, the woman said. "Then send six Cokes, and lots of ice, and I'll pay whatever," I said. The woman laughed.

I had brought nothing to read with me. Ever since I was ten and stopped talking for four years, reading had been a queer experience for me. When I was mute, I worked so hard on experience and word meaning that I relied heavily on television. Never mind that television often got pronunciations and emotions wrong; it caught Idi Amin and three popes in a row with dead-on, cold accuracy, and to my way of believing that meant that I could count on it for truth. Books, on the other hand, were full of open stories that teachers saw only one way. I thought J. D. Salinger wrote about nothing but loneliness, but my English teacher thought I was missing the point, gave me a C+ on my paper, and I quit getting involved with books right then and there. I'd listen for whatever the teacher believed was true about a story, and I'd write it back for her, and I'd get good, silent, acquiescent grades, and for me books became nothing more than repositories of other people's interpretations. I never let myself feel anything from a book again, approaching literature the way I approached geometry, as a puzzle to be gotten through. I still read, but only with a purpose, looking for facts. It was possible to find facts in fiction, names and appearances of characters, descriptions of Los Angeles in the thirties, Paris in the eighteenth century, and years later I could show myself to be well-read by saying as little as, "This place makes Oran look positively antiseptic," and anyone force-fed Camus in school would laugh, not with humor but with pride of recognition.

I put on the television, and it was full of the amphetamine-fueled and bloodless death of Saturday-morning fare. Finding no cable box, I leaned on the button until I reached black-and-white. An old episode of *Superman*. I loved the part where he flew through the clouds. When I was small, I fully believed he was flying. Then, before my parents were dead, someone told me he wasn't flying at all, that it was trick photography in a studio. Soon thereafter I sat in the television room in Poppy's house, my parents now dead, and squirmed around trying to figure out how the cameramen did that; after all, the cape flapped all around his body. I was living in Washington when I finally, happily decided that George Reeves stood tippy-toe on a soundstage with electric fans blowing down on him from above, his arms stretched over his head; that was the image superimposed over film of clouds. When I read in a magazine a while later that in fact George Reeves had done all his flying on his belly in front of a kinescope projection, I was furious and unbelieving, and whenever I saw the show I watched for the times when he would fly, still convinced he couldn't have laid flat. I watched *Leave It to Beaver* and *Dennis the Menace* and drank Coke and peed and listened for the phone, then I bathed and dressed and peed again and put on make-up, posing at all moments in case Maxim had tricked the desk clerk out of my key, and it was getting close to nightfall in the eastern end of the central time zone, and I began phoning his room. No answer. I was shaking with caffeine and sugar and emptiness, sensing I might never stop and I would be able to do nothing about it. I turned on the TV again, watched *Lifestyles of the Rich and Famous* until I was sobbing from hyperactivity, dialed his room again. I let it ring ten times, hung up, dialed again, let it ring twenty times, hung up, let it keep ringing nonstop, and then I couldn't hang up, couldn't leave the phone for even a second, couldn't call room service, couldn't pee, couldn't change the channel, and I lay on the bed for two hours like that, trapped now by the downspiral of metabolized sweets, a taut bladder, and a basketball game on television. All I could hear was the rhythm of the phone ringing in his room, and when he rushed in breathless and answered at two minutes to seven, I was beyond expecting anything.

"It's Eleanor," I said.

"Pardon?" He was breathing hard, hearing little.

"Eleanor. Eleanor Rushing. Can you talk?"

"No," he said, laughing, still breathless.

"I'd really like to see you." He asked me where I was. I told him I was in my room, I gave him the number, "Go up three floors and take a left when you get off the elevator." He asked me what I was doing in Nashville. "I wanted to see you," I said.

He was silent for a moment. "I don't understand," he said. I asked him to meet me for dinner. Someone was picking him up out front in ten minutes; I just happened to catch him in his room. After dinner, I said. If it's not too late, he said. It's important to me; no time's too late, I said. He said he had to be out early in the morning; any time after eleven was too late for him. Fair enough, I said, figuring he'd be out of there in ten minutes, anywhere in Nashville in thirty minutes, putting him at seven-thirty, two hours maximum for dinner; who could talk religion for more than two hours without realizing he was a fool? Talking religion was like talking to a psychiatrist; if it went on for more than forty-five minutes, the person talking would begin to hear his own words, fatuous, repeating all

the dilemmas that had stumped better and more con-
founded minds for years, and then he'd have to retreat, because nothing was going to be solved.

Maxim would be heading back to the hotel by nine-
thirty. "Fair enough," I said.

Free to leave the room, I went downstairs and ate in the
restaurant. When I love a man, the only time I come un-
tethered is when I know he's beyond reaching me. I float
loose, I'm nowhere, I have no worries. I ate alone with no
shame, staring straight ahead, not reading, not speaking,
letting the time go by slowly, as if my two hours were a
large, smooth piece of hard candy.

When he didn't call my room by ten o'clock, I phoned
him. He was already asleep by the sound of him. "Oh,
God, I forgot," he said, his voice thick and sorry. "I am so
completely exhausted."

"You sound pleased."

I could hear his rustling around, sheets tangling in the
dark, then the tiniest click of a lamp switch. I closed my
eyes. I could almost smell him, the heady musk of a man
who falls into bed without washing, the faint smell of wine,
hot bread, garlic on his breath. "This's been a good trip," he
said softly. "Worthwhile. Very worthwhile." I told him I'd be
down in a minute. "No, no," he said, we could meet for coffee. In the coffee shop downstairs, twenty minutes. He was
going to go into the bathroom and erase all those groggy
scents, he was going to splash cold water on his face, and
everything he saw would be magnified, icier. I raced for the
elevator, pressed the button; middle of the night, it took forever to come, and I took the back stairs, made it to his room
in under a minute, knocked on the door. He didn't answer

right away, and I knocked again, ready to use my key in one more minute. "Coming, coming," he said, with the perplexity of someone who's sat around all day with nothing happening, then suddenly has doorbells and phones and alarms ringing all at once. He opened the door, no chain, puzzled, flipping his bathrobe tie the way men always did in movies in the 1950s. I cocked my head at him and smiled, and he stepped aside, and I walked into the room. It smelled of sleep, of a body's sweet effluvium let loose from under covers. He closed the door, and I reached up and kissed him, full and gentle on the mouth. His robe fell open, and he was naked, and the weave of my dress was so thin and fine I could feel every rill of his body, and he was hard, and then he pulled back, throwing his robe closed, bending forward as if I wouldn't notice that he was excited. "No, this is not right, not right at all."

"You don't have to worry," I said, stepping back for him.

"I'm not worried. This isn't right. I'll have coffee with you. I said I'd have coffee with you." He was sitting down now, on the edge of the bed, knees crossed, not looking at me, and I felt sorry for him. I told him I'd call room service. "Are you crazy?" he said.

"We'll have coffee. We'll just talk and have coffee. Okay?"

"Are you crazy? I call room service in the middle of the night, and I ask for two cups of coffee, and they bring it up here, and they see me with some woman in my room, and this is where everybody stays when they come on church business; besides, who drinks coffee in the middle of the night anyway?" I laughed. "Look, I'm not joking, you need to get out of here," he said.

"There's an enormous conceit in thinking that everyone is noticing what you're doing," I said.

"In my line of work, it's no conceit. I can't even go into K&B and buy Kaopectate without a rumor flying through the church that I'm not coping." He looked up at me. "What am I telling you all this for?"

"Because you know me."

"You need to get out of here."

"We'll go for coffee," I said. I was getting what I wanted from him. Making love wasn't that important; I could lie in my bed at home alone and slip a kitchen spoon handle in me and think about him and get all the pleasure I needed. He told me he'd meet me in the coffee shop, and I told him no, that he might fall back to sleep. I said it good-naturedly, a woman who knows what a man might do in a given situation, so he let me sit on his bed while he went into the bathroom and splashed water on his face and slipped into his trousers and shirt and socks. He was hiding flesh, protecting both of us, and I appreciated that. When we walked together to the elevator, he used no stealth, a clean man, willing to walk right out there in front of bellhops, room service, assorted Methodists, and God.

Twelve

At the Paris Peace Talks a lot of the posturing and squabbling had to do with the seating configuration, and I'm surprised since that time no one's done serious studies about what happens when two or more people are positioned around a table. One of the findings would be that a square table, two and a half feet across, is perfect for ideal love between two ideal-sized people. Any smaller, and there's no wishing, no tension; any larger, and the distance is good for business, nothing more. A round table with a diameter of two and a half feet doesn't work; ambiguity lies in edging around the perimeter, with no limits. The corners are important for holding onto.

Maxim and I sat at a two-and-a-half-foot-square butcher-block table in the coffee shop until almost midnight. He drank decaffeinated coffee with cream; pale, kind, mother's breast coffee. I drank five cups of regular coffee, black, and it went through me with no impact, no shakiness, no terror of plummeting from a high place.

"So tell me what's on your mind," he said after we'd given our order. His voice was like that of a doctor who's been wakened in the night when he's on call.

"Don't be ministerial with me," I said, pleasant, too.

"I thought you said you wanted to talk to me."

"Yes."

He said nothing, waiting for me, waiting for the coffee, pouring in cream and stirring, looking at me. "How are your meetings going?" I said finally.

"Good, good, very good. Worthwhile, I think." I asked him what they were about, and he looked at me queerly, as if he expected me to change the subject. "Missionary work," he said with finality. "I knew it," I said, loud enough for our waitress to look up from the copy of *Us* she was reading in the smoking section. No one else was in the place, not even a cashier, and she was chain-smoking and drinking a can of Tab. Maxim tilted his head to the side, questioning, more for the waitress's benefit than for mine. "I *knew* you were generous."

He was pleased, hearing compliments, without a public, in the middle of the night, and he blushed, making me glad he knew when to be flawed.

"No, seriously. The first day I saw you, I knew you knew things no one understood. But the way you *said* them! You can put yourself on other people's level. I swear, you could get anyone to believe anything."

"Thank you." He didn't look at me, but concentrated instead on stirring extra cream into his coffee. Counter-clockwise, white blending into almost white, filling the cup to the brim; he took a sip, added another tiny carafe of cream; eventually he would have all cream with a molecule of coffee. He looked up and said, "But I'm not out to convince anyone of anything."

"I find that hard to believe."

"Then I'll have to convince you," he said, and smiled.

From then on, I had no doubts. There across the table, he was full of absolute joy, the sort that only comes when a person discovers he loves someone for the purest familiarity, of seeing himself in another, of having struggled against others' plans so he could be ready for her. He told me about the missionary program as if he were filling me in on matters I fully understood, this business of going to the hurting corners of the world and being good, expecting nothing, not counting heads for God. "There's a message in that," I said.

"Precisely." He ordered two more cups of coffee, calling the waitress over as if we were ready for champagne now.

"I love you," I said after a good silence.

"That happens." His voice was low; he was studying his spoon as if he were going to have to pick it out of a lineup and lives depended on his getting it right. He looked at me. "It'll be all right," he said. I memorized his face, open and true, for dreams.

I said, "You're being pastoral again."

He furrowed his brow, pretending he didn't understand, and I laughed until I choked. Anyone else, anyplace else, and I'd have thought him foolish and been embarrassed for him; because he was so out of character I found him funny. He tried not to crack a smile, to make the extra point of going deadpan, but he couldn't help it, watching my snuffling little fits; I drank water and lost control, dribbled water out my nose, laughed with that feeling of primordial summers spent filling my sinuses from clear pools, and he broke into a self-conscious closed-lip smile. "Can you believe this?" I said, cocking my head to the side and laughing some more.

"Frankly, no." The smile was gone; he was being funny again.

I tipped my coffee cup toward him, a salute. "And what do you think is the nature of love in the western world?" I felt exquisite. "I believe de Rougemont."

"I believe you've drunk too much coffee."

I held the cup right in front of his eyes, my hand as steady as that of a model pointing a pencil at a computer chip on television. "I suppose I could interpolate a great deal into that answer, go on about external stimuli in a postindustrial age, but I think you're just trying to get out of answering the question."

"It's about one o'clock in the morning," he said.

"It's 11:44."

"Close enough."

"Not really."

Now that he knew what time it was, he began thinking about what time it was. "You want to go to bed," I said.

"Yes," he said. "Well, no. Well, yes, I need to get some *sleep*. I'm not up here for the fun of it."

"You knew I'd come up."

"No."

"You thought I might come up."

"I don't even know who you are."

"Like hell you don't."

He signaled the waitress, asked for the check. "I'll take that," I said. "No, you won't," he said. He snatched the check away from the waitress, who was standing with fist on hip, as if this was what she expected from having to work the night shift. He handed her a ten-dollar bill and bolted out of the coffee shop. "Hey, thanks, padre," she called after him, and I ran behind him. I had twenty-three seconds in the elevator, assuming it didn't stop at any floors, that was plenty of time; the doors closed on us and he backed into a corner. People only back into corners in elevators when they expect to be crowded. I moved forward toward him, leaned up against him, kissed him full on the mouth, coffee on coffee, and the elevator opened on his floor and I didn't let him move, pressed my floor; by the time the door opened again (eleven seconds) he was sodden with me and I took him by the hand to my room and this time he made love to me (three times before 2:23), white light and sweet spit and come and I looked at the clock before I fell asleep with him still inside me. When I awakened at 9:30, he was gone.

Without getting out of bed, I phoned his room, let it ring twelve times. I figured he was in the shower. I waited five minutes, tried again, waited ten minutes, and then he picked up. "Yes?" "Hi," I said. "I can't talk to you right now." "You have a meeting at 10:30," I said. "I have church at 10:30." "Ah," I said, "I should've known."

"You seem to know a great deal."

"I know everything," I said, then hung up, gently, seductively.

I was in the front pew when he walked in with the minister and took a seat at the side of the pulpit. His eyes scanned the crowd, looking for me, and he found me quickly, knowing to start at the front. I smiled at him, but he looked away, not wanting to let on that we were together. I could imagine how news traveled among people with the same large pool of beliefs; some woman in the congregation would have gone to college at Newcomb, been paired off with a roommate the way colleges did thirty years ago, protecting Jews from Catholics and Catholics from Protestants, and everybody from African girls, and now that woman would have children at Tulane and a few old friends in New Orleans, and of course she'd know what church her friends attended, and before the morning was out she'd be on the phone saying, Did you know your Dr. Walters showed up in Nashville with this gorgeous woman; is he divorced or what? I saw no sense in letting word get back to Maxim's wife until he was ready to tell her himself, and I was willing at that stage to go slowly, to let him leave his family without scandal among small-minded people who'd punish him out of pure envy.

He didn't participate in the service. The minister, Dr. Don Robertson, introduced him, then launched into a sermon about missions, about doing good for its own sake, and now Maxim sat still and straight in an intricately carved chair at the back of the podium, an example of how humble a good person can be, his eloquence greater than Dr. Robertson's, Maxim's full absence of color—white hair, white skin, white eyes—a quiet rebuke to all those women out there in hot red nubby-wool suits and thick aquamarine-and-gold jewelry. A phony stained-glass window filled the entire wall behind the pulpit, full of fast-food restaurant colors, Jesus on the cross; even Jesus's skin wasn't absolutely white but Crayola flesh, and I tried to imagine a window with the same picture lines drawn in lead, the spaces all beveled clear glass, full of prisms, sun colors but no others. I thought maybe when I got home I'd take a class in stained glass, making ever-larger panels, if not in flawless clear glass, then in single colors, all translucent white, or maybe stygian red. I stared at Maxim, hearing little of what the minister was saying, imagining what Maxim would say when I brought him to my studio in the garage and unveiled my crystal Jesus. At the end of the service, I moved up next to him in the receiving line. He whispered to me that I should get into the line, but I reached across him and offered my hand to Dr. Robertson, so Maxim told him I was a major contributor at Uptown United Methodist Church in New Orleans, and Dr. Robertson said, "Well, naturally you'll join us for lunch," and Maxim said, "Oh, no, she has an afternoon flight," and I said, "Oh, I'll make it all right, I'd be delighted." I took my place between the two men, and as each person passed through the receiving line I said, "I'm Eleanor Rushing from New Orleans, and wasn't that a wonderful sermon," and I could tell Maxim heard me, having known all along I'd say the right thing.

It happens everywhere, at church, at lectures by famous doctors, at autograph parties for big authors, that the first and last to leave are the old ladies. The ones who leave first are busy spreading silly chores out across their days, and they will live forever, but the ones who linger have illusions about powerful people, and they slip away from reality so fast that parts of their bodies quit working, one by one, until they die looking perfectly healthy on the outside. At Dr. Robertson's church, three women, all with deep rouge tugging at their cheeks, stood to the side, jockeying with one another for last place, waiting to talk to him. They figured if they nattered at him long enough, they'd become part of his life so in turn they'd become holier and more interesting than their friends. Maxim and I stood and smiled, him with the familiarity of experience, me with a great deal of knowledge of human behavior. To the women, we looked as if we were standing by with awe and envy, but Maxim and I had a private joke, and we watched until we, too, had these women as parts of our lives. When Dr. Robertson went for his coat, Maxim motioned me to the side, and I thought he might kiss me there in the dark church. A church is an excellent place for making love, full of filtered light and warm air that rises high. But Maxim said, "I think it would be an excellent idea if you went back to the hotel now." I reminded him that I'd accepted a lunch invitation; to leave now would make everyone talk about me. "No one will talk about you; no one knows you're invited except Don, and Don's the one who invited you to begin with." I told him I'd seen him tell his wife to set an extra place, and Maxim asked me how I knew what he'd said. "I know wives; I know what men say to wives, too," I said, looking him straight in the eye. "Jesus Christ," he said, right there inside the church. His face was absolutely white, and I patted his arm. "Trust me," I said.

"I don't like this," he said.

I spent what seemed like hours in the kitchen with Juliana Robertson. I'd never been in a kitchen with a white woman before. I'd never seen a white woman's hands touch raw meat. I'd never seen a white woman wash out a deep pot that had cruciferous vegetable scum around the edges. I was used to seeing brown arms elbow-deep in flour, I was used to seeing ashy dark hands with nails yellow from bad nutrition and mean detergents. But Juliana had slender, busy hands with pink-polished nails, and I leaned against a counter and talked to her and paid attention, for the first time, to the miracle of putting a crunchy crust on a piece of chicken.

"I've been to New Orleans once," she said.

"I don't remember seeing you in church," I said.

"Oh, I went down there back when everybody wanted to be 'Easy Rider,' you know, back before I signed on to behave in public." She laughed, and slogged a raw chicken breast in a bowl of egg, then took the eggy flesh in her fingers, dropped it in a bagful of cornmeal, picked up the whole nasty mess, and slid it into a skillet of oil.

"You did drugs?" I said, knowing the answer; people who did drugs and gave birth to babies could do things other people couldn't do. They had nothing left to be squeamish about. Dancing around the kitchen with egg and cornmeal paste all over your hands is nothing compared to sucking your own blood back into a hypodermic needle or lying on a table with your legs in the air while half a dozen people stand around and watch your private parts rip open. "I smoked dope. I suppose anyone born between World War II and the Korean War smoked dope; no big deal."

Nineteen-forty-three: Maxim was born before the cutoff. Juliana made it sound like an absolute rule; I'd have to ask him. "Even your husband?" I said.

"Even Don," she said, her voice wistful. "But to tell you the truth, I think he was more philosophical about it than anything else. You know, trying to decide what's truly bad; it seemed like an evil you could talk about afterward, and not be damned ashamed of yourself." She giggled.

"I've never done any mind-altering drugs," I said, not bragging, just stating a fact.

"Trust me, it doesn't alter your mind. Maybe it kills off a few brain cells, but who needs more brain cells?"

"You still do it?" I had this image of the Robertsons and Maxim, people of the sixties, figuring things out when I was newborn, getting together now to smoke marijuana and get over having signed on to be more virtuous than everyone else.

"Lord, no," she said. "The day Don walked into divinity school, that's the day he gave up vice." She giggled again, as if she and her husband broke certain archaic Tennessee laws every night in their own bedroom.

Having seen the ladies who wanted so badly to touch Don Robertson, I knew Juliana didn't want her old stories to get out. I asked her why she would tell me these things. She shrugged.

"You've got worse secrets," she said.

I couldn't help smiling and turning a proud pink. Something about having others notice what passes between you and a man strengthens it, as if the pleasure he takes in you is so enormous that no one can miss seeing it. At least no one lusty and sensitive can. "It's pretty obvious?" I whispered. She nodded her head vigorously. "You're not the first person I've had stand up in this kitchen trying to pass herself off as a pillar of the church."

"Thanks."

"Hey, ease up, I'm only kidding." She rinsed her hands off, wiped them on a paper towel, took me by the arm. I looked at the clock over the stove. I'd known this woman for forty-five minutes. She was getting cornmeal and sal-

monella on my white dress, but I didn't try to pull away.
She cocked her head to the side. "You don't know too
many women, do you?" she said.

"Oh, I know enough." From television, books, and sitting quietly, I knew how women behaved. "I think I prefer
men, nothing personal." I smiled at her, embarrassed.

"Big mistake," she said, smiling back.

I thought about that for a while, and I watched her as
she moved around the kitchen. She could have been blind:
she knew where things were without looking, pots, pep-
pers. I couldn't see the point of it, spending an hour fixing
food that no one tasted, then cleaning up the mess afterward, only to be back where she was when she started. It
was one thing to get paid for doing that sort of work, and
surely Naomi was grateful, unencumbered with the brain-
fill of reading, to know enough by heart to earn money fixing food and cleaning floors and sheets. I'd spent so much
time trailing after Naomi, watching her smooth rhythms,
thrilled when she cleaned a piece of glass perfectly, that I
knew it took a lot of remembering to do that sort of work.
I was lulled, too, by watching Juliana, though I didn't trust
she'd dice an onion or wipe a counter with the precision I'd
grown to expect from Naomi. "Want something to do?"
she said, holding a stalk of celery toward me with one
hand, a knife with the other. I looked at her blankly. She
lay the celery down on a cutting board, made two cuts
from its head to its toe, then chopped all along its length,
every quarter of an inch, letting three fine cubes fall with
each chop. I took it from her and began to work, and soon
I felt the way I'd felt in Dr. Vigilante's office; with a
bracelet on my wrist, I'd be so involved in twisting that

bracelet and studying its links that I'd think anything. "You can't worship women," I said.

"Of course not. They're too damn familiar. Men are like mutants that you want to put on altars and dance around naked and wave torches at."

I laughed. "Not very many men. Men like Maxim. Men like Don, maybe, but, really, not a lot of men."

She pointed toward the living room where the two men were. "Those two fart and ooze ear wax like everybody else. You're bound to have illusions at this point. Sorry, but I see it all the time."

"You see idiots fawning and fantasizing. What I have with him is something altogether different. On a higher plane, you know. Spiritual almost, just this perfect connection. I don't think I've ever had anyone so completely in love with me before. See, maybe the difference is that you're not talking about women that make men fall in love with *them;* you're just talking about wishful thinking. I understand Maxim, and he knows it."

"How long have you been together?"

I knew to the day how long it had been since the City Council meeting, but I knew better than to measure anything out in days. "Months."

"I rest my case."

I finished the stalk of celery I was working on, then quietly laid the knife down on the cutting board and left the kitchen, shaking celery water from my hands onto the floor as I walked. Let her clean it up.

When we left late that afternoon, Juliana pulled me into the kitchen. She handed me a piece of paper with her name and two phone numbers on it. One had (h) written next to it, the other (w). "Sorry about what I said," she said. "Call me if you ever need to talk."

I took the paper, smiled as if she were handing me a diploma, shook her hand, let her hug me. I'd have to find someone who could tell me what (h) and (w) meant.

When Don dropped us off at the hotel, Maxim sat in the car and told me to go up to my room, that he wanted to finish up business with Don. I waited in the lobby, and he came in a minute later, saw me, walked right past me toward the elevator. I followed him in. He looked at me for my floor number, and I pushed the button myself, amused because the only other person in the elevator was a boy about ten, too young to reach conclusions or judgments. Maxim put his hand out to push the button for his floor, but I beat him to it. The door closed, and he said, "From here on out, I don't want to see you, understand? If you're on my flight, don't get in my taxi. Don't sit in my row. And for God's sake stay away from me when we get to New Orleans." I looked at the boy, and as I expected he was paying no attention. The door opened at his floor.

I hadn't done a thing wrong at the Robertsons'. The meal had gone flawlessly; for Don I'd shown myself to be curious and innovative about the church, a woman with deep pockets to whom Maxim naturally would give prestige; that was the way rich people with nothing else to do were always treated by non-profit organizations. If Maxim was distancing himself now, it was from nerves. Maybe his wife was coming to the airport. "I understand," I said before he got off the elevator.

Thirteen

People don't change after they achieve full adult height. That's why, when Ellis Ryan stood up to speak before the City Council, I knew before he opened his mouth he would build what he said on six layers of meaning, though I hadn't seen him since I was in high school.

The Thursday after the trip to Nashville, I was curious whether Maxim was going to speak in front of the City Council this time. I phoned the church and said I was the clerk of council, wanted to get all speakers lined up for a long docket; when was Dr. Walters planning on coming down? "Aw, honey," the secretary said, "he got his appointment book with him. That gonna be a problem for you?" She was so round-toned, polite, I could tell she was one of those old people who, if she ever heard a white person's voice emanating from City Hall, would do anything in her limited power to be encouraging, as if Mayor Morrison might come back from his 1964 plane crash. I told her no, we could squeeze him in; no need to ask him, no need for me to check back, I was just trying to get as many speakers set up as possible.

I'd take my chances, since I wasn't going to miss the meeting anyway. The council was having public hearings on the Mardi Gras ordinance no one honestly wanted. It called for desegregating the carnival krewes, opening them all up to Jews, blacks, and women. Never mind about Zulu and Venus, none of the complainers cared about getting rich white men into places they'd never go. What they wanted was to break the hard line drawn around the fancy clubs, a line that gave New Orleans its distinction as a fully preserved colonial civilization. In truth, the flat-out hatred of whites by blacks kept the city alive and hopping with excitement, and no one wanted to give it up. Certainly not the whites, probably not the blacks. New Orleans never had exploded the way other cities had, and I remember my mother saying that after Martin Luther King was shot Naomi refused to go down to Canal Street to protest. "'Shoot, it too damn *hot*,'" my mother would mimic her, and after that, whenever she wasn't in the mood for something, my mother'd say, "Shoot, it too damn *hot*," then rip back with laughter. Maxim would have ten words that would cut through everyone else's shyness about the matter, and I couldn't wait. Maxim didn't appear, but Ellis Ryan did.

Ellis was a Deke with John Paul McCloskey, and now he was an attorney who showed up in group shots on the society page during debutante season, smirking to show he knew he was foolish. What had startled me about Ellis when I was younger was that he was not wonderful looking but a young Morley Safer, with droopiness in his face before age could take a toll. His lips were thin, and his chin was narrow, and he felt free to rush Deke and get accepted.

Living so close to a rich boys' university, I'd always assumed that fraternities judged by looks the way the SS had, taking as their own those with square jaws and light eyes and mesomorph bodies, sloughing off for the ashbin anyone who fell short of standard. But Ellis Ryan had had money and Dekes in his family forever, and Ellis Ryan had grown up thinking he could reject people as easily as the next guy. I thought his hangdog little face gave him a quiet advantage, of seeing the possibility of being hurt. I knew he didn't care if more blacks and Jews and anyone else who'd grown up with black hair and smelly rituals joined his krewe. But his talent for talking in layers tended to put him in charge of things, and here he was, speaking on behalf of men who'd always had strong jaws and rich daddies and definitely wanted nothing ever to change. For them, Ellis was trying to make a new club, a men's club, of the City Council, created ad hoc then forgotten, a club that pulled into a tight little circle and excluded women, thereby setting up the means to exclude everybody. It didn't bother him a bit that the council was now chock-a-block with women, tough, biting women who made the foolish, lisping men on the council sound half beaten to death every time they talked. I always had liked Ellis because he could be such a thoroughly bad boy. He had that Morley Safer glint in his eye, and no matter how sympathetic I might have been to the person he was making squirm, I had to enjoy him, the way everyone enjoyed Morley Safer.

He walked up to the microphone, gave his name, his occupation, attorney, then let full silence fall before he made his opening. Copying Maxim. "Let's talk bathrooms," he said, and the chambers popped and tingled with the laughter that comes when people sit next to other people they'd like to beat the shit out of on the street. "We'll start with the easy ones. You ever been on a Mardi Gras float?" he said to the council, most of whom grew up excluded from being on Mardi Gras floats. They stared blankly at him. None of them was on the phone today; this was too interesting. "Well, you know as well as I do that there's more beer than water on a Mardi Gras float." Pause. "At least when we pull out of the den." Punch, a break of laughter that all came from the same place. He was going to make the chambers one big fraternity smoker, taking everyone back to poo-poo jokes, the fetid mucilage that held together most associations: everyone was once four years old. "No, seriously," he said, letting us all know he respected the rhythms of Jewish comedians. "We've got one john on a float. We've got one dressing room at the den. You can be black or white or Jewish or Italian, and it doesn't matter." I could picture the images in the back of his mind, of circumcised Jewish knishes and uncircumcised brown jelly rolls; he was probably among those who'd mixed up Rex to satisfy their curiosity about what other kinds of men looked like at the urinal. "I think you'll find that the true problem with this ordinance is that you want to put women in men's organizations. That's a fundamental invasion of privacy. I'm not speaking as an attorney, I'm speaking as a person." I laughed, expecting all the self-bashing lawyers to get the joke, but mine was the only voice hacking through the chambers.

Of course he came nowhere near where I was sitting when he finished talking. I didn't have spiritual connectedness with him, because all that power was directed toward Maxim; that was what had drawn Maxim to come sit next to me the first time I'd seen him in a City Council meeting. If I concentrated hard enough, I could pull him downtown from wherever he was, but I preferred to stockpile the energy that drew him for the truly important times. Having him come speak in a public place wasn't of any particular value to me that day. If he'd shown up it would have been good, but I preferred the times when we met in places he chose. He knew I went to City Council meetings, and the idea of him following me to one without my having wished him there didn't excite me.

As soon as Ellis sat down, I got up and walked across the front of the chambers and took the seat next to his. People did that all the time, showing off their loyalties by scurrying around like upright-walking cockroaches, wriggling and leaning over and whispering to an important person long enough for everyone to notice, then sliding into place as if they were the most lithe, smooth creatures ever to participate in city government. I marched over, said nothing until I sat down, not even excusing myself for having to step over him. "Hello, Ellis Ryan," I said low. He turned, moved his head back and forth, like a radiologist reading film over a twenty-five-watt bulb.

"Oh, Christ, Eleanor Rushing," he said pleasantly, glancing down at my ring finger. "Yep, Eleanor Rushing."

Ellis was the boy who took me in for my abortion when I was fifteen. He went to Woolworth's on Oak Street and bought me a fake engagement ring, he told me how to make myself up to look twenty-one, he pretended he was my husband when I went into the Delta Women's Clinic on a Thursday morning when I was supposed to be in school and he was supposed to be in Introduction to Logic. His was an act of charity, of community service, like other fraternity boys' can-shakes on neutral grounds.

John Paul didn't plan to move into the Deke house until his sophomore year, but he spent so much time over there his freshman year that I could usually find him. It was easy enough to walk over to Henry Clay Avenue on a Saturday night after Poppy was asleep and walk right in the front door of the fraternity house if a lot of music was blasting out onto the street. It was possible in a crowd to appear to have come with any boy, to drift and drink and pretend to take a toke off someone's joint, and the first few times I went over there I kept myself hidden in motion, watching John Paul, seeing how awkward he was. He preferred being alone, but he hadn't lived long enough to realize the difference between what was common and what was comfortable. I watched him drink beer as if he were a chemist who'd found a compound to transform him into a man of pure magic, eternal and powerful; he tipped his head back, poured, and waited, over and over again, until he no longer knew where his feet were going, and the stumbling around gave him permission to say anything he felt like. The more he drank, the more dangerous the people were that he spoke to: first quiet, sober young boys, then thick-necked man-boys, then nervous thin girls, and then I watched to see what scared him the most. Tall girls with sun-lined dark hair, girls who'd have played lacrosse if they'd been born in the East; instead they drove red MGs for power. I wasn't surprised, because I'd been following him around the campus after I got out of school in the afternoons, and

I'd seen what girls he'd look after with longing as he walked from class, as he wandered around the bookstore fingering jiggers and decals and key rings, all with TULANE on them, souvenirs a boy might take back home to Texas. Those girls were like me, and it wasn't a matter of falling in love with the familiar; he was searching for me directly.

Since that time I've occasionally found myself at parties. Having arrived alone, I've had the choice of busying myself at eating and drinking, or finding someone to talk to, or moving from room to room as if any second I would find the person I was looking for. Instead I've remembered that I didn't feel lonely following John Paul, having something to do. At any party where I have no one to talk to now, I single out someone and move along the edges, smoothly, smiling, feeling good, learning things, watching. Quite a lot of what I know about the way people act comes from this effort of making myself busy, finding some bit of understanding to take home afterward. It makes little difference whether some woman has taken my arm and confided that "he's only three, and he gets the most adorable little erections!" or instead has told another woman, holding *her* arm, while I've listened from six feet away, my back turned, taking it all in, smiling in someone else's direction.

"I know you, right?" Ellis said, coming up next to me in a thicket of tall boys.

"You're Ellis, but you don't know me." I'd learned most of the older boys' names, because the freshmen got such a terrific kick out of bellowing out their names from across the room, as if that meant full acceptance.

"True," he said, and that was the first time I noticed he liked himself a lot for a droopy-looking boy. He asked me whom I'd come with. I told him John Paul McCloskey, knowing when a lie is too hard to trace. "Makes sense," he said.

"What's that supposed to mean?" I was tall, but he was taller, and I had to shout, concentrating so much on being heard that for a moment I quit being a watcher.

"You're exact opposites." He offered me a joint, and I pretended to inhale slowly, taking in as much cool air around the tip of the cigarette as I could. I sipped beer the same way, looking good, looking old, keeping control.

"You don't know a thing about me," I said.

"Oh, I think I do." His eyebrows danced, and I believed him.

"Tell me one thing. Like tell me my *name*." I was trembling, wanting to be caught out by someone so much more clever than I was that I'd have no comebacks at all.

"Christ, who cares what your name is? You're completely inscrutable, and J.P.'s completely transparent; that's the sort of stuff I *know*."

I'd only recently learned what "inscrutable" meant, but he sounded as if he'd been tossing the word around for years until it was soft and malleable, and I was impressed. "I think you're going to be a lawyer," I said.

"I *know* I'm going to be a lawyer."

Back to watching, right then I saw John Paul coming toward us, and I pushed away like a swimmer on the last lap, knowing only how I had to move, nothing more. It was late, and he wasn't very sure on his feet, and I reached him before he could come close enough for Ellis to hear anything he said, and I pivoted him with the grace that drunks sometimes have and led him away toward the front porch. He moved as if he'd been expecting me. "Eleanor?" he said happily when we were out on the porch.

It was the time of year when oak pollen covered every-thing, making cars and benches dirty and ghostly, and lazy yardmen realized the grass was growing again and came around in their trucks. Out on the porch the air was cool and clean and smelled of grass and rich dirt churned up by lawn edgers. I stood away from John Paul, who reeked of beer and nerves. I folded my arms across my chest and nodded, and he said, "I keep thinking I see you here."

"I'm here." I wasn't sure how much people hallucinated when they were drunk and stoned. One night I'd walked past a boy who was sitting on the bottom step of the stair-case, and I heard him tell a girl as he handed her a joint, "I can look at my foot and I can make it as big as this room." She had sipped at the cigarette, waiting for everything to dissolve around her, and I had walked on, certain I wasn't ready to know how limited the possibilities were. I wanted to think that right now I could pretend to drink and smoke and be wild and hazy as the rest of them, while keeping perfect clarity, keeping, too, a chance for no con-trol at a later time.

"I mean, I think I see you all the time. Here, you know, at parties, or maybe I saw you at one party a dozen times, I don't know, but then I think I see you everywhere else, you know?"

"A lot of girls look like me."

"Yeh, yeh," he said, half satisfied, and he leaned back against the rail as if it would hold him. I watched, wanting to see if he'd fall over softly into the camellia bushes, doing the damage I expected of boys his age. The rail held with his weight, accustomed to brutal boys, and he pushed himself forward, leaving a good sneaker print. "No, I think I see you. For all I know, I want to see you."

"I'm here," I said, feeling dramatic as hell.

"What're you doing here?" His eyes were closed, and he was rocking back and forth, with nerve that comes of not looking another person in the eye.

"I'm with you." You can tell a dog, a drunk, and yourself just about anything, Naomi once told me.

"No, you're not," John Paul said. He was grinning, and then a look of horror came over his face, and he turned so pale I could see it, even with no more light than was filtered in from street lamps, the moon, and smoky rooms. His hands flew up in front of him, as if he suddenly found himself in pitch-black space, he reeled back, and then he threw up all over me. I'd never seen anyone else throw up before, except on television, and I'd always thought it was a noisy process; I certainly had thought I'd been audible all through my house the few times it had happened to me. But John Paul made no sound, as if he were a full two-liter plastic bottle that someone had held upright and squeezed with all his might. Nothing came up but beer and bile, covering the front of my clothes, neatly missing John Paul, whose head cleared as fast as his stomach, giving him the reflexes to jump back two feet before it all splashed from my dress onto the porch.

Anywhere else, someone would have scurried out with mops and sympathy, but no one noticed me or the porch. John Paul led me upstairs, careful not to come too close, leaving the puddle for someone else to discover, probably tomorrow.

From the moment we reached the top of the stairs we were in the process of making love. Like sleepwalkers, moving without thinking because everything about us smelled so bad, we didn't think about modesty, and fully sober I let him lead me into a big institutional bathroom and deftly remove my clothes, holding hems with two fingers as if they were soaked with an indelible stain that would show up on his hands for days afterward. His hands were warm, and he washed me off with a soapy cloth, a cloth he found on a shelf with a price tag straight-pinned to its edge, some boy's mama's idea of guaranteed good hygiene. "I'm really sorry," he said every few minutes, running the cloth over the outer contours, thigh, hipbone, breast, where a sopping dress would cling, and then he found me a Fruit Of The Loom undershirt, size XL, and a pair of boxer shorts, size 32, both wrapped in plastic, probably bought by the same mama who bought the washcloth, and he helped me step into the pants, gently lowered the shirt over my head, as if he were my older brother, my lover, my sick daddy. He saw the goose bumps on my skin, could have seen my nipples shriveled up like golden raisins if he'd had the nerve to look, and he found me a blanket, this time an item well used, with the musk left from a boy who probably woke up in the night from time to time sweating and flopping, and shocked by a mean hard-on. I sat on a bed with only a bottom sheet, clean for the occasion, and it occurred to me that if I had to do my own chores I'd never use a top sheet, either. I folded myself up under the blanket, trying to get warm, lay down in a little ball, and John Paul turned off the overhead light and tiptoed out of the room.

I saw no clock in the room, and I had left my watch in the bathroom, and it didn't matter what time I was home as long as it was before first light, so I had no means of telling how long he was gone. I fell asleep the way I can in a strange room. Naomi had always said that was the way I managed around strangers when I was small, falling asleep so I wouldn't be so lonely for my mother, even before she died. "Babies do that, you babysit a child's never seen you before, I guarantee you that child going to fall asleep just to spite his mama when she come back," Naomi said. I thought that when I fell asleep in strange places I went down to some special animal level, dreaming the simplest dreams, but hearing everything, picking up on every movement, ready to strike out in self-defense. John Paul came into the room, smelling sharply of Listerine and softly of Camay, and he slipped into the cot with me, and I knew he was there, and I remember everything, his pink soap-bar slipping between my legs, up inside me, lathering on me, leaving another puddle for tomorrow. I wakened every hour, and he was still beside me.

When I thought morning was close and John Paul was gone, I slid out of the bed and took a trench coat from the closet. I couldn't find my shoes or my watch, and I let myself out of the house barefoot. Two boys were sleeping downstairs on their backs, arms flung wide, unafraid that some bird would come down and eat their entrails, and they didn't stir as I passed, didn't move as the front door clicked open. I found ELLIS RYAN IV on a nametape in the coat when I woke up in my room at home at ten minutes before noon.

FOURTEEN

Ellis asked me what I was doing at the City Council meeting. I said, "I come to *every* one; if you did, too, you'd know that."

"I know better than to ask why." He wasn't whispering, though the chamber was fairly quiet; he wanted to prove something to whoever listened, perhaps that he knew me well. I couldn't blame him, because he was approaching that age when people would give him a second look if they saw him with a pretty woman, wondering what he had to make up for his droopy face. I gave him a broad, public smile.

The women on the council were bickering among themselves, poles apart, three of them not caring whether they were left out as women, long having had ways of breaking down back doors or going through front doors on the arms of powerful men. The other two wanted to kick down all doors and let the tired, huddled masses rush through, happily imagining black boys with faces dusted in powder riding as pages on the king's float like gilded lawn jockeys, Jewish girls with red fingernails curtseying at the balls, slipping and letting out raucous laughs. The women on the council talked through their teeth, grinding the enamel on their molars, their voices loud and full of furious politeness, and I said to Ellis, "I've always dreamed of a catfight up there." He let out a whoop of laughter, and the chambers fell silent for a moment. My councilwoman, who was talking at the time, cast her eyes in his direction and said, "Ellis Ryan, I'd expect better of you," and Ellis held up his hand, palm toward her apologetically.

When the council took a break for lunch, Ellis stood up over me, asked me if I wanted to go get something to eat. I told him I was expecting someone, and I stood up and looked around the room, though I'd have sensed if Maxim had walked in. It was part instinct, part his godliness that made people turn, as if the vacuum made by his purity would suck them in. He's not here yet, I told Ellis, and Ellis scanned the room as if he could tell who was missing.

It was ten minutes to three, the only part of day when it was possible to eat a meal at Galatoire's without standing in line or arriving unfashionably early, and Ellis wanted to go there. My father had liked Galatoire's so much he'd eaten lunch there four times a week, reducing himself to eating plain lamb chops after he realized too much good, complicated food would make it impossible to appreciate. I'd been to Galatoire's for lunch when I had my eleventh birthday and Poppy had some notion I'd start talking if I had crème caramel with a candle in it. Even the waiters were embarrassed by my silence, and after that the only times I ate at Galatoire's were when I decided to go out for dinner alone for quiet celebrations of anniversaries known only to me. I matched the date, December 22, against my chronologies, finding a meaning. With Christmas coming so soon, it was an easy time to check back on, because people can always remember what they did, day by day, over any given Christmas holiday, and I've lived few enough years to recall them all. I'd always considered December 21 the anniversary of the moment I crashed through the soundproof shield of mutism, because it was the winter solstice, and I'd been looking at the sky with John Paul; it was fitting, especially with the palindrome of numbers, 1–2–2–1, and I went to Galatoire's ten years later to mark the anniversary. But technically I'd gone downstairs after midnight, gone outside with John Paul after midnight had passed in every U.S. time zone, so the true anniversary, of the beginning with John Paul, the end of being safely silent, was today.

"Did you ever know I stopped talking when I was ten?" I said as I hurried to keep pace with Ellis, a man who probably only slowed down when he was billing a spoiled client. I'd thought we were going to ride, but I liked moving at an important clip on foot through the business district.

"Everybody knew that; it's sort of the only interesting story J. P. ever told, and I think he told it about a thousand times." Ellis began to recount the stories boys told to bond in meanness, one freshman's tales of a Cajun roommate who had a harelip and went to Mass every morning. "Want to go to Mass?" Ellis said "Mass" with a whiny puff of air straight out his nose, and I could imagine boys sitting around perfecting their ability to sound as if they'd been born with a cruel natural slice through their faces. "You ever meet Reefer from Roanoke?" I shook my head no; it was a name anyone would remember. We were stopped at a crosswalk on Canal Street and all the other people were dodging across, but Ellis waited, not out of respect for the lights but to get his story out whole. "Reef swore he backed over a drunk with his car six times in a parking lot and got away with it." I gave Ellis an oh-please look. "The dead guy was white," he said, as if that made a difference; it was the attitude I'd noticed in myself when I'd seen cowboy movies and been unfazed when the cowboys were shot as long as the horses were unhurt.

"I think I started talking on this day. Today. December 22."

"So talk."

I laughed and couldn't think of a thing to say. We opened the door to Galatoire's, and the smell of hot French bread and rich people wafted out, giving me a cradling sense. A number of tables were empty at that time of the afternoon, and we were led to one that was right next to the wall. Those mirrors on almost every wall above the wainscoting give you nowhere in the restaurant to completely avoid seeing yourself. At the tables set right against the mirrors, part of the meal would have to do with watching your companion, aware of himself, then watching yourself, aware of yourself. I liked the way I looked in these particular mirrors, because their slight smokiness gave me a more ethereal appearance, flawless and very cold.

"McCloskey never came back across the parish line after you got him," Ellis said, putting back a dry martini and chuckling. I'd ordered a Pimm's cup, but I was sipping, as if I were back at the Deke house, keeping control.

"I didn't get him."

"You *got* him all right," Ellis said.

"He got *me*. Jesus, you tell a guy he's gotten you pregnant, and you've gone through this terrible *ordeal*, and you're still bleeding like crazy, and he goes running to his parents, and the next thing you know they've shipped him off to Massachusetts or somewhere and even your best friend won't give you his address." Patti Ann and the boys in Deke and everyone at Tulane closed ranks around John Paul after I called his mother to try to get her to punish him for what he'd done to me. I had to write a letter to him in care of Tulane, let it get forwarded, have it sent back with a notation in his handwriting "return to sender," so trite I almost lost interest, and then I knew he was in Worcester, and I narrowed down the search until I found him at the fraternity house at WPI up there. He'd been expecting me, because no one would call him to the phone even when I waited a week and called back and said I was Patti Ann, his sister, and there was a terrible emergency. I planned to fly up there over Easter, then I decided a boy who wrote "return to sender" on a letter was a boy who got all his emotional cues from pop music and I wasn't going to let him love me anymore.

"I paid the clinic, what more'd you want?" Ellis said.

"You were a great social chairman," I said.

He began running his finger around the edge of his glass, as if he wondered whether a person could leave Galatoire's after a single drink, then whether I was someone who stumbled into enough legal complications to be worth cultivating. "I paid because I felt bad for you. And so maybe I'd get my coat back." He smiled, watching himself for style and technique in the mirror out of the corner of his eye. He was pleased with his performance.

"I could've paid for it myself, you know; it was the principle of the thing. They ripped my guts out. John Paul should've felt something, too."

Ellis tilted his head to the side. "They didn't rip your guts out." His voice was gentle, as if he were afraid of what he was saying.

"How the hell do you know? Christ, they put you on this table, and they give you this paper bag to breathe in and out of, like it's going to do anyone any good to hyperventilate, and then they rip and scrape and suck until you think you are absolutely going to fucking die." I talked behind my hand, not wanting to make a scene.

"You didn't have an abortion."

I studied him to see if he was joking, but he was looking me straight in the eye. "Ellis, for God's sake, you were there."

He shrugged. "Look, let's drop this." Typical male behavior, according to everything I'd ever read; go just so far with something, then run like hell.

I shook my head no. "I was pregnant, Ellis, I mean very pregnant, throwing up all day, you know, the kind of pregnant that doesn't go away without doing something about it. You don't see me with a child, right?" The baby would have been in middle school, almost as old as I was when I was pregnant, and I wondered if I'd have been dead when she was ten. Of course it was a girl. "What do you think, I took your two hundred dollars, slipped out the backdoor, and waited two hours?"

"I really don't want to go into this."

I caught my reflection in the mirror; my face was pink, and I looked sort of romantic. I half hoped someone was watching. "You're accusing me of stealing your two hundred dollars. You talk to me." I couldn't figure out why I was so angry, because two hundred dollars wasn't a big deal; in fact, pulling off a prank like that was a fine stunt, one I wouldn't mind being wrongfully accused of.

"I'm not saying you took my money. The clinic took my money, and you went in there, but you didn't have an abortion. You weren't fucking pregnant."

I felt like crying, remembering how I sat in the tiny dressing room with other women, each taking her turn, each coming back with tears streaming and a big smile, willing to tell everything to the ones still waiting, half out of bravery, half out of the meanness that comes on days when you've been badly hurt. "It is like the worst cramps you ever had multiplied by a thousand; you feel like they are going to suck your brains out," one woman said, and then she sat down on a bench and put her head in her hands and cried so piteously that the rest of us forgot to be frightened for a while. The doctor had been African, needing little English, and like the rest I held that paper sack over my mouth with one hand, squeezing the social worker's hand with the other, and the pain was so intense I never forgot it; I bled all afternoon, afraid I was going to die.

Ellis reached over and patted my hand. "You don't remember what happened, do you?"

"I remember everything."

The waiter came, and I ordered Chicken Clemenceau, the only thing on the menu I'd ever tried. My parents always ordered it for me when I was small, protein and potatoes, and it never occurred to me to order anything else.

"Eleanor, they came out into the waiting room and got me."

"No, they didn't."

"Yes, they did." He signaled for another martini, and when it came he drank it down in one gulp. "Christ, it was embarrassing. If you want to know the truth, I was a fucking virgin when I was twenty-two years old, and these people come out and they say, 'Are you this girl's boyfriend?' And I say, 'I'm her husband,' remember, because we figured you'd pass for older if we pretended we were married? And they took me into this little office, and this woman who is as officious and sanctimonious as hell starts saying, 'Well, did you consummate your marriage?' and I didn't know what that meant, for Chrissakes, and she says, 'I mean, did you achieve penetration?' and I may be as cool as the next twenty-two-year-old guy, but in front of this woman I am about to die of humiliation, and I say, 'Of course. She's pregnant, isn't she?' And the woman says, 'No, she's not. In fact, she's a fucking virgin.' Well, she didn't say 'fucking,' but she wanted to."

With one hard tug, I swept the linen cloth off the table, with the thick water pitcher and glasses and ice and silverware and breadcrumbs and butter pats; I saw the olive from Ellis's martini fly across the restaurant. "You are not funny, Ellis," I screamed. And I walked out of Galatoire's.

FIFTEEN

When I got home that evening, Naomi had left me a message: "L.S. 593–0841." Shaky, round handwriting; handwriting is only as complicated as the last year a person has spent in school. New Orleans housekeepers have a style, as identifiable as that of eastern boarding-school girls, and Naomi had it. I dialed the number, curious, and no one answered, so I waited until Naomi came in the next morning and asked her. "He say his name L.S." Ellis? "That what I *told* you." I didn't phone back; it was then I realized Ellis probably had been in love with me for all those years, and he was jealous of John Paul. If he knew what I had with Maxim, he might do something crazy; Maxim wasn't hiding out in the empty middle of Massa-chusetts but was standing up innocently in front of a hun-dred-fifty people every Sunday, unprotected, easily assassinated. I tried to remember whether I'd given Ellis any indication of whom I was waiting for at the City Council meeting. I'd said only that I was waiting for some-one. And Ellis hadn't seen me at meetings before, so he hadn't witnessed the moment when Maxim and I were to-gether the first time. Still, Ellis was a crafty man, an attorney who knew how to find queer fragments of information, using computers and yellowed archives and detectives, and that morning I phoned Maxim to warn him.

"Please don't phone me here," he said when he picked up the line. I'd refused to give my name to the woman who answered, and all I'd said to him was, "Hello, Maxim."

"I think you're in grave danger," I said. He didn't say anything. "Someone knows what's going on between us, and you need to be very careful."

"Nothing is going on between us."

"Is someone with you there in your office?"

"No." That meant yes.

"Maybe it'd be better if we talked in person."

He was silent for a moment, sifting through all the homilies and histories of divinity school, looking for that nugget of psychology that had been thrown in to keep the church competitive in the marketplace. "Why don't you come in to my office?" he said finally. I told him to name a time, and he flipped some pages noisily, suggested Tuesday morning at ten. I told him he might be in danger up at the pulpit Sunday, especially with the Christmas crowds; maybe we should meet today. Or possibly tomorrow, Saturday. No one would be around on Saturday. "Meeting a woman alone at the church on a Saturday wouldn't look very proper," he said, and I told him I understood, that I'd come in this afternoon. One o'clock, he said, and I knew from the comics that secretaries always take long lunches on Fridays before three-day holidays.

When I arrived, a party filled the office, and the warm air smelled of cinnamon and pine and rose-based perfume. All of the women wore little plastic corsages with holly leaves and jingle bells and tiny reindeer and peppermint canes, the kind of items they sell at the checkout counter at Walgreen's at every season, pumpkins, turkeys, and pastel eggs; I'd assumed only kindergarten teachers wore them. They were all dressed in red or green, their bubble rumps stuffed into skirts worn only once a year. Whenever I saw women like that, I tried to wonder what their bridal announcement pictures had looked like in the *Times-Picayune*, because such women always were married, yet I'd only see a fat bride about every month or so. Even now, when a lot of black girls were putting their pictures in the paper. A table alongside the wall was covered by a paper tablecloth with garlands of green drawn along the edge in dye that would fade and run if someone spilled punch on it. And from end to end was set enough food for ten times as many people, platters piled high with chocolate doberge squares and ham finger sandwiches, bowls brimming with cashews and red and green M&M's, a tray covered with cheddar cubes and saltine crackers, a punch bowl with Hawaiian Punch and lime sherbet. A prom spread. It gave off no smell; it was possible not to be tempted by it if a person didn't look at it. But the women and two custodians stood around the table as if it were a shrine, as if they were waiting for visual cues, going back and forth between sweet and salt with no worry of what was stuck in their teeth.

Maxim wasn't among them, and I waited for someone to notice me. A tiny woman who was chubbier by far than the rest was upending her punch glass, wattle pulsing, and I came into her line of vision. When she asked me if she could help me I recognized her voice as that of the person who'd answered the phone earlier. I told her who I was, that

I had an appointment with Dr. Walters, and she offered me food. She had half a sandwich stuffed into her cheek balloon, and she was working hard at being polite when she wanted to be let loose at the table like an untrained puppy, and I found her quite winning. I smiled and took a handful of cashews, and she poured me a glass of punch, assuming salted nuts would do to me what they did to her. She swallowed her cheekful and told me I could go in, just knock, and I popped a nut into my mouth, in so doing giving her permission to take a handful of M&M's and fling them into her mouth, dropping none. I told her again that I was Eleanor Rushing, asked her name. Mary Cook, she told me, with chocolate on her teeth. I pictured her with a white apron, a chef's hat, a spoon and ladle, a great commercial smile, her own logo, and she must have read my mind because she said, "I know, I know," and rolled her eyes.

I closed Maxim's door tight behind me, then pulled a small wrapped gift out of my shoulder bag. He said he couldn't take a gift from me, and I told him sure he could, probably half of his congregation gave him presents for Christmas, right? Especially the generous, heavy supporters, right? "Tax breaks," I said, "nothing unto Caesar. Right?" and he smiled.

It was a Rolex wristwatch, and he put it down with two fingers, as if he'd just unwrapped two open vials of potassium cyanide and sulfuric acid. "You know there's not a thing on earth I can do with this," he said.

"Tell everyone it's a fake."

"Isn't that sort of self-defeating?"

"It keeps excellent time. People never know if your watch is keeping time or not; nobody's going to say, 'Hey, for a fake that thing sure keeps perfect time.' See, I'm giving you a private luxury. I'll be the only one who'll know. And you."

"I don't want to know. I don't want to have a Rolex. I don't particularly *approve* of people who have Rolexes."

I was wearing a Movado myself; he wasn't insulting me. "So sell it, give the money to charity, make of it whatever you want, it's yours."

"The spring raffle! You'll get complete tax credit, of course."

"No."

He gave me a questioning look.

"Just no."

He closed the box and tried to hand it to me, but I pushed it away. "It's a lovely gift, thank you," he said.

I still had the cashews and punch cup in one hand, and so far nothing had spilled, and I felt as if I were armed. Once a person has left Galatoire's with glass shattered and silver nicked and water all over the floor runners, it's easy to consider smaller messes, red punch all over sermons and newsletters. I put the punch cup down gently on his desk, sure he knew an act of kindness and control when he saw one, and I put the handful of warm nuts into my mouth, leaving my hand oily and salty. I could still do private, unseen damage with fingerprints.

As I sat and chewed the nuts into a sweet paste, I stared at Maxim; he said nothing, and I could hear happy fat noises outside, noises that meant no one was listening to us. I stood up, feeling better to the point of good now, and I walked over to where he was sitting. I put my hand on his shoulder, and he rolled back a few inches in his desk chair.

"I'm just concerned," I said. He rolled back farther, so he was looking up at me as if from a wheelchair. I leaned over a bit so the front of my blouse gaped enough to show a rim of slip lace, and he rolled back still a few more inches, a man who knew how to line things up so people watching him were sure he only saw what he was supposed to see. I sat on the edge of the desk, like the long-legged women in trouble who turn to hardboiled detectives on AMC, and I began to tell him about the danger he was in. "Ellis has been in love with me since we were kids, I know that now; he acted like an insane person yesterday at Galatoire's. He made me so thoroughly furious I dumped the table on him."

"At Galatoire's?"

He was jealous, let him be jealous. I smiled. "At *Galatoire's*. I'm sure the waiter called the police; it'll be a long time before Ellis tries to eat in there again. I know he called me afterward, so he didn't go to jail or anything, which means he's quite free to wreak any havoc he wants."

"Ellis. Ellis Ryan?" He was almost whispering, as if his mouth were too dry to talk.

Adrenaline shot straight to my scalp, and I could imagine the first quarter of an inch of my hair stood straight up. "You've heard from him already?"

Maxim shook his head no. "He's in the congregation. With a wife and three children."

"Oh, God," I said. "He could come into church anytime, and no one would suspect him, you know."

"Suspect him of what? Of being a sincere worshiper?" Maxim laughed, pleased with himself.

I said, "This is serious." I wanted to slap him or kiss him so hard my teeth would tear his lip.

"Ellis Ryan is a respected attorney. And not the passionate type at all, from what I've seen," he said. "Doesn't he do tax law?"

I shrugged. A lawyer was a lawyer, filling a social slot. Unless I needed him for some reason. "You don't know much about human nature, do you?" I tried to say it lightly, not wanting to hurt Maxim's feelings. That was supposed to be part of his job. "Ellis has been a good boy all his life, even when he was in trouble he was a good boy. Now he can't take it anymore. Like you."

Maxim stood up. "This is going too far."

I stood up, too. "I don't think you understand. I don't think you understand at all." I needed to protect him and couldn't. It was a feeling I'd never had before, certainly never seen in anyone else. When I was small, I was always in the presence of an adult, never scraped or bruised, always cooperating in my own safety, and then suddenly I could run around in the dark and no one tried to stop me. The only people who protected me were paid to do so, and if they wanted to take their pleasure from me, touching or taunting, that was quite fine, no problem, no one ever knew, and I certainly didn't tell, because then Poppy might have clamped down on my safety, investing more money in it, and I'd have lost all liberty.

"You need to go now," Maxim said softly.

"No." I rubbed my eyes red; what would the people outside think of him, sending a woman out brokenhearted at Christmas? I'd tell them I lived alone, and they'd wonder more.

A frog chorus of laughter at nothing came through the door, happy people in a closed circle, and I gave Maxim a look of pure unhappiness. "This isn't a time of year to be so terribly, terribly sad," he said softly, and though I hadn't cried from feeling since I was ten, I could force tears easily. I made the noises of pain I'd allowed when I was a mute child; I'd gone on and on, and Naomi had said, "Little racket as you ever make, you think I'd be wanting this, but you don't shut up, I'm going to smack you."

"Shh, shh, stop, stop," Maxim said, cradling my head against his chest, muffling the sadness for everyone, and I put my arms around his waist, and then the door opened behind me, and I didn't look up, but I could feel him waving the person out with great urgency. Whoever it was must have backed out like a British servant; it was over in seconds, but the kind of seconds that everyone picks apart, like the Zapruder film.

"Well, now I've gone and done it," I said, stepping back. "Now everyone will know."

"There's nothing between us. I haven't even done wrong in my dreams."

"What about Nashville?"

"What *about* Nashville?"

"Maxim, no one is listening to us."

"Nothing happened in Nashville that I have any reason to keep secret."

"Even Juliana Robertson knows."

"What?" He grabbed my shoulder hard, and I put my hand on top of his hand. He pulled back.

"Remember when we had Sunday dinner at their house? How I stayed out in the kitchen with her for all that time? She was one sharp lady, and she said she could tell that we were lovers the minute she saw us walk into her house."

"We are not lovers." He was using that voice that plays to the acoustics, calling God and everyone else who's awake. I looked in the direction of the door, expecting the silence of eavesdroppers, but the party was in full din, with what sounded to me like a number of conversations that start once everyone's sure no one's left out.

"No one's listening," I said.

"You're not listening!"

"Look, I don't think you have to worry. Women come in here all the time and pour their hearts out, right? I've been to the church, I've made a donation to the church, as far as anyone knows, I'm just here for counseling. Okay?"

He let out a little cough and shook his head; his eyes were closed, and I wanted him to feel better, so I reached up and kissed him. "No!" he said.

"All right, all right," I whispered, and then I put my finger to my lips, began to tiptoe out of the office. "I'll watch Ellis for you, don't worry," I said, wondering as I spoke how I'd manage to do that. I wasn't used to being invisible. He nodded, with relief. I put the Rolex in my purse; he saw me do so and said nothing.

I singled out Mary Cook when I was leaving. I took a handful of sandwiches, wrapped them in a paper napkin, knowing Naomi liked pig meat, knowing, too, that Mary would be flattered. I told her I'd like to do some volunteer work around the office; she would not resist a skinny woman who ate ham sandwiches. Mary was happy and trusting, as if the mayonnaise had half stopped the blood flow to her brain. Probably she'd have been willing to let a rheumy-eyed derelict come in and lick stamps for her.

"Sure, baby," she said, hugging me so I had to bend over. "You have a Merry Christmas."

I was home in ten minutes, and Naomi already had taken a message from Maxim. She'd written nothing down; this was the sort of message that made her too curious to do anything more than worry at it like a bad shoelace knot. "I know Dr. Walters no doctor, but he sound like this some sort of *emergency*."

I stood right there in the kitchen and used the sky blue rotary phone that had been on the wall since before I'd moved in. I knew the number by heart, knew the pattern, two long spins, high numbers, then a one, a short chop, back and forth, but I missed the rhythm, hung up, tried again, missed twice, my hand was trembling, and I had to give Naomi the number, ask her to dial. She got the wrong number. "You did that on purpose," I said. "What I'm going to get a wrong number on purpose for, you want to tell me that?" she said and marched out of the kitchen, though she had a pot of water on the stove that was about a quarter of a minute from a rolling boil. I dialed slowly, smoothly. It rang more than ten times, and I thought maybe I'd gotten Naomi's wrong number. When someone picked up, though, I could hear the same timbre of holy merrymaking I'd heard outside Maxim's door, and I asked for Dr. Walters. It was Mary, but she wasn't in the spirit to recognize voices right then.

"I understand you want to volunteer at the church," Maxim said when he came on the line. I told him yes, I thought it was an excellent idea, though I apologized for having come up with it on the spur of the moment like that. "I don't want you working here," he said. I asked him how we were ever going to be together, knowing no one was listening in on the extension, or I'd have heard party fragments, like bits of confetti and popped balloons, coming over the lines. It wasn't possible for him to tell, though, because the same noise was coming through his door, into his other ear. "I know you're doing your best," I said, and he was silent. "I'll wait, you know," I said softly, then hung up, letting him go back to the same sort of Christmas he'd been having for so long that if someone so much as substituted Triscuits for saltines from one year to the next he'd have been perplexed. I understood his wife and Mary Cook, their hungry mouths needing him, Jack Sprat, to feed them, keep them in patterns, but he was going to break out eventually. What he felt for me was too strong.

Sixteen

I hated obstacles. Let them stand. Anyone who didn't know me would have said I was spoiled; a born prettiness and too much money gave me an attitude that everything I wanted would come easily or it wasn't worth having. But I had decided obstacles were nature's way of saying I wasn't supposed to have something good at that very second—appreciation for music, shoes that came in my size, a belief in God; why struggle? Instead I saved up all the energies and poisons most people have to expend every day striving for what they want and shouldn't naturally have at the moment. And when it absolutely came time for me to have to have time with Maxim, I didn't need to make any philosophical shifts. All my life I'd been stockpiling my share of drivenness, so each obstacle was no more than a bit of gravel in the road.

I wanted to be with him every minute of the day. We were druidic like-spirit forces, drawn together, not needing to touch. It didn't matter whether we spoke or even whether he knew I was around. That is the substance of love, merging experience so there are no secrets, no mysteries, no differences. If a fire truck roared up St. Charles

Avenue at 2:15 in the afternoon, and I was in the church, and Maxim was in the church, then we had the identical moment, of interrupting and listening, waiting to see how long it took for the siren to fade, waiting, too, to see if it stopped out front of the church or maybe in the next block, then speculating for a few seconds on what changes that might make in our lives. If a custodian ripped up the wandering Jew in the side bed of the church because he thought it was a weed, Maxim would have had a pang of regret, a moment of annoyance, a flit of guilt over berating a person with few advantages and little knowledge. I'd have seen the ragged and ripped purple leaves, piled on the sidewalk and already darkening in the sun, and I'd have had the exact same reactions as Maxim. For that I needed to be around him, so I stood behind an oleander across from the church as if waiting for a ride on the side street, until I saw him leave, went in and told Mary Cook I was going to help around the office: Dr. Walters had said he needed me for more important business, but I had argued with him, told him being around the church gave me serenity, and he had allowed as how stuffing envelopes could be a very relaxing way to spend free time, so here I was. Mary had put me to work, almost apologetically, giving me donation thank-you cards to type on an old portable, and when Maxim had come back in two hours it was too late for him to do anything but enjoy my quiet presence; I didn't look up when he walked in, showing him no one would ever know he loved me, and from then on I was a terrific source of joy to Mary Cook, who hated repetitive chores. I kept her busy with keeping me busy, so after a while I was weeding the mailing list for the first

time in ten years, looking for dead people, then I was creating new files, streamlining billing, learning everything
there was to know about the church, though I never let on
that any of the millions of particles of information stuck
with me. I even knew Maxim's salary, and that is one of the
most powerful facts to share with another person.

On regular, ordinary days, I had a child's sort of peace,
mother nearby, no fretting, no fear, but when I was away
from him at night I had a child's sort of nightmares, too.
Maxim went home at suppertime, and the sky was already
dark, so close past the solstice, and all I could do was
hover. I found a perfect place in his backyard, an open
shed, where no one would go at night or in winter. From
there I could see into the kitchen, through archways, almost clear to the picture window at the front of the house.
I couldn't see him at all times, but he had to move back
and forth across the light field, and I knew what he was
doing almost every minute. If he went out after dinner, I
could move silently up the side alley before he was in his
car, hide behind tangles of mean pyracantha, and I knew
by the way he dressed whether he was out for the evening
or off to Walgreen's or the Winn-Dixie; I could tell where
he'd been, too, by what he returned with, a single plastic
sack from the drugstore, a centerpiece of balloons from a
testimonial dinner. I was having chances to move around
the church office more, seeing schedules no one thought
meant a thing to me, and often I knew where he was going
at night before he left. I was compiling statistics and facts
so that, soon, I'd be able to get about more freely. I knew,
for instance, that on Tuesday nights he went to the drugstore, as if someone in his house had a prescription that

had to be filled once a week. The nights were cold and wet, and I put a blanket, a thermos of hot chocolate, a flashlight, and a magazine in my car each morning so I could be comfortable in the shed until Maxim went upstairs to sleep. On nights when he had nowhere fancy to go, he went up to bed at precisely 9:45. The lights stayed on downstairs; I could see his wife cleaning corners of the kitchen, moving slowly, staying up much later than he did, and I was pleased. When I knew how firmly the pattern was set, I began going home at 9:45, going up straight to bed with the must and dirt of Maxim's small city square still on me. A child with a transitional object, sucking in the scent, I could fall asleep with no sense that he was any distance away from me.

The shed was full of garden things that gathered cobwebs while waiting for good intentions, a sack of rich dirt emptied by about a cupful, large clay pots for plants that were still sitting crimped at the roots in smaller pots, trowels and rakes someone had used once before hiring a black man to do the hot work. I saw through the kitchen window, and recalled from the night of my accident, that the Walters house was full of plants of sentimental value. Many still had foil and ribbons on them, their leaves sparse and dwarfed and brown. Gifts that in any other house would be trashed for neatness or kept for superstition; here they were kept out of politeness and reverence. Mrs. Walters watered them every Wednesday night, holding the plastic watering can over each plant for a count of five; never mind the difference between begonias and bromeliads, all plants were equal in the sight of God. It wasn't even a fair way to treat children and parishioners.

That Wednesday night, Maxim had just gone up to bed, and I was thinking about gathering up my things as soon as the upstairs light went out. I saw Mrs. Walters knock over a blue-and-white ceramic pot that a few weeks ago had been brimming with narcissus and now held nothing but long brown leaves bent with their own weight. There was no reason for her to have that particular accident, except perhaps that she was being too careful: I think she was *supposed* to have that accident right then. She screamed "shit" so loudly I wanted to hush her from back of the property, then she was crashing out into the yard, running for a new container as if she'd just broken a full goldfish bowl. I had no time to move, no time to react, and when she saw me in the dim light with my drinking cup and blanket, she judged only by the contours and went hustling back into the house. "Maxim!" I could hear her across the yard. "There's a homeless person living in our shed. Maxim!" He came lumbering down the steps, and I heard him say, "Well, I'm sure he's harmless," using his pulpit voice, straining for the damned in the last pew, and I bolted. I left behind my things, an L. L. Bean 100 per-cent wool blanket, a stainless steel vacuum bottle, a copy of *Vanity Fair*, and a Coleman lantern. When I reached my car, I began to laugh, all by myself. Maxim would sit up with his wife tonight, trying to figure out where they got a homeless person with such refined taste. Only when I tried to put the key into the ignition did I realize I was trembling so badly I couldn't do it, not even with two hands.

I went back the next night. Maxim hadn't mentioned his yard squatter when he was at the office, but he rarely spoke of personal things there, and when he did he might talk about seeing *Unsolved Mysteries* on television, he might tell everyone he had drunk a quart of water for hiccups, reminding them that in some ways he was ordinary, but not in very many ways. It took me weeks to learn his wife's name was not Margaret, as I'd read in the back issues of the *Times-Picayune*, but Peg, a nickname used for so long it appeared on computerized mailing lists. I found it in the files, time and time again; Maxim never referred to her by name. I hated Peg, a fat-headmistress, skinny-fishwife name. To my knowledge, Maxim never called her by name at home, even when they were alone; he simply made certain they were in the same room, with no possibility he was speaking to someone else, then he addressed her, as if she were a mother-in-law about whom he'd never made a decision.

I tiptoed into the Walterses' yard right after Maxim went home, figuring they'd wait until the same time as last night to trap me. And there in the shed was a shrine to charity. The floor had been swept and mopped, and my blanket now covered a small, clean mattress. A tray with sandwiches and fruit sat on top of the blanket, and when I opened my thermos I found it was filled with hot café au lait. A Bible lay open to Luke 14:7, with a Post-it note designating chapter and verse in case I had any doubt, and the *Vanity Fair* was nowhere to be seen. A humane trap, like the ones animal-rights people use to catch mice and then set them free in the park.

I pitied Maxim's wife so much that I sat down on the mattress and ached for her. She couldn't help being simple, it wasn't her fault she'd been a phase in his life, filling in the time when what he wanted was a firm, sexless woman who'd never behave badly but also would never have a penetrating thought. When he was young, spirituality probably had meant no more than mindless faith, having so little insight that one believed whatever was said with the most emphasis and propaganda. Later on, when Maxim began to learn that only some of us are spiritual beings, with powers to tap into one another, he began to see his wife differently, an uncomprehending little person, much like the small boy I once heard say to his mother in a McKenzie's bakery shop, "I don't believe in God, but I believe in Jesus." The mother ordered a dozen Prussians and asked him offhandedly, "And then who is Jesus?" "Jesus is God's baby brother," the boy announced, and while the salesclerk scowled the mother laughed with delight.

I sat on the mattress for quite a while, thinking about nothing, seeing little activity in the house, then I decided to drink the coffee. I knew nothing was poisoned, because they weren't that sort of people, even if she knew I was the one in the yard. I took a sip; it wasn't coffee with hot milk but rather a thin instant half whitened with Coffee-mate, sweetened with sugar. I checked the sandwiches. White bread, that was all right, she used white bread for her family, but between the slices was bologna red with nitrites, slathered with warm yellow mayonnaise. The banana was getting black, smelling like anesthetic, singing to fruit flies, the apples small and mealy. This was jail food, Ozanam Inn food, the world's leftovers, served up in the name of kindness but ready for the Dumpster. Who did she think she was? I thought about trashing the place, pouring coffee onto the mattress, smearing the walls with mashed banana so the shed would smell like garbage for months, but there was no dignity in that, so I packed up my blanket and lantern, discreetly emptied the vacuum bottle into a wormy camellia, and marched up the alleyway, lantern lit and swinging, footsteps reverberating, and only when I was too close to the front to turn around did I realize a scuffling had begun inside the house, of people who'd been waiting halfheartedly for the mousetrap to snap, and now were determined to come running to see while the body was still warm and the blood was still fresh.

I kept walking with the boldness of ownership, never considered turning back or running. When I reached the front of the property, the Walterses' front door swung open, and Maxim and his wife pressed out onto the porch. I noticed that the wife turned around and waved someone else back into the house, the boy Max, probably, as if she were protecting him from seeing terrible ugliness. I stopped where I was. "Oh, my God," Maxim said when he saw me. His wife looked more wounded than surprised, as if she'd given alms to a rich man and hadn't yet heard of a parable saying that was not only perfectly all right but in fact worthy of a cautionary tale. She looked toward Maxim for an explanation, but he had nothing to say. "We have to be together," I said to her. She moved a bit closer to her husband, though it wasn't a conscious act, and said to me that she didn't understand. "Maybe you'd better ask him," I said softly.

"I don't know her, I mean, I know who she is, she comes to the church all the time, but I don't *know* her," Maxim said, pretending to act as if I were crazy. I wasn't hurt. Maxim was growing toward a level of honesty that had to invoke cruelty, but he wasn't there yet. That was one of the reasons he needed me so much, to teach him how to tell the truth everywhere, not just in front of great crowds of people. If he could stand up in front of the City Council or the full congregation of Uptown United Methodist Church, not needing to look anyone directly in the eye, and say, You are all missing the point, then he was a man who'd one day tell truths that listeners, standing alone in front of him, couldn't squirm out of, couldn't pretend were for the man three rows back.

"Maxim'll tell you in his own sweet time," I said to his wife.

"Tell me what?" I thought I caught a tremor in her voice. A woman has to be very deluded not to notice when a man doesn't love her anymore. She may not be able to pull the fact all the way up to spoken words, or idle thoughts, or even deep night bad dreams, but when she starts to get close to hearing it from somewhere else, all her ductless glands start secreting green fluids into her body; she shakes and fiddles so she can't ignore the fact anymore.

Maxim pulled her over to the other side of the porch and began whispering. Her hip went up, and her hand went on it, and he kept talking, and then her hand fell to her side, and I began walking toward the porch steps. She turned to face me, and she folded her arms across her chest, and I was at a small disadvantage, carrying a heavy blanket and a lantern and a thermos tucked under my arm. "What're you telling her?" I said, not accusing, just asking.

"I'll be happy to tell you the same thing. I'd like for you to stay away from here."

"You believe him, don't you?" I said softly to his wife. She nodded vigorously. "Well, I'm not going to call him a liar. He's not a liar, he's a serious truth-teller. I guess you've known that for a long time, though maybe you're so used to it you don't remember anymore. But if Maxim doesn't want me here, it only means he wants me somewhere else. We're lovers, you know."

She looked at him, and he shook his head. "We are *not* lovers. I don't know what this woman's problem is, but, Peg, I'm telling you the truth. I don't even know her." Peg.

"How do you explain Nashville?" I was close to screaming. "You remember he went to Nashville? You want to know what hotel he stayed in? You want to know what room he stayed in? You want to know whom he made love to in that room? Just ask. Just ask!"

"I mean it, Maxim," his wife said.

"Miss Rushing. You have to the count of ten."

"Miss Rushing? Miss Rushing?" This was a lie. This was not his name for me.

"You are trespassing. *Miss Rushing*," he said, and I could tell now he wasn't really calling me that. I felt an instant calm, and I gathered up my things so I wouldn't trip on the blanket and started to leave. "It's all right," I told him.

SEVENTEEN

It wasn't a déjà vu, a sense of everything around me be-coming so familiar that each detail was expected, ren-dered in the brightest colors, each word as known as a film script. Rather, it was a mix of disparate elements that can come together only in a dream, a place of such safety it is possible to touch villains and perhaps even kiss them. When I arrived at the church office that morning, I hadn't yet spoken a word to anyone, so I was as full of sleep as I might have been if I'd walked around for two hours with my eyes closed. Maxim's door was open, and as I passed I looked in out of the corner of my eye, and while I couldn't see Maxim, I could see Ellis. A dream with my dead mother in front of my English classroom, a dream with Saddam Hussein crawling gently into my bed in Poppy's house, smelling faintly of smoke and nothing else. The right person in the wrong place, the wrong person in the right place, either way I lay through dreams with little more than a smirk of curiosity. I'd often wondered, upon waking from such a dream, whether I'd like to have had a camera trained on me while I slept, and I considered vol-unteering for one of the labs at the medical school, but I figured that in a sterile setting I'd have white dreams, no facial expressions.

Mary Cook saw me come in, and she told me to go into Dr. Walters's office. She had the smallest hint of a smile, but that, too, would be expected in a dream.

I walked in like a moving spectator, unafraid for myself because the two men had nothing to fear from each other. Maxim motioned for me to sit down, and when I did Ellis pushed the door closed. Slow motion, dream motion, my senses were dulled, as if I were on a landing jet, breathing used-up air, hearing only through eardrums thick with pounding. I looked from one to the other, and neither spoke, and time didn't pass, and then Maxim said, "I think you know we have a problem here."

I looked toward Ellis, smiling, expecting him to give me a godless sort of look, to try to draw me into a conspiracy against soft men. But he had no expression at all, and he said, "We think you need help, Eleanor." Like a schoolboy, without the taunting in his voice, saying, You need help, when in truth he meant, I can't figure you out because you are so much more complex than I ever will be that I am afraid of you, I'm afraid of what your existence means about my own simplicity. "You don't need to feel threatened by me," I said to Ellis.

"*I'm* threatened by you," Maxim said to me, then he turned to Ellis. "She's positively everywhere. Night before last, Peg goes out into the yard, and there this woman is, in the *dark*, scares my poor wife half to death." As if he hadn't tried to tell this story to Ellis only moments before; why else was Ellis there? Maxim was a teacher, enunciating all a child's offenses over her head at some other adult.

"Don't treat me like a child."

"She throws everything off a table at Galatoire's. Can you imagine, Galatoire's?" Ellis said. "Naturally they didn't make me pay for the breakage, but only because they felt so sorry for me. Thank God it was the middle of the afternoon. Almost no one was in there. Just tourists, or I'd have had to leave town."

"Like you've never cut up in public before," I said, giving Maxim a hopeful look. This was going to take a long time and, with a triangle, allegiances were going to keep shifting. "When he was in college . . . "

"Acting out in public is half of what you do in *college*," Maxim said, and Ellis nodded eagerly.

"I never acted out in college," I said. It was true. I couldn't recall speaking to anyone in class. I lived at home, sat through lectures, answered questions, wrote papers, took tests, even went to the library, but I had no audience, knew no one by first name, had nothing I cared about shallowly enough to make a spectacle over.

"Maybe that's your trouble," Ellis said, and Maxim scowled at him. "Sorry," he said to Maxim.

"We'd like you to get psychiatric help," Maxim said.

At that the dream state dissolved into red. "You can't do this. You've committed adultery, and I haven't. Look it up, you're both so goddamn legalistic. *You're* the one who's broken a rule, and now you're going to walk around and pretend I'm crazy so you'll get out of trouble. This is something straight out of Kafka." College was fresh on my mind, classroom pain, learning of spiraling helplessness and afraid to volunteer a word. "Look, Maxim, you knew as well as I did that your wife was going to find out what was going on. You knew it! But did you get ready for that possibility? No. You got caught, and now you're trying to look so innocent." My voice softened all of a sudden. "What you've got to realize, you *are* innocent. We were supposed to be together. We're going to be together. But if you go running around trying to tell everybody I've done something wrong, you're admitting that *you've* done something wrong. And you haven't. Really, you haven't. Just take it easy, Maxim, I told you it'd be all right."

I didn't look at Ellis because I couldn't let myself be bothered by his feelings. He didn't deserve much from me, ganging up like that, believing in the power of men who stuck together. He wasn't going to make me love him by allying himself with a very strong man, chorusing in that I was crazy, trying to force me to depend on him. A man who would take a girl to an abortion clinic, then tell her almost fifteen years later it never happened, was a man who'd tell a woman they were going for a drive in the country, then leave her in a hospital with electrode burns on her temples.

"You have to stay away from here," Maxim said.

"Could I talk to you alone?" I said.

Maxim shook his head no, without hesitating, without looking toward Ellis for a legal opinion. "Fine," I said. "Just fine." I turned to Ellis. "Maxim and I are lovers." Ellis didn't flinch; he was a man who spent time in courtrooms and over card tables, where any expression could cost him. "We met in the fall, and we both knew from the very first second. Now Maxim's an important man, he's in the limelight, people are always watching him, judging him; they're just waiting for him to slip up." Unlike Ellis, interchangeable with a thousand other attorneys, leaving a space on a letterhead when he dies, a space a typesetter can fix. "So we have to be discreet, you know?" I was burning up, like a tattered-poor child taunted on the playground, wanting to spit back. Ellis gave me a blank look. He couldn't read my mind.

"Ellis is here to help you," Maxim said. I told him I didn't want him here, and Ellis stood up, shrugged, and slipped out the door. Now we were getting somewhere; maybe I'd seen Ellis as meaner than he was. I stood up, too, ready to lock the door behind him, and Maxim moved quickly between me and the door, hands splayed across the exit behind him as if he had suction spiders on his fingertips. "You have to get it into your head, we are not lovers."

"He can't hear you."

"He's right outside the door." Maxim suddenly had a funny look on his face, the kind a speaker gets when he loses his place, finding himself so deep in a daydream that he hears only the fact of his silence. I waited, he said nothing, trying to get back in his mind to the point where he became lost. "I'm telling you that because I don't want you to think he's not listening," Maxim said. I smiled at him. "Oh, God," he said, "everything is so terribly twisted." I shook my head no. He shook his head yes. I wanted this to be the time when he told the private truth to someone besides me. "Tell me so Ellis can hear it," I said. "That's all you have to do. Maybe he'll hear it, and maybe he won't. But *you'll* hear it, and you'll believe you have a witness, and then everything will be all right. I promise you. Everything will be all right." I was happy, with no catch in my voice, no change in my color, just happy.

Maxim said nothing, instead opened the door, and Ellis was standing outside. They changed places, Maxim walking out and Ellis walking in, moving their bodies with athletic swagger, as if they were team members who'd been coached to act as if they were equal, secretly believing otherwise.

"Okay, look," Ellis said, positioning himself behind Maxim's desk and leaning forward. "I'll put it to you straight." I sat down, knowing that signaled he'd say everything but what he meant. "You have to stay away from Dr. Walters. Period."

"I'm sure that's what you think."

"I'm sure that's what *he* thinks."

"Right." I wondered if Maxim was standing outside the door, full of regret.

"Eleanor, I'm here because I'm a friend of yours."

"No, you're not."

"Think what you want to think. The point is, I'm also here because I'm an attorney."

"You're a *tax* attorney."

"Well, a brain surgeon can remove an ingrown hair. I can file a restraining order."

"Thanks," I said. "I am truly flattered." I started to giggle.

"Will you get help?" His voice was low and ridiculously kind, as if he worked for the ACLU.

"I don't need help. I'm in a bad situation, but you don't go running to a psychiatrist because your circumstances are messed up. As long as you can live with them. And I can live with this for a while. I'm patient. This'll all work out, Maxim just has to be ready for some major changes, I understand what he's going through. I have to wait. And I'm good at that, you know."

Ellis was holding the edge of the desk tightly, keeping his hands off me. "Christ, Eleanor!" He screamed so loud that I imagined Jesus on the altar cross falling from his pinnings. The door opened and Maxim walked in. Ellis told him to bring Mrs. Cook in, and Mary waddled in, trying not to smile, pleased to death with herself. She was going to have to be the most secretive woman in New Orleans now. "I'm telling you this in front of a witness," Ellis said. "I'm asking you nicely to stay away from Dr. Walters. I mean far away. No hanging around the church. No sneaking around his house. If you show up again, I'm ready to take legal action. Okay?"

I turned to Maxim. "Is that what you want?" I said. He nodded his head. He looked terribly sad.

EIGHTEEN

I haven't figured out distance yet. I once believed the only true closeness came skin to skin when not so much as a swatch of fabric, a molecule of air, came between two people. Then I learned that in the physical world opposites attract, so it is possible for a woman and a man to be making love, convexity into concavity, when they are both mute and thoughtless and actually far apart. Too, I've lost a sense of what geography can do, because letters and telephones and the fact of airplanes can make distances have no meaning; it is possible for a man to orbit the Earth and tell a woman in Houston his most intimate thoughts, provided he doesn't mind electronic interference and millions of voyeurs. Every single day Maxim was spending most of his time within a few city blocks of where I was spending most of my time, but all the rules of overcoming distance were broken. Mary Cook and Peg Walters and fancy telephone equipment and the violation of a few postal laws put a chasm between me and Maxim so wide it made me miserable.

First I tried the telephone. I asked for him straight out. No. I disguised my voice. No. I asked Naomi to make a call for me. She refused. I waited several days, tried again with a new voice. Mary asked a dozen questions, what was my name, I gave her Naomi's name, why was I calling, I told her I was a member of the church, she said no, I wasn't. "Listen, Eleanor, we are having to be horribly rude to everyone who calls here. Please stop," she said. I began trying the house instead. Peg answered, and I hung up. I tried at different times, different days of the week when I knew he was home, and he never picked up. Then one night she picked up the phone on the second ring and said, "Miss Rushing, we know it's you." "Beg pardon?" I said, using a whiskeyed black voice. "We have a new phone system, we know it's you, and we won't pick up again when we see your number." I waited until very late, went to the pay phone inside the Winn-Dixie. "Maxim, I have to see you," I said when he answered the phone. I heard his wife ask him who it was, then the receiver slammed down.

I tried writing him letters, but the mail system is more imperfect than the phone system when it comes to getting around threatened, unscrupulous people. A woman will rip open a man's mail, she'll sign for a certified letter, then tear it out of the envelope as soon as the mail carrier leaves. She may very well toss it out unopened, but few women are that uncurious, especially when they think they can learn the secrets of women they envy. Either for copying or for using against them. Knowing that the same women who answered Maxim's phones intercepted his mail, I made my first letter as simple and clear as I could and mailed it to the church, where I thought everyone would be too superstitious to break secular rules. "Know that I'm waiting for you. E." A pronouncement to Maxim and everyone else, in case they had notions that I was easily destroyed. I heard nothing from him, and I knew there were many possible reasons, that he wasn't ready yet, that Mary Cook had raised a ruckus, that Mary Cook hadn't let him have the letter at all. I took my time, trying to figure what sort of letter would meet all possibilities, and finally I talked a circle around the matter to Naomi, who had sense about everything. I moved the facts, said I was complaining to the manager of a store, phoning him, sending him letters, and his secretary was standing in the way. I didn't know if he ever knew I'd tried. Naomi asked what I was complaining about. Keep the analogy perfect, I figured, and I told her I was banned from the store, and I had the feeling that security had made the decision without telling him. "You been shoplifting or what?" Naomi said. "Jesus, Naomi," I said. I told her no, that I had pissed off a salesclerk, not being ready to leave when the store closed. I was beginning to enjoy this. "I'd have bought a lot of stuff, but no, she's one of these women, probably has a husband who hasn't had a raise in years, resents the hell out of women who don't work, but face it, only people with other people's money go shopping these days anyway, she's going to get up every morning and know she'll be furious all day. I said, Give me ten more minutes, I swear, and she calls security."

"Call the manager."

"I told you, I can't get through."

"So write a letter."

"I *told* you, I wrote a letter. Christ, are you listening?"

"You granddaddy don't pay me to sit here and be your lawyer, no." I said I was sorry. "So what you put in the letter?" I told her I'd written him that I needed to speak to him. "That's it?" That's it. "Lord, girl, I maybe written five letters in my *life*, and somebody else done the typing for me, but even I know you got to spell it all out. You spell it *all* out, you tell the man everything, you keep a copy, you send it return receipt, send a copy to you lawyer, they take notice. I guarantee you, the man be on the phone direct the next day." I gave Naomi a hug and ran off, thrilled to have direction.

I lay on top of my bed and closed my eyes, and I had a pencil and tablet of paper lying next to me in case the ideas came. It took me two full days, no eating, no sleeping except catnaps that came when the ideas drifted off into full-blown scenes. I went to the Tulane Law Library once, rumpled and bleary-eyed, with the plan that I'd show up Ellis for the eternal fraternity boy he was. The law librarian was used to people who looked like me; she asked no questions. I found the part of the Criminal Code Procedure about peace bonds, and right away I learned that Ellis knew no more about criminal law than did anyone else who watched *America's Most Wanted* every Saturday night: restraining orders were for domestic squabbles. But the law was so dry and picky and difficult to put flourishes on, and I tired of it quickly. I went back home to bed and began composing a terribly sad letter, then I dozed off into the letter. A splendid red-haired woman in a turquoise suit with big gold buttons came into the dream, and she felt so sorry for me. I strained through the dream to get her name. Grace, she said. A last name, I needed a last name for the letter, now she was writing the letter. She didn't give me the name right away, but let me fuddle around with choosing one. I went through Nabokovian names,

jokes strained through several languages, then I remembered Maxim had gone to Yale and might have learned
about butterflies and philosophical puns. Smith? No.
Jones? No. The woman and I laughed together at that one.
You can use Grace as a last name, if you want, the woman
said, as long as you don't make me a man. Hailmaryfullof,
a good Catholic friend, so there, Maxim. Mary Grace, no,
too much like a nun; she wouldn't understand passion.
Wake up, get a book, she told me finally, and I walked over
to my bookshelf, where half the books were paperbacks for
college survey courses, and I closed my eyes and plopped a
finger down on a book spine. *Don Quixote.* Dulcinea, I
liked that. Dulcie. Dulcie Grace, sweet mercy, better than
Nabokov. She would be a psychiatrist. And an old friend
of mine.

> *Dear Dr. Walters:*
>
> *As you and I both know, Eleanor Rushing is a most
> unassuming woman, a person of significant talent and
> wisdom, whose life is marked by a desire to be quiet
> about her assets and, moreover, by a willingness to
> retreat from confrontation. As a medical specialist and a
> personal friend and admirer of Ms. Rushing, I am
> taking it upon myself to write this letter, because I
> believe it will be beneficial to both of you, and I know
> that she is not the type to press an issue.*
>
> *Ms. Rushing has shared with me the details of your
> relationship, and I'm sure you are willing to admit that
> you have told her that sexually and emotionally you
> have never been happier than you have been when you
> and she are together. She is a complex, insightful*

*woman, one who shares your intellectual and spiritual
depth, and as such she understands, too, that it will take
time for you to break tiresome old bonds before you can
make your relationship public. However, I'd like to
remind you that when you and she traveled to
Nashville, Tennessee, together, you were met with open
approval and acceptance by the religious leaders who
spent time in the presence of you and Ms. Rushing as a
couple. I think you will find that when you publicly
acknowledge your love and commitment to this woman,
you will see that your congregants and fellow
community leaders will applaud your decision.*

*At this time, you are running a serious risk of
alienating the one woman with whom you are going to
spend the rest of your life. Succumbing to the pressures of
such people as Mr. Ellis Ryan—as well as the meddling
of your office staff and your wife—is only placing you in
a position of destroying the most exquisite relationship
you have ever known. I urge you to get in touch with
Ms. Rushing as soon as possible. I hope I will have an
opportunity to meet you in the near future.*

*Sincerely,
Dulcie Grace, M.D.
Adjunct Professor of Psychiatry,
Louisiana State University Medical School*

I went over to the Tulane Library, flashed my alumni
card until a gray-faced graduate student was plucked from
the stacks to supervise me on the word processor; he didn't
care what I wrote as long as it didn't involve moving para-

graph blocks or shifting into and out of italics. I practiced
an illegible signature for half an hour. When I put the final
period after M.D., I began to giggle, right there in the library. I imagined myself with a great pouf of red hair, a thin
wrist jutting from a turquoise sleeve, with a costly gold
bracelet to match my gold buttons. No one paid attention
to me; the place was full of people with delusions.

I went straight to the post office with the letter, giving
myself no time to lie around and pick at it. That was the
way I'd been in school, taking the first draft as the best effort; anything else lacked truth. I put no return address on
the envelope, then sent the letter certified mail with my
home address on the card. A terrific feeling of control
came over me as soon as I walked away from the counter
at the post office; an answer had to come in a matter of
days. That sort of power gave me freedom. I was not going
to hear anything for at least two days, so for two days I had
the kind of life I imagine old people have when they retire,
working toward nothing, taking an earned pleasure: they
live in dust-free condominiums and spend all their time
going to movies and reading foolish books and eating out
in restaurants, waiting to die. There is no purpose in a day
except to fill it. I walked everywhere, not for health or
good looks, or even to be seen in the park or on the avenue,
but rather for the fun of spying on strangers, following bits
of talk between women in sweatsuits chugging along in
pairs, peering in picture windows on back streets, trailing
a postman to see what sorts of addresses were on the most
mailing lists. I saw a lot of proxy statements on Valence
Street, on Jefferson Avenue I heard about the man whose
wife had planned his funeral just hours before his doctor

gave him cortisone and saved him from an iatrogenic death, I saw a living room decorated in only teal blue and white, walls, pillows, paintings, no bravery, on display for the street. I saw three movies and ate fried oysters twice, and then two days had passed, and I went home to wait.

No one phoned, no receipt came in the mail, and I lay in my bed and waited patiently. Naomi came in once and flicked a feather duster over me, Just checking, seeing if you was alive. The mail came between 10 and 10:30, and when the card didn't come I could go back and lie down, accepting the chance that a certified letter might take a full week to travel ten blocks.

The notice came back six days after I mailed the letter. I could see the green card mixed in with the white envelopes and the four-color catalogues, and I grabbed it without looking at it and scurried to my room. "You look like a squirrel with a pecan," Naomi called up the stairs after me.

It was signed by "MCook" the day after it was mailed. Good enough. The letter was for all of them. Mary Cook could open it and read it and get the message that the word was out on how meddlesome she was. If she were crafty, she'd seal it back, pretend she'd never seen it, give it to Maxim. But Mary had that dullness very friendly people have: there was a chance she'd get the letter and throw it away. If I didn't hear from Maxim by Monday, I'd have her on grounds of violating federal law. I lay down on my bed, waited for the phone to ring, half hoped it wouldn't, found myself full of relief when it actually did ring and I could hear Naomi shrilling at her grandchild.

On Tuesday I took my copy of the letter and the postal receipt and went to sit on the wrought-iron bench outside

Walgreen's. It was after nightfall, and I'd brought nothing to read. I was accustomed to the silent tumbling of thought, as if I were a lone trapper in the Northwest Territory spending the entire winter in a lean-to.

I listened to piped-in radio, Magic 101.9, piped under the walkways, kept track of time, and pulled back deeper into the darkness the longer I was there. People often passed me twice or more, losing each other, failing to make up their minds. This Walgreen's was not what a person would expect in New Orleans, a city of rich whites and poor blacks. At this Walgreen's blacks pulled up in Jeeps and Volvos, too; whites dragged over in shower clogs covered with the dust of Tchoupitoulas Street as often as blacks. I knew that, inside, the lines were full of people judging one another and saying no to their children. Passing me, they judged me, maybe I was a whore, maybe I was someone forgotten. It seemed Maxim would never show up, and when the radio said it was 8:35 I decided to give up if he didn't come by nine. I knew only that he came home every Tuesday night with a Walgreen's bag. It was possible he went to the one on St. Charles Avenue, but that one was for derelicts and tourists, a drugstore that probably never filled a prescription except in an emergency. His car pulled up one minute later, and I watched him being absurdly polite in a traffic maze where there are no rules outside of pure aggression. A white woman driving a new silver Lexus zoomed into the parking place he was going to take, and he kept on going, without so much as a tap on the brakes. He had to go almost to Blockbuster to find another spot, and I screamed at the Lexus woman, "You stupid bitch!" then began walking in the direction Maxim had driven.

Suddenly I was shy. I suppose it had something to do with the dark. The lack of clarity, maybe, that comes from not necessarily being recognized, or not being understood, when one of the senses is compromised. Or it could have been the audience of strangers, judgmental strangers. As it was, I found myself out of his line of vision as he emerged. I wasn't ready to move, to speak. I knew he was going into the drugstore and I'd have a second or third chance; I considered for a second that I should hide in the colonnade and follow him in, make it look like a huge coincidence. But he walked right up to me, stopped two feet in front of me, as if he had a Mediterranean's sense of personal space. "Yes," he said.

"I sent you a letter," I said, and I held out my copy for him to see.

"I have to have a prescription filled." He stepped around me. I told him I'd go with him. He said he'd prefer I didn't. I asked him why. "You're supposed to stay away from me, that's why." His voice was low, as if he didn't want us to be caught.

"I've been sitting here for over an hour, and I haven't seen a single Methodist," I said.

He laughed. "And what does a Methodist look like?"

I smiled with pleasure over myself. "You know, middle of the road. Only extreme people come here."

He looked around, remembered where he was, started walking again. I took his arm, asked him to wait, and he stopped. "I got your letter."

"No, you didn't."

"What?"

"Mary Cook signed for that letter." I waved the return receipt at him. "She threw that letter away after she read it. That's why I have to talk to you. It violates federal regulations to open someone else's mail."

"She's my secretary, for heaven's sake. She's supposed to open my mail. She does open my mail. But she doesn't *read* it. And she certainly doesn't throw it away."

"So what'd the letter say?" I folded my arms across my chest, blocking him, though he could have gone around me.

"You know what the letter said."

"But I don't know that you know."

Maxim got a wild look in his eyes, as if he were ready to forget all his holiness and be a terrible young boy again. "I don't have to go through all this," he said. He looked around, saw no one who could help him. I pointed behind him. "There's a security guard right over there," I said. He turned and looked, then he seemed to relax, remembering I was his partner. "Please go home," he said. We were at the door of Walgreen's, and from time to time someone walked out and washed us in cool, antiseptic air that smelled vaguely of candy wrappers.

"Why do you come here every Tuesday?" I said, needing something.

He considered for a moment, like a child who can't think of a good reason to be selfish. "I'm a diabetic. This is the way I manage."

"I didn't know that." I felt sick. Not that he was flawed or that he was in danger, but rather that I hadn't been thorough. A fact like that could leave me full of mistakes, give us moments when he had to work around a secret. Sugar in his coffee. Christmas chocolates. Dulcie Grace. I didn't like the possibility that when I was thinking about one thing, he was thinking about another. "You should have told me."

"Why?" He opened the door and walked in, and I had to skitter and sidestep to keep up with him as he moved toward the drug counter. The store was crowded for a weekday, brimming with pastels and golds and sweets for Easter.

"Did you have it as a child?" I said, imagining him small, towheaded, and disappointed. That was another gap, the pictures of him when he was young. Living in the South, where people rarely came from somewhere else, I'd always known others as they edged up through the generations. I suppose that was necessary where so many weaknesses, overbites and drinking problems, pool in the genes. Maxim came from away, like a full-grown street dog whose first scrappy garbage days are anyone's guess.

"Yes, I had it when I was a child." He gave the druggist a plaintive look, but the druggist didn't react. He was used to people pacing that twenty-square-foot patch of linoleum, eyes rheumy, fists clutched over cramping bellies, getting remedies for ailments that sometimes were their own fault and sometimes were not. A druggist had to hand over lithium and Dilaudid as if they were sugar dots.

A woman came up behind us lugging a shopping basket full of name-brand supplies. The Lexus woman, who would pay extra for Whiskas cat food at a drugstore on a Tuesday night. I turned away, not forgiving her, and I heard her say, Hello, Dr. Walters, as if she called him Maxim everywhere else. Maxim gave her a hearty greeting, not by name, and I settled back, edged away farther, once again his partner, confident and understanding. I considered buying a new toothbrush. So many colors, neons and primaries, far away from the Easter displays, and suddenly it was important that Maxim know the color of my toothbrush. I studied the colors for image, for memorability, settled on lavender, trudged past Maxim and Lexus, more Nabokovian names of principle, handed the druggist the toothbrush and a five-dollar bill. He had no expression, and I wanted to say, I know you didn't take organic chemistry for this, but I preferred listening, said nothing, smiled sympathetically, and a bit of fuddlement crossed his brow.

The Lexus woman began whispering to Maxim. She was tall, shorthaired, pinheaded, and she was breathing right in his face. I figured her breath smelled of rotten fish the way Maxim pulled back, though he was straining to hear her, standing so no stinking puff of secrecy leaked in my direction. She had the posture of a tattletale, and he glanced toward me. He nodded, she spoke, he nodded again. "She cut you off in the parking lot," I said. The woman turned in my direction. "You shouldn't have done that," I said to her. "He's the type who forgives everything. You took advantage of him."

She looked at Maxim as if he were her husband of twenty years, and now I detested her. "I didn't know it was you," she said. "As a matter of fact, I didn't know it was a *car*. I wasn't looking." Coy. Maxim said he knew, he knew, his voice so tired, the way a voice can be under fluorescent lights. This was a woman to impress: she was so vigorously careless, with her money, with other people's space, that she'd be a fine church supporter, making contributions so she could show up on newsletter lists, volunteering for committees so she could serve cake and punch, never thinking someone might be a diabetic.

"Who is this?" I said to Maxim. I hoped she'd find out that he had no earthly idea.

"Why?" he said.

"He doesn't know," I told her. "He just naturally *assumes* you have power over him."

"Are you crazy?" she said.

"Am I crazy? *You* buy cat food in the drugstore, for God's sake."

"They *sell* cat food in the drugstore," she said, then looked at Maxim. "Who is this?"

I wished him to say, Why? One word, one breathy syllable, that was all I needed from him. It would mean a filament of pure spirit hung taut between us. He looked at me, he knew what I wanted, his lip curled a bit with the temptation to go along with me, and he shook his head no, with the smallest motion, ten degrees rotation; only I could see. I gave him a go-ahead smile, and he said to me, "Get out of here before I call security."

"No," I said, liking the idea of playacting without children's rules: children say, Okay, you say this, then I'll say that; without such conventions the next line is anyone's guess.

"This is not a game." He almost called me by name, but he stopped himself.

"I want to talk to you privately."

"You can't."

"Do you want me to call the guard?" the woman said, deciding she wanted to play, too. Now this was a child's game, we were on the level where it was all right to leave someone out because we hadn't reached the age of reason. On the playground, no one was allowed into a game just because all the players were generous. I'd been on both sides, left in before my parents died, left out afterward. I'd decided long ago that the only people worth talking to were the ones who'd been in both places. This woman had never been left out; she'd been born entitled, and she'd acted accordingly for almost forty years, from the looks of her.

"Call the guard, call the guard," I said, taunting and singsong. The joy of being a child! I could see why some people never give up meanness. "Who the hell do you think you are?"

"I'm Louise Ryan," she said, with the assurance that that would mean something to everyone.

"So?"

Maxim grabbed my arm and pulled me to the side, over by the vitamin racks. Rows and rows of light plastic brown bottles; they'd make a horrific clatter if they fell, even full of cotton. "Louise Ryan," he said. "So?" I said, loud enough for her to hear. "Ryan, *Ellis* Ryan," he said.

I looked at her, and something fell apart inside of me. She was terribly unattractive, her face lined with the arrogance that comes of lying around costly sun places all her life. She was a holding-back woman, holding back Ellis so he wouldn't dare touch me for fear of coming home and having her scream at him. Holding back Maxim the one night I could see him alone. She figured she owned men, her daddy was probably very rich. If your daddy's very rich, you can be Queen of Carnival, even if you're plain and pin-headed, provided, of course, that your daddy isn't too busy hopping on planes with your mother, biding his time until he dies, instantly or slowly. "Christ, I hate you," I said to Louise Ryan. Maxim made the tiniest gesture to the security guard, who'd been waiting for this moment, having done nothing but be a deterrent for as long as he could remember. He came over and gently took my arm, tugged me in the direction of the door. I saw the manager, and I pulled my arm away, though I kept walking toward the exit. I waved my toothbrush at the manager. "I bought something, you know," I said. "I bought something."

NINETEEN

Except during City Council shenanigans, generally I don't enjoy the law. I imagine some day it will be truly elastic, changing every single minute, adaptable for every person. It will take the technology of a second-by-second referendum, so laws can reflect everyone's opinions at a given moment. Until then, laws will be written on paper and usually won't change from year to year. That means a handful of people have access to the statutes and precedents, and they go around controlling everyone else. The process server came to my house the next day, knowing the law, thinking I was going to run from him.

I was in my room, trying to figure out what to do with a three-month-old Rolex that had never been out of the box, sitting instead on my dresser and making me terribly sad when I looked at it. "A man want to see you," Naomi said through the door. I asked her who he was. "I don't know, but he got a good suit."

"Lord, Naomi, you let a man into the house because he has a good suit?"

"He white."

I told her to send him upstairs; if he killed me, it would be her fault. She refused, never having given up on teaching me manners. "So what's his name?" I said. She shrugged, scurried down the steps, clumped back up, breathing hard with annoyance. "He don't say. He got papers, though. I got a feeling he the sheriff." I looked at her blankly. "What you done now?" she said, then I realized it was a message from Maxim, and I ran downstairs, skipping steps, knowing the stairs so well I could have run down them with my eyes closed, certain from habit and the sound of the wood exactly when I reached bottom.

The man began to laugh. "Eleanor Rushing?" he said.

I nodded; I was trembling with the excitement of a boy who's about to be punished by the teacher he has a crush on.

I signed for the summons, and the man left, shaking his head. "Twelve years, and I never had that happen before," he said to Naomi. "Except once. This woman was adopting a baby. But that wasn't criminal court. You know."

"She a little different," Naomi said, and I ran up to my room before she could turn around.

"I want to think you some kind of witness," Naomi said through the door.

"Leave me alone," I said, opening the door for emphasis. I hadn't looked at the paper yet; I wanted to learn every particular.

"I ain't studying about you. Let you grandpoppy ask you the questions. I got bathrooms to clean."

"Not mine."

"You want me to do yours last, I can do yours last. But you don't let me in, you can clean it yourself."

"It's never dirty," I said.

"You think you shit don't stink." Naomi trundled off down the hallway, pleased to pieces with herself. "You think you shit don't stink," she said over her shoulder and laughed.

"Jesus!" I said, loud enough for her to hear, and slammed the door good-naturedly.

My copy of the notice to appear wasn't as personal as I wanted it to be. DO NOT FAIL, it said, telling me when to show up. As if I were a common criminal. The charges were second-degree harassment, which sounded about as strong as skeeting a water pistol at a presidential motorcade, easily misunderstood. No name but my own, the deputy clerk's, and the process server's was on the paper at all, and that annoyed me. I wanted details, I wanted to know who my adversary was. Maybe it was Ellis and his wife, not Maxim, and I wanted it to be Maxim. There is no greater sexual tension than that of the courtroom, from what I've seen on television; I've even expected the male district attorney to mount the female defense attorney and ride her as if he were a crazed stallion right in front of the bench. I've never understood how divorces can actually go through when people do so much tearing and scratching at one another in a courtroom. Maxim would sit on one side of the room and I on the other, and I would cross and uncross my legs, letting a heady scent of Anaïs Anaïs escape from my inner thighs. He was a man who strained for virtue, but he was still a complicated mass of protoplasm, driven by the secretions of endocrine glands. It's possible Jesus had an erection during the crucifixion, though when a boy in Patti Ann's Sunday School class asked about it, he was sent home for a month. I phoned Ellis, and the switchboard put me right through.

"I've somehow been expecting you," he said.

"I just have one question." I didn't mind being predictable, but only if the predicting was being done by someone very canny.

"Let me guess."

"Whatever you guess, I'll say no."

He laughed out his nose, filling the phone with static and germs. People with children always have germs. "Whatever you say, I'll probably answer no, too," he said.

"Good." All I had to do was ask the right question, and I'd get the answer I wanted. "I got a summons today. But it doesn't say who the . . ." I couldn't think of the word. Complainant. No. I knew I'd first learned the word on *People's Court* on television: each of the two adversaries stood behind a lectern that had a plaque on it. I closed my eyes. Ellis let out a little bill-by-the-quarter-hour sigh. Defendant. Plaintiff.

"But it doesn't say who the *plaintiff* is. Is it your wife?"

"Of course not."

"Good," I said and hung up gently.

I went shopping for weeks. Some women actually do that: they're known by name in every store in the city and surrounding parishes, and I began to recognize a few of them. They all wore red lipstick in public, terrorizing salesgirls. It was possible to spend an entire day looking for nothing more than a pair of earrings to go with a lavender dress, only to decide the lavender dress did not slip into a vee at the crotch when I was sitting down, effectively putting me back to the start, returning the dress, the accessories, the shoes. When I found myself with only two days before the court date, I decided to become systematic. Lavender was foolish, matching a toothbrush, black was foolish, too—any woman could create illusions in black, and most men knew that—then I remembered white. Any shade of white. I brought home fourteen ensembles, six pairs of shoes, only three pairs of earrings. If my trial went on for weeks, filled with the screams of a jealous wife and postponements during the search for Dr. Dulcie Grace, I'd have enough white clothes. I decided on a single-breasted cream jacket with matching skirt and a cowlneck cotton sweater of the palest beige. Instead of the earrings I'd brought home, I pulled out a pair of intricately carved ivory ones, slender African woman forms with pendulous pimple breasts and rounded bellies; my mother had had them in her jewelry box when she was killed. The elephant would have died of old age by now anyway; I would certainly say that if anyone asked. I tried on the outfit, marched downstairs to ask Naomi what she thought. "Either you look like you getting married, or you look like you about to get crowned homecoming queen," she said, her voice full of criticism.

"In other words, like a sweet little virgin."

"Maybe you a virgin, but you not little. Or sweet."

Poppy hadn't said a word to me about the summons, and I was beginning to be grateful to Naomi, but the morning of my court date he knocked on my door at seven in the morning and said, "Get up, you have to be downtown by ten, and I'm going with you." He walked off, not bothering to find out whether I'd heard him.

I understand why attending one's own funeral is such a popular device in literature, theater, and situation comedy.

It's a chance to hover over the crowd, a child's seraph, in white, hearing only good things. But the thrill of watching is sexual, seeing that level of yearning. At the outset, the gathering in Judge Paris's office was like a wake for me: all my most important people, unable to think or talk about anything but Eleanor Rushing. Judge Paris himself was godlike, not in a green pastures way, but in my notion of pure sensuality. He was a few years older than I was, having reached the point in life when one could say he was of indeterminate age, he was not too tall and of easy musculature, and his dark hair was long and streaked through with natural silver. He was the sort who could come into my story as a stranger and fit right in, creating no imbalance. Ellis was there, and Maxim, and Poppy, of course; I expected all of them. I was tumescent with attention. But after about ten minutes Peg Walters walked in, and Mary Cook, and then Naomi. Naomi was dressed for church. I counted the house, figuring up sides, and it seemed possible for one sickening moment they were all pulled together against me, so many people who loved me, set against me by the strength of law. All it takes is the invocation of a statute, and everyone gets power to wield, so they crowd together with the pleasure that comes from being part of a clique. I looked around the room and made myself burst into tears, and when no one came over to sit by me, I looked up at Judge Paris, hoping he'd see what was going on and send me home to bed. "Are you represented by counsel?" he said to me, and I looked at Ellis. "Are you here for me?" I said. "Not really," he said. "Are you here for him?" I said, pointing at Maxim. "I'm just here," Ellis said, and I stopped the crying.

Judge Paris had grown up in New Orleans from the sound of him, the port accent, the slightest wheeze from years of breathing wet, carcinogenic air. This was going to be an informal hearing, he said to me, and then the room divided along the subtlest of lines, the men relaxing with relief, the women sitting up stiff and straight with disappointment, as if they'd come hoping to witness a hanging. Even Naomi.

Maxim started to tell his story, and I wanted to be certain I caught his eye at every opportunity. It would be hard for him to look anywhere else, because it was a dark room full of dark people, lit on a Louisiana budget with sixty-watt bulbs, paneling buckling, everyone in somber clothes even though Easter had come, and in New Orleans one dresses by the rules of the North, never mind that it was eighty degrees outside. "This woman has been harassing me," he said. "I've known her for a few months, and she has pursued me everywhere I've turned."

"Wait a minute," I said quietly. "How is he going to tell the truth when his wife is sitting right here?"

"He's *supposed* to tell the truth," the judge said.

"Maybe he won't be able to."

The judge told him to go on. The law was painfully impersonal, though I'd always thought I wanted it that way. Maxim had a sheaf of paper in his hands, and he looked down at it. This was a man who could stand in front of the City Council and his congregation and from his head deliver ideas so full of loops and whorls that only the super-intelligent could follow. "She followed me into the drugstore. She *lived* in my backyard. She took a job in my office, even though I told her not to. She showed up in

Nashville when I went up there for a meeting." I looked at his wife out of the corner of my eye. She was believing everything. Maybe she wrote Maxim's notes and insisted he use them exclusively; I wished I could see them, but the paper was opaque, probably the good stationery she never used, and besides, he had it half folded onto itself.

"He's making it sound like there's something wrong with all that," I whispered.

"Shh, shh," the judge said.

"Look, my wife understands what's going on, but there's no reason on earth that anyone else would. This woman is going around telling people we're lovers. Even in Nashville, where I have an impeccable reputation. I suppose Jimmy Swaggart can get away with all sorts of bad behavior, but I can't. Particularly when I haven't done anything wrong." He smiled at the judge, who didn't react. The impersonality of the law was wonderful.

"Do you have reason to believe she'll harm you?" Judge Paris said to Maxim.

"Harm my reputation, yes. Seriously harm it."

Judge Paris rocked back in his desk chair. He had a certain exquisite wickedness to him, as if he'd gotten all his misbehaving out of the way before he was thirty, then had had to live it down from time to time. I'd never heard of anyone in his age group who hadn't smoked marijuana and then grown up to have any sense. "What about physical harm? To yourself, your family?" This was a man who saw murderers every day; I felt bad for Maxim.

"I think this might be a fatal attraction," Peg Walters said.

"I wish for your sake that it were," I said and gave her a look of sympathy.

"One person at a time," the judge said, sleeptalking. He turned in Maxim's direction.

"Any danger?" he said.

"She was on my property," Maxim said, as if he were trying to be helpful. The judge suppressed a yawn; I could see it in his nostril wings.

When it was my turn, I spoke from deep, accurate memory, needing no mnemonics; I had even the most forgettable dates sharp in my mind for easy accessing. "We met in the City Council meeting of October 13. Maxim spoke for seven minutes, sitting down after delivering the most poignant commentary of the meeting, at 10:29 A.M. He chose to sit next to me, and the attraction was immediate, intense, and reciprocal. We agreed to see each other at a later time because he had pressing commitments. I wasn't able to ascertain what those were, because of the urgency of his departure. I remained at the council chambers until a 9:46 P.M. adjournment. The cable access channel has this meeting on videotape, if further evidence is required."

The judge's office was deathly still, no one was taking notes, no one was breathing deeply, everyone was looking at me. I hadn't faltered on a single syllable. I caught Maxim's eye, and he shook his head no, and I went on.

"Nashville," I said, after I'd given every other detail of our relationship; I'd skipped my auto accident, because judges don't believe in fate. "Nashville," I said again. That was a trick I'd seen Maxim use to get attention, and it worked. Maxim crossed his knees, and I knew the anthropological origins of that gesture.

"I had told Maxim that I'd get in touch with him after I saw him the night of November 17. But I phoned—as promised—when he was leaving for Nashville, so he invited me to come up with him. We flew up on the same flight, though I'd booked too late to get seats together." I looked at his wife, and she was making a huge effort to look straight at me and not listen. "We had separate rooms." I smiled at her, but she didn't react. "Not because we were hiding anything. On the contrary, he took me wherever he could. And that includes an intimate meal at the home of Don and Juliana Robertson." I was relieved I hadn't contacted Juliana when I thought this might be a drawn-out proceeding. She'd be a good witness later on, when I really needed her. "Anyway, I simply took my own room because I was recovering from an automobile accident."

"Jesus," Naomi said, and the judge scowled at her as if they were old friends.

I looked around the room and realized no one was sexual except the judge, and I knew nothing about him. The other women were used up, two white women with fat bellies that had filled with babies too often, one black woman who was wizened and ashy with years of resentful work; all of them shriveled inside. Ellis had probably never made love in his life, going straight from beer-burp sex to cramming himself into a woman who douched with alum. Maxim hadn't known slow good love for months, scared as he was, and though he'd had the loyalty to go to bed hours before his wife, he deserved to ache for me. I sat back, took a deep breath, and decided to tell the story that would have men putting their hats in their laps and women wanting to hurt me from envy.

"When a man venerates you, you know," I said slowly, "he's almost afraid to touch you. Maxim and I made love in his hotel room and in mine, and each time he treated me as if I were a delicate icon. So precious he dared not wear a molecule off me." I looked at his soft preaching hands with their even nails, and his wife followed my gaze before she could stop herself. "He *never* touched you the way he touched me," I said to her, not unkindly, and she recoiled.

"We're looking for facts," the judge said softly, as if he were in a hushed movie theater where no one dared chew popcorn during the love scene for fear others would hear the saliva sloshing around.

"That's probably a fact," I said, but the judge didn't smile. I took the hint. "Okay, facts. The night of November 20, a Friday, Nashville, Tennessee. Really the morning of Saturday, November 21; it was after midnight. In his room, from approximately 1:15 until 2:45 A.M. He was busy all day Saturday, but we made love again in my room Saturday night, three times between 11:48 P.M. and 2:23 A.M." I looked at Judge Paris. "That better?" I said. He nodded, and I looked at Maxim's wife, who was perhaps the only other woman with whom Maxim had ever been in bed. A strange sort of sorority builds among women who've slept with the same man; that's why polygamous families in Utah are so happy. She was white in the face the way people become when they are ready to vomit. "Are you going to be sick?" I said to her, and she shot me a look of pure hatred. Maybe I had gone too far telling how often Maxim could make love to me in less than a three-hour period. Even when she'd had newness on her side, she'd surely never drawn him down that far into a well of senselessness.

"Who initiated contact?" the judge said.

"That sounds like you're talking about some business deal," I said.

"Well, this *is* a legal proceeding."

"It shouldn't be."

"But it is." Judge Paris was getting annoyed. He'd probably seen too many judges on television, with their terrible scripts.

"There're a lot of ways to initiate contact," I said. "Especially when two people know each other so well. Haven't you ever sat by a telephone and actually *willed* someone to call you?"

"No," the judge said.

"Really?" The judge and I were on a date, or having a job interview, and no one else was in the room.

"Let's put it this way." I hated when men said that. "Did Dr. Walters ever phone you?"

"Yes."

Maxim stood up, another person who'd been forced to watch too much foolish television. "That's not true. I've had enough of this."

"You did, you know," Naomi said shyly. Everyone turned to look at her, as if she should know being a truth-teller was out of line here. Naomi looked down in her lap, stripping herself instantly of a hundred years of history and righteous anger. Never mind that a minute ago she'd probably forgotten what color she was, the way it is possible to do when everyone around you is of another race, as long as your own hands don't flutter up into your line of vision.

"Christ, Naomi, tell them." She shrugged. She was the tiniest person in the room, all bird bones and poor posture, and with her black-don't-crack face she could have passed for a twelve-year-old girl if enough shadow fell on her. "I know you took at least one message," I said, more for the others' benefit. Naomi looked up at me, her expression not so much pleading as weary, and I said, "It was right before Christmas, remember? You thought it was some kind of an emergency, the way he acted."

"Can she do that?" Ellis said.

"Just tell us what *you* know," the judge said to me, and Naomi slumped back, relieved, sure she had disappeared.

"You phoned me right after the Christmas party at the church," I said to Maxim. Sometimes I see value in reciting exact times and places, but a lot of power comes from ambiguity, the way it triggers other people's imaginations. I liked to think that right then Peg Walters wasn't feeling so sure of anything.

"Yes, well," Maxim said.

I turned to the judge, as if he and I were the only ones able to track logically. "This is all a side issue," I said. "To give you a straight answer, there are two people in this relationship. One of us is a man in the public eye, a man who is decent enough to remain in a lifeless marriage. But a marriage nevertheless. Now for all intents and purposes, I live alone." I looked at Poppy, to see if he'd react. His eyebrows went up a bit, as if the idea had never occurred to him before but, now that he thought about it, he had to admit it was true. "And I'm a terribly private person, even the cashiers at the Time Saver don't recognize me from one visit to the next. Given those circumstances, naturally

I'm going to be the one with flexibility, of adjusting my schedule around Maxim's. If I made contact, it was because I was in the position of *having* to."

"That doesn't make any sense," I heard Ellis whisper to no one in particular.

"That's because you don't think much of women," I said.

"Hold on, hold on," Judge Paris said. I caught Naomi's eye. Now that she was a spectator once more, she was having a fine old time, suppressing a smile, getting ready to go home that night and tell anyone who'd listen what kind of foolishness rich people spent their free time on. She'd have every detail down perfectly, even Mary Cook's hot-pink Thom McAn three-inch heels that looked as though a three-hundred-pound duck had worn them before her, the small toes abrading every curb. "Have you ever physically threatened Dr. Walters or any member of his family?" the judge said to me.

"No."

"She threw our cat out into Prytania Street once," Peg Walters said.

The judge held his hand up, silencing her, pretending what she'd said had been backspaced over. He asked me if I had anything I wanted to add.

"Well, I can pretty well sum this all up for you." Judge Paris smiled, a little indulgently, I thought, but I let it go. "Maxim Walters is in love with me, and I'm in love with him. Given time, he'll find means to be with me the way he was in Nashville. He knows I understand that right now he has to mollify his wife and his staff and all the people who depend on him—and he also has to work through the tough business of being a spiritual leader who made a secular mistake when he was a very young man. He may be here in your office today, but that's because of all these people"—I waved my hand over Ellis and Mary Cook and Peg Walters—"and he knows that I know what he's doing. He knows I'll find ways to be with him. Maxim, I understand." I looked straight at him, and his eyes were shiny, white opals hit by sunlight through shallow water; that was all the assurance I needed.

Twenty

When I finished speaking, the chamber fell silent until Mary Cook said, "I've just come as decoration," then giggled, looked around the room with eyes wide, got no response, shrugged. I sat back with the comfort of a wise child at a puppet show.

Peg Walters had heard the word *harm,* and she'd fed it into her mind to see what it would attach itself to. "She dressed herself up like a bag lady, and she hid in my yard until I came out, and then she scared me to death. A person ought to be protected from being scared to death. It's like dropping water balloons off a highway overpass, a person could get killed just from being surprised, you know."

You weren't going fifty-five miles an hour across your backyard, I wanted to say, then I imagined Peg Walters, a human Volkswagen, churning over the St. Augustine, broad little tires spinning up the dirt, permed hair bouncing, and I started to laugh. I could see Ellis was fighting a smile, and Judge Paris frowned at me.

"All else aside," Peg said, and her voice had the timbre of a peckish child, "she was trespassing. There are reasons for people not trespassing, you know. She could have been hurt." I caught Naomi's eye, her Lord-give-me-a-break expression, and I smiled. Peg Walters saw me, and she began to scream, "This woman is insane. Look at her!" I was still smiling, the way some children smile when they see blood coming out of someone else. "She threw our cat into Prytania Street."

"Wait a minute," I said. "When did you see me throw your cat into Prytania Street?" Being in that room was making me picky, and I didn't like it. The law usually gave me fits, in part because for me it was so twisted in on itself, like a nasty ganglion, that I could never pull an intact thread out of it, but this much I knew: you're not supposed to tell about something that you haven't seen yourself. For most people, it's hard enough remembering whatever has come directly through the senses, never mind tales that have passed through someone else's desire to embellish or detract.

"I didn't see it, but Maxim did, and he told me, and I don't think he's the type to make up something like that," she said to the judge. The judge asked me if I'd thrown the cat into Prytania Street.

"The cat was on my lap, and I stood up, and it ran out into the street. Something it probably did on a regular basis. Probably still *does* on a regular basis." I knew she was trying to give him the impression their cat was now nothing more than a lump of tar in the street, thanks to me.

"Our cat never goes out into the street," she said. Judge Paris asked her if there was anything else. She laid harm over her recollections of me as if it were a celluloid transparency, and I knew she wished she had the list Maxim held in his hand. Maxim had folded the paper into eighths by now, running his fingernails along the very edge to tighten the fold. When I did that as a child there would be a rim of dirt on the fold, and I could never figure out where it came from. Even across the room, I could see that Maxim's folds were clean. "You know, I think she staged that accident, Maxim," Peg Walters said.

"I was driving a new Mercedes," I said to the judge, trying not to sound rattled. It wasn't a lie.

Peg Walters was excited now. "Seriously. Everything that happened. That was no accident. You let that guy run into you on purpose."

"You weren't there," I said, reminding the judge. "And his insurance paid."

"That's harm," Peg Walters said, ignoring me. "Lucky the man behind her was wearing a seatbelt. She could've seriously injured someone."

"We're trying to see if circumstances warrant keeping Ms. Rushing away from your husband, Mrs. Walters. We're not trying to take her off the streets."

"Well, she's shown she has the capability to hurt people. *I'm* probably the person on earth she wants to hurt most," she said.

"That's not the way things work here," the judge said.

"Can I get her on defamation of character?" I said to Ellis. He shook his head no.

"Lot you know," I whispered.

"I want to speak." The voice came from the corner where I'd quit expecting anyone to be. A primal voice, so familiar it was the baseline against which I measured all others, the one I considered accent-free, the way Alabama children and British adults perceive their own voices.

"Sir," Judge Paris said to Poppy—then I knew without doubt the judge once had been a very bad boy who knew how to turn a rampage off on a dime.

"I'm her grandfather, she's lived with me since she was, what, Naomi, seven?" He looked at his watch.

"Ten," Naomi said.

"God, Poppy."

"Since she was about ten. Her parents were killed in an automobile accident, and she hasn't been the same since." I shook my head vigorously, no, at the judge. "I'm not sure what to say in proceedings like this," Poppy said, "but I want to ask that you take her condition into consideration. Look at her. Please don't send her to jail." The judge told Poppy I wasn't going to jail, and I let out a sigh of relief. "We're here about a restraining order," he said to Poppy. "What about a peace bond?" I said. What do you think about taking away television privileges until I do my homework, sir? "But money means nothing to Eleanor," Poppy said. "No one posts peace bonds anymore," Ellis said. I tried to get the judge's eye, but he was being neutral.

I told Poppy as we were walking to the car afterward that it was very clever of him, telling the judge that. "You *don't* care nothing about money," Naomi said, missing my sarcasm. She was walking alone ahead of Poppy and me; she might as well have been walking ten paces behind, a heavy trunk on her back, embarrassing us. I ran up to walk alongside her.

Maxim and his women were parked in the Saratoga Garage, too. Mary Cook was eating a Baby Ruth from the vending machine while they waited. I've never understood fat people, or even people who smoke cigarettes, which are supposed to make you as helpless as if they were a narcotic. It seems to me that if you see yourself eating too much, and you look bad from it, then you tell yourself to stop, and that's it. I feel funny around fat people because they don't have any self-control. Once Patti Ann and I spent a day together, taking in the same amounts of food, using up the same amounts of energy, and in the late afternoon we sat down at a table with a full bag of Hydrox cookies, and I ate three, washed down with milk, and felt satiation coming on. But Patti Ann kept on eating, a beatific expression on her face, as if the Hydrox were chocolate communion wafers stuffed with sugar glue, dulcie grace, and I asked her what the hell she thought she was doing. "The more you weigh, the more you have to eat," she said matter-of-factly. "I just keep going until I run out."

Peg Walters walked over to me. "You don't have any more chances, you know." I looked at her blankly. The judge had said I had to see a psychiatrist, and Poppy had agreed eagerly, and as far as I was concerned I was no more responsible for what happened next than a man let off a murder charge on an insanity defense. I'd sat in that office and had every bit of free will plucked off of me. "To save a thousand dollars—which you'd have gotten back—you made me look like a crazy person," I'd said to Poppy when we walked out. He could have posted a peace bond, *I* could have posted a peace bond, and then I could have been more careful in finding ways to see Maxim, and the most it could have cost me was a thousand dollars, if I were caught. "I don't think that's how it turned out," I said to Peg Walters, then I turned on my heel and walked away from her.

We drove in silence. Naomi was riding in the front seat, because I was terrified of being killed while Poppy was driving. He was such a silent man that it was hard most of the time to track his deterioration, but on the way downtown I'd noticed how terribly old he was, how, in spite of anything he might want to do, he couldn't drive a car safely anymore. He stayed in the left lane, six inches over the center line, and each time he passed a car that was on the right I took in a great whistling rush of breath until he hollered at me, "I was driving forty years before you were born."

"Mr. Rushing, I never driven a car, but I do know you supposed to stay on you side of the line, and you *ain't*," Naomi said, and Poppy pulled the wheel to the left.

"Christ, you're a pair of liars," I said. Naomi turned around in her seat; she wasn't wearing a belt, and she could have come right over easily. She gave me a look of disgust, and for a second I felt like a small child, riding in the backseat of her parents' car, fussing for attention. "You can drive," I said to Naomi.

"No, I can't. You want to tell me where I'm getting a driving license? You got to pass a test, for starts."

"You probably drove without a license."

"Suit yourself," Naomi said.

We were stopped at the corner of Claiborne and Martin Luther King, the latter of which Naomi still called Melpomene, mel-fa-mean. It was supposed to be the most dangerous intersection in the city, the gateway to a stygian stretch of barrooms and wig parlors; cars careened down off the overpass, still full of high-speed motion from the interstate, and routinely broadsided rusted 1970s Chevrolets that came screaming in low gear out of the projects. I'd often seen homeless men lying on the neutral ground at the foot of the overpass, so still they might have been dead. I never saw dead dogs and cats along there, because dogs and cats were too smart to hang out where there was absolutely no food to be had. "Why'd you pick a car wreck in there?" I said to Poppy. He caught my eye in the rearview mirror, and I looked away so he'd concentrate on getting through the intersection alive. At most intersections in New Orleans you were supposed to count to three before pulling off at a green light; it was practically a law. At this corner, it was better to count to ten, then ease out slowly; there was still a terrific risk. "They died in a plane crash, remember?" I didn't suspect him of senescence, but I was willing to let him try it.

Poppy hit the brakes in the middle of the block, in front of the Holy Tabernacle Church. The church was marked by a huge, hand-painted sign, brown on white. Poppy was in the center lane, and he pulled over to the right, without looking, and cars braked and zoomed around him as if they were in midtown Manhattan traffic and expected no less.

"Your parents died the same day a plane crashed, but they weren't on it," Poppy said gently.

"Why would you tell me something like that?" I was burning with adrenaline, frightened, the way everyone was picking on me, with no purpose except to confuse me.

"It's *true*, that's why," Naomi said.

I began to cry, honestly cry, a little believing child in the backseat, told she'd be left alongside the highway if she didn't behave. "I didn't do anything wrong," I said, sobbing as if I might never breathe again.

"No one said you did," Poppy said. We were still parked next to the church, and three black men walked past, all in threadbare white undershirts, the uniform of the up-to-no-good. "I think you better turn you motor back on," Naomi said; Poppy ignored her, and the men kept walking. He reminded me of Ronald Reagan, a man who'd lived such a long life of comfort that he couldn't imagine harm coming to himself, and didn't really care about harm coming to anyone else.

"They died in the crash of Eastern Flight 66, nonstop from New Orleans to New York, it was in all the papers," I said, snuffling with fear.

"Find it for me in *one* newspaper, and I'll believe you," Poppy said.

I told him to drop me at the public library. No, he said, he had to get back downtown, he was late, Naomi was late, streetcars weren't running very fast now, it was time to get up to the house. I fished in my purse for all my loose change, found a considerable amount. I let myself out of the car, and Naomi hollered that I was going to get my white self killed, to get back in that car right now. "Let her go," Poppy said, as if my getting my white self killed might solve a number of the problems that plagued his old age. But even a white woman can pass through any part of town with no trouble if she is crying out of control and carrying nothing more than a hot fistful of dimes and quarters. I jogged to the library in my Ferragamo pumps, setting foot on broken sidewalks no white person had touched for decades, and I arrived soaked and stinking from nerves but unharmed.

Their names were not on any lists in the *Times-Picayune* from June 25 and June 26 of 1975. I went up to the periodicals librarian and asked her why a name might be left off the list, and I could tell she had no idea. "The first day, maybe they didn't have complete information, especially in 1975, but the second day, they should have had all the facts. Though you know how the *Times-Picayune* is." I tried the old *States-Item*, I tried the vertical files, no mention of my parents in the crash of Flight 66. The microfilm was getting all twisted up, but it didn't matter to me, and the librarian came over, wanting to rescue the film; librarians are proprietary about the things in their charge, as if a hundred years from now they'll get credit for neatness. She suggested I check the obituaries for that week, but the microfilm was tangled and creased, and I wasn't in the mood for obituaries. I started to walk out. She called for me to wait, like a car salesman with a better offer. I stood a few yards away, watched her fix the film with fingers so deft that she once must have taken a course in lacing celluloid through balky machines.

"Okay!" she said. I tiptoed over as if I were visiting the snake house at the zoo. Her index finger, silhouetted and distorted with its half-chewed nail, bounced up and down on the screen, larger and smaller, in and out of focus. Obituaries were in such tiny typeface; I could approach slowly, see as little or as much as I wanted. I found my mother's name first. AT ROCKMONT, TENNESSEE, ON TUESDAY, JUNE 24, AT 9:15 A.M. I stopped, found my father's name, AT ROCKMONT, TENNESSEE, ON TUESDAY, JUNE 24, AT 9:15 A.M. I was faint from the news of their deaths, as if this were the first time knowing it. I told the librarian quietly that I'd seen enough, and I backed up a foot until the foggy type was completely blurred. She asked me if I wanted a photocopy.

"What for," I whispered. "Just asking," she said, injured. I apologized, fished through the coins in my hand for a dime. "It's okay," she said, "I understand."

I took the streetcar home, and it had only five riders far past Lee Circle, going uptown that time of day. The side-to-side rocking, unbroken as we moved past stops without slowing down, lulled me; the windows were down, and the air cooled the sour perspiration on my skin. I could have fallen asleep, even on the low wooden seat, but too many cars tore across the avenue after it narrowed at Louisiana, and when we reached that point I found myself watching, hoping we would smash broadside into anyone inconsiderate; even the near-misses, heartstoppers, were good enough.

Poppy already was gone, and Naomi was in her uniform, and maybe the entire morning had been a rich dream. I checked the back closet, and Naomi's church dress was hanging there; I could see the white powdery half-circles inside the armpits. She was having a cup of coffee in the kitchen. "Lord, you shot my nerves bad," she said when I came back into the room.

"You didn't exactly add years to my life," I said.

Naomi sniffed with indignation. "People like you live forever."

I stood over her. "That decaffeinated?" I said.

"Hell, no."

I laughed. A good-sized puddle of coffee filled Naomi's saucer, something I'd never seen before. If I tipped even a spoonful of coffee out of a cup by accident, she'd slip a paper towel into the saucer, "so you don't go dripping." Naomi was dripping each time she took a sip, and it didn't seem to matter to her in the least. "Tell me everything," I said.

"What."

"Tell me why the paper says they died in Rockmont, Tennessee."

"Because they *did*."

I took a big draught from her coffee cup, never mind that it was two-thirds down and probably full of spit. "They died in a car crash and it was you fault. Ten years old, and you as good as killed them; that's half the reason I don't blame you for nothing since. You grandpa, either, if you want to know the truth."

I asked her what I'd done, knowing nothing, imagining anything, a child flinging herself over the front seat and turning the wheel toward a mountain, the same child, back a few frames, loosening the lugnuts on all the tires. I held my breath, the way one might when hearing a detailed, bloody description of one's mother's death in childbirth: it had a lot to do with me, but I was blameless for what happened before I knew what I was doing. "I don't know. I wasn't there."

"You drove me home. I think you drove me home."

"Well, now that a switch, yeah. You *think* I drove you home."

"Okay, I *know* you drove me home."

Naomi took the coffee cup away from me, looked down inside it with disgust, then slid it into the sink at just the right angle so it clattered but didn't break. Chipping the crockery was one of the small compensations in Naomi's life. She told me to look her in the face. I stared into her eyes, and I realized that when I was a child I had known them well, the jaundice yellow that never went away and never killed her, the egg-white scar on her left iris from having been in the way of a BB gun when she was three. I probably hadn't looked her in the eye since I'd asked her all the questions about her scars and scabs more than twenty years before. "I never been in Tennessee. I don't never want to be in Tennessee. Matter of fact, I never been past Hattiesburg, Mississippi, in any direction, and that's fine with me. They put you on a plane, in Nashville, come to think of it. I been to the airport with you grandpa that one time. I don't think *he* ever been in Tennessee, neither. No point in it."

"They died at the same time," I said. Nine-fifteen, not even a minute apart. I'd seen the obituaries after multiple-fatality car crashes, and only occasionally did the paper list identical times of death. Usually one would say, ON THE LAKE PONTCHARTRAIN CAUSEWAY AT 4:45 P.M., and another would say, AT EAST JEFFERSON HOSPITAL AT 5:10 P.M., and then it was easy to put the entire story together, that one had died instantly, and the other, perhaps still conscious, had been rushed off the bridge, knowing what had happened, only to slip into cardiac arrest and be declared dead at the emergency room. I learned a lot from the obituaries, not so much facts, but rather what the structure of drama was all about. The funerals usually were set for the same time, the same parlor.

"So?" "So plenty." "So how'd they die?" "Head-on collision." "And where was I?" "I figure in the backseat." Naomi was getting fidgety; that wasn't her first cup of coffee of the day. Her foot was jiggling under the table at such high speed that she was driving me crazy. "Stop it," I said.

"You stop it. You making me half insane with this. Everything I know is this: the doorbell ring, and it's early enough in the morning you grandpa shouldn't be out yet, and he not saying a word, so I leave the room, and then he tell me, 'Naomi, you better sit down.' So I sit down in the living room, matter of fact, first and last time for everything, and he tell me you mama and you daddy been killed in a head-on crash, and you okay, except that mess on you face, couldn't be better, and the girls done seen it say you fooling around. That's it."

"You're lying," I said, though my hand went up to my face. Naomi had driven up to Rockmont, Tennessee, in a green Mercedes and had told me that my parents had died on Flight 66, and then she'd ruined my life, and of course she wasn't ever going to tell the truth. It was far too late for her to get fired or prosecuted for what she'd done to me, but it wasn't too late for her to be disgusted with herself.

"I'm lying, then everybody else lying, too. You call that fat little friend. She tell you. I believe she *seen* it." Patti Ann McCloskey? She nodded. "Patti Ann McCloskey is an almost-thirty-year-old woman who's been mad at me half my life."

"Yeah, but like the judge say, people *supposed* to tell the truth."

TWENTY-ONE

When I was fourteen and called Patti Ann's house for the first time with my new voice and adolescent chattiness, I said, "Can I talk to Patti Ann?" and her mother said, "I don't know, can you?" "*May* I speak to Patti Ann?" "Who's calling?" "Oh," I said, "I guess you don't know my voice yet." "You are supposed to identify yourself when you call people. Say, 'Hello, this is Eleanor, may I please speak to Patti Ann?'" I heard Patti Ann in the background. "Jesus, Mama, she's never going to talk again at that rate." "Don't 'Jesus' me," her mother said. After that I always identified myself when Mrs. McCloskey answered, though it didn't take long for her to start hanging up on me when she heard my voice.

"Hello, this is Eleanor," I said, nearly thirty years old and still jittery with her. Other people's parents were the reason half the girls I knew moved far from town, while the other half stayed home and became imitations of their own mothers. She didn't hang up. "Eleanor Rushing," I said. "Yes?" Polite. I let out a sigh of relief, and I thought I heard a tolerant little sniff.

Surely Mrs. McCloskey had become one of those women who were so bored they talked nonstop, but not so bored they asked questions. I could picture her, in her house, the furniture in the same places with the same upholstery, her hair sculpted last Friday at Aida in a full-blown bouffant flip, with color; she was perfectly content to sit on the phone reciting the produce prices at Dorignac's to her friends, occasionally taking a break to tell about Mrs. Joseph's son who was back in DePaul's after stopping his medication; the catatonia was so bad he was being nose-fed. In New Orleans it was possible to pick up a good sick story once a day if you stayed in touch. I preferred eavesdropping; it was easier than sitting with a phone receiver pressed to my ear, building obligations to other women.

I hesitated. "I suppose you're calling about the baby," she said. I opened my mouth, but I couldn't figure out whether to say yes or no that quickly. "Just dreadful, simply dreadful. We had no earthly idea, you know, at her age, who'd think to look for something like that? I tell her it's the pollution in Baton Rouge, I've been telling her that for years, but maybe now's not the right time, you know?" I sat back fascinated, as if I were looking through a kaleidoscope filled with bits of pale glass; every now and then a shard of familiarity would move into my line of vision, and I'd remember it, in case another fragment of the same color followed. "How is she?" I said, turning the cylinder of the kaleidoscope a quarter of an inch, listening for the tumble of glass. "It's a boy. Oh, you mean Patricia. I guess you can't get used to her name, either. I don't think I ever called her Patricia, not even when they brought her to me in the hospital." Mrs. McCloskey began to cry. "Oh, he's so perfect, you wouldn't believe anything could be so wrong. All his fingers, all his toes, what'd God give him fingers and toes for, I'd like to know?" I told her how sorry I was, and she stopped snuffling. "I have to get control of myself, I know. I just can't go up there. I mean, I went up there last Thursday, but she delivered so quickly that by the time I got there they already knew. Just a brainstem. They can just tell those things, Lord knows how. I don't want to know how. I came back Saturday. She's so out of it, there's nothing I could do anyway." I wondered about my mental picture; when had Mrs. McCloskey had her hair done?

I went to Baton Rouge Friday morning. I wish I were one of those people who lop off part of the past, hacking back through the years to get to the good portions as if time were a piece of bruised fruit, still sweet close to the heart. I'd like, too, to be someone who right away understands pain and runs straight for it. But in truth I was sure Patti Ann was sitting in one place, her belly sliced open and rudely stitched up, ready to answer my questions. I figured when I arrived at the hospital I'd see the baby and come to some understanding of why children mattered. To me, children had had so little experience there was no room for regret, for them or for anyone else, if they didn't survive. Infants, in particular, had seen lights and heard muffled, unintelligible sounds, and it was hard to imagine being sorry to leave just that. A baby with nothing more than a brainstem was like a buckmoth caterpillar lying on the sidewalk. I had seen the caterpillars every April showing a collective intelligence perhaps, making rings around the oak trees as they moved in single file toward the ground for no reason except to be stepped on. I'd considered their worth, their symmetry, their ability to annoy great numbers of people, but ultimately I'd had no compunction about smashing any that lay in my path, watching the dark brown liquid explode gently across the sidewalk.

Patti Ann already had checked out of the hospital, but she was in fact sitting in one place, having waited for days for the baby to die. I found her subdivision after stopping at three filling stations: the map I had of Baton Rouge in my glove compartment had been drawn before her neighborhood was anything but raw, happy land, full of snakes and ozone. The houses were all different from one another, but they were all made of flesh-crayon-colored brick, none more than a single story, and even with beveled glass here and wrought iron there, they were indistinguishable. I would have hated to be a small child trying to find my way home from school.

The woman who answered the door was slender and sad, no more than five feet tall, with a round belly under a loose T-shirt; it was as if Patti Ann had allowed all her old joy and adipose tissue to pool in a sac in front of her, attached to her body but not really part of her. "Holy shit," she said softly, once she had looked at my face long enough to figure it out. "Holy shit." She didn't hug me. We weren't that sort of friends, thank goodness.

Patti Ann wasn't supposed to move around at all. She had a black woman floating and tending through her house, but I had a feeling this was the way life always was in her house. "He died last night," she said, letting herself down gingerly on a stretch of sectional sofa. "I wanted to see him," I said, and it was true.

"He was a perfectly normal child, everything he did was involuntary." She was trying to smile, but the tears were spilling freely.

"God, same old Patti Ann."

"Patricia." She was shy, as if she hadn't had to try it on with too many people who'd known her before.

She lived in a subdivision, and all her furniture came from the same tree and bolt of cloth; this was a life for a Patti Ann. "Patricia. That feels truly strange. Sort of like trying to call your mother Barbara after I've been calling her Mrs. McCloskey my whole life."

"She's being *hor*rible," Patti Ann said loudly. For a second I worried she'd wake the baby. The hush in the house was that of a house with a new baby; few lights were on, and the drapes were drawn. The housekeeper tiptoed through the adjoining hallway, nothing in her hands. "Mama stands there in the hospital and she half tears her hair out, and I expect her to double over any second and tell me she's ripped out her stitches from her C-section; she's forgotten I had anything to do with this, except maybe as a bad girl who broke her favorite netsuke or something. She's not even coming up for the funeral. Christ, I think she figures they're going to do like the vet, you know, incinerate the dead dogs and put the ashes out for the garbage." The housekeeper cut through the hallway again, caught my eye, shook her head, kept on walking. Patti Ann sobbed noisily, then she caught herself. "I have to be careful," she said. I nodded. I wasn't very good at these things; I was used to hearing about tragedy second-hand, waiting in line and listening to other people's conversations.

It took until nearly midnight for me to remember what I'd come for. For a house with a death in it, Patti Ann's was immensely quiet. The phone didn't ring, no deliveries came to the door, and I wondered whether this was social convention's way of telling her that her baby indeed had not been a person. Her husband came home, having busied himself for as long as possible with the paperwork that comes equally with every death, and right then there was nothing to the man. He moved in a dream state, not expecting to wake up, a small pale man who looked enough like Patti Ann for me to think she had fallen in love with the thoroughly familiar. He asked for nothing to eat, and Patti Ann had never considered food, or drink, either, except to get a glass of water, from the maid, from the tap, Baton Rouge river water, to wash down Percodan as often as possible. After her husband drifted out of the room, I asked her what the baby looked like. All those recessive genes; in Louisiana, the death of such a truly white baby was a rarity, and I felt like knowing. "Where hair grows, there isn't any head," she said, and I ran to the bathroom and threw up.

Vague with drugs, yet frantic with sleeplessness, Patti Ann talked about the past month as if we had no previous catching up to do. I wasn't bored, even when she began to repeat herself, and I thought perhaps I'd been missing out on something for quite a while. Her past month had been full of hope, and that was what I'd failed to understand, this business of thinking from the moment of conception that a child will bring you pride and kindness later on. "You pick out talents for them before you pick out names," she said. When she fell silent, as if she were going to go into one of her old snoozes, I began working my way around to asking her my question. "I outlived my parents," I said.

She stared at nothing, as if she hadn't heard me. "Well, you sort of *guaranteed* you'd outlive them," she said after a while.

I sat bolt upright, losing the contagion of her painkiller haze. "That's what everybody says, right? You know what I say? I say this is beginning to sound like one of those myths, you know, the hook on the door handle? Somebody makes up some sick story, and by about the third telling it's true."

"Oh, for God's sake, Eleanor, I was there."

"You were there? *I* was there.'"

"Well, you've always been there physically." She giggled, as if the liberties allowed in childhood when you're trying out new words still applied.

I knew she had fresh, raw stitches in her body, and if I went too far she'd pop along the seam like a biscuit can. "You're not funny," I said evenly.

"Sorry," she said, beginning to cry. I expected her to furl into a ball. "You were really a little kid, anybody would've done the same thing." I shook my head no, I remembered nothing. "You were leaving camp," she said helpfully.

"They were already dead when I left camp." Naomi at the riding ring, telling me, Mrs. Carlton coming into my cabin, bumping her head, I remembered everything.

"Look, you have been going around for nearly twenty years saying your parents died in a plane crash. Well, less than that, since you didn't tell *any*body *any*thing for four years. Though I think you told me. Though I don't know how, except that I always knew what you wanted to say anyway." I shrugged, as if to say, If there are any lies, maybe they came from you. Patti Ann smiled, still reading my mind. "All I can tell you is what I remember. They shipped us both off to camp, remember?" I nodded, but I didn't remember her going. "Well, I didn't give a rat's ass either way about going, but you were thoroughly pissed off. Like they were sending you to the gulag or something. Anyway, you get up there, and the place truly is fascist, with all these college girls with their North Carolina accents thrilled out of their minds that they can boss us around in private and then act all yes-ma'am Southern Baptist in public." This much was true. Two girls from Mary Washington College, Kelly and Christine, had lived on the porch of my cabin and ordered me around with absolutely no love. "So *you* figured a way to get out. You know, I've got to hand it to you. These days everybody's screaming 'child molester' for absolutely nothing, and back then I don't think it'd even been invented, and here you were, only ten years old, and you pulled this thing off. Old Carlton kind of deserved it, if you want to know the truth. After all, *she* was the ultimate fascist." I shook my head, yes, no, yes, she had been mean, no, I accused her of nothing, yes, Naomi put her hands on me, no, I hadn't told Patti Ann about Naomi, Mrs. Carlton had been cruel to Naomi, where did she get all this? "To this day, I don't know where you got the idea," she said. That she molested me? I said, disgusted by the image of dry, thick, snobbish Mrs. Carlton touching me; making up that story and holding to it was sickening when the truth about Naomi was enough. Someone else must have done that, I said. At least a dozen girls at camp were from Washington, D.C. You had to be sophisticated to live in Washington, D.C., going to private school with girls whose fathers were vice presidents and senators; much sick imagination fermented in those circles. "Well, I remember sitting around just listening to *you*. 'How about she does it to me in the shower? No, wait, who'd believe that? A campout. Nah, I say she did anything on a campout, people'd know I was making it up. Mrs. Carlton's never been in the woods in her life.' Jesus, they were impressed." You're making this up, I said. "You know I wasn't mean. I wouldn't have wanted to *destroy* the woman. Not to mention how I'd've upset my parents."

"You want something to eat?" she said, feeling better now that I was feeling bad. I shook my head no; my throat was closing up. I followed her as she padded into the kitchen, set herself at the table with a half gallon of mint chocolate chip ice cream. She dangled a cooking spoon over the container. "I thought the baby would come out asking for vanilla. I mean, I think I ate it every day. I figured my breasts would give out vanilla ice cream. Cold." She looked down at her chest. It was still big and lumpy under her shirt. "I guess I'm never going to eat vanilla again."

"Sure you will. Your mouth forgets. My mother ate smoked oysters every day and threw up every day when she was pregnant, and she told me that while she was *eating* them."

"What did she have to forget?"

"Sorry," I said.

"I saw it," she said, dipping the spoon deep into the ice cream, then filling her mouth until I thought the spoon would rip it at the corners. "Like it was fate or something. Well, actually not. I mean, *you* were supposed to go on that trip, too, so I guess none of us could get on the road until they packed you out of there. God, you had so much crap. Like you got the camp list in the mail and went out and bought everything on it. You know, I think it even said 'stuffed animal for your bunk,' and somebody went out and bought you this stuffed white bear. I mean, brand-new, for God's sake, like if you got homesick or something you were going to sleep with this brand-new bear that didn't even smell like anything except the inside of a department store." She was silent for a moment. "We bought him a bear, you want to see it?" I shook my head no; I didn't want to go back into a nursery where I knew there had to be wallpaper with ducks and an empty crib, and the white bear. I remembered my bear; it had a pink ribbon around its neck, probably 50 percent off after Easter. "You don't have to come into the room," Patti Ann said, and she lumbered off like an old woman. She came back empty-handed. "He's packed up everything already," she said. That's probably good, I said. "Probably," she said.

The canoe trip, I said. My heart wasn't racing at all; rather, I felt like one of those cars that used to be shown in commercials: a raw egg is perched precariously inside while the vehicle rolls over the roughest terrain. The egg remains intact. A wonderfully peculiar detachment comes when you expect the other person to lie.

"Yeh, it *was* a canoe trip. See? Matter of fact, maybe if there hadn't been those canoes on top of the truck, nothing would've happened. I mean, we could see you, and you could see us, but your father probably couldn't see squat.

God, were we pissed at you. I don't think any of us really wanted to go home, but you made it feel like you'd gotten something that maybe we ought to be jealous of. You ride there in the backseat of this big air-conditioned Mercedes, and it's already hot out in the middle of the morning, and we're sitting in the open back of this truck that's probably had horse manure in it, and you keep sticking out your tongue. I mean, everybody saw it, and we kept hollering to Kelly, 'don't let them pass,' and I swear Kelly speeded up, and we could see you hollering at your dad, and your mom was turning around telling you to cut the crap, probably, and you kept after him, and then finally I think he must have wanted to pass us and shut you up and get you the hell home, and he couldn't see around the truck, I swear that's it, unless he had some death wish."

"Why are you doing this?"

She shrugged. "This is not exactly the best time in the world for me." She was getting ready to cry again, reading my mind.

"You don't have to take it out on everybody else."

"Jesus, Eleanor," she said, "I'm the only person who never picked on you."

"What's that supposed to mean?"

"Look, you couldn't help it. Well, technically, it was your fault, but after a while, it *wasn't* anymore."

"What."

"The line, honey, the line."

I looked at myself in the glass on her microwave oven, saw no line. "The doctor told me it was invisible," I said.

Her voice became soft. Tired. Motherly. "You were ten years old."

My hand went to my cheek, and I felt the scar, a ten-inch ridge, once a slice uninterrupted by features, by eyelid, by nose, by upper lip. "No."

"I'm sure men get used to it," Patti Ann said.

"They don't see it. I know they don't see it. You're just saying that."

Patti Ann dropped the full spoon, spattering everything in its path with mint chocolate chip ice cream. "You didn't come up here about the baby, did you? How'd you know about him, anyway?" I told her I heard from her mother. "My mother wouldn't call you."

"How do you know?" I said, almost believing her mother had called.

"You know what the trouble with you is, Eleanor Rushing? The trouble with you is you need too much protecting. Well, frankly, right now I'm not in the mood."

"Hey, I'm really sorry about the baby. I really am. But you don't have to be so mad at me." It was three in the morning, 3:07 to be exact, and I walked out, leaving a thin trail of creamy green mint droplets. I could get to New Orleans before daybreak.

TWENTY-TWO

There's magic in geography. Geography is precise and magic breaks rules, but I believe it anyway. The continental divide is a good example. Right at that point, rivers flow east or west, depending on which side they lie on, and of course scientists know why. But if a person is traveling from California to New York and flies over that demarcation line, odds are that she will be transformed in some way, from freewheeling and slightly crazed to mean and hungry for order. I've heard of that happening, and so far no one's gone looking for exact reasons. I reached the halfway point between Baton Rouge and New Orleans, 42.3 miles on the odometer, out in the middle of nothing on an interstate that could have been crossing any low-lying patch of the United States, and suddenly I knew what was going on.

Somewhere along the line my story had been rewritten, maybe by rumor, maybe by someone who didn't wish me well, and now all the wrong facts were taken by everyone to be true. That is what used to happen with history: tiny mutations came into every telling of a story until it was no longer recognizable. When I was small, I thought about

Jesus and about how little I'd have wanted to be him. What's the point of being known, after all, if people two thousand years later have no idea what you looked like? He might as well have been anyone. That's why people needed to believe in a second coming. It should be different now: two thousand years from now, people will find evidence that Mikhail Gorbachev had a cruel red stain on the top of his balding head. Gorbachev can slip quietly into history knowing he isn't interchangeable with whatever images artists feel like making of him. He does not need a resurrection or even cryogenics.

Maybe Patti Ann and Poppy and Naomi and all the rest truly believed my parents died in a car crash that I caused. Maybe they all wanted to make me crazy. It didn't matter. I was living in Louisiana, and I couldn't get away from people who'd known me since I was small. I was driving through St. James Parish, with well-meaning liars in any direction I might want to go. It wasn't possible to have a relationship with Maxim when I was going to turn around at odd times and find Poppy and Naomi saying, Oh, she different, or She hasn't been the same since, or even Patti Ann saying, You know what the trouble with you is, Eleanor Rushing? They had a lot of nerve, pretending they knew me. Naomi cleaned my bathroom, and Poppy did my taxes, but that made me about as well delineated in their minds as Jesus was. I was going to go to Tennessee, not the eastern part, where contorted old stories floated alongside the highway like ghosts, but rather to Nashville. Only the Robertsons knew me in Nashville. Juliana and Don Robertson were people Maxim could be honest in front of, because they knew the truth and found it quite right, that he should be with me. Maxim had to go to Nashville on a regular basis, and I would be perfectly content to live my days out, waiting for his visit every few months, instead of scurrying around New Orleans like a tree roach at night. Eventually he'd see Nashville for what it was, a spiritual boomtown, where churches could treble their congregations in weeks and chalk it up to practical planning and the favor of God, both of which Maxim had acquired at Yale. He needed to be at the center, and Tennessee was the center of something, probably of concentrations of people, or why would Federal Express fly every package through there? Maxim was wasting himself in New Orleans, a dead end at the water's edge, a place where people came to die, sometimes from the moment they were born.

I owned almost nothing. In fact, it's surprising, now that I look back, that I never chose a peripatetic life, limiting myself to a bag of favorite clothes, going from place to place, leaving behind anything that didn't strike my fancy at a given second. I slipped into the house long before Poppy was awake and went through every niche and drawer in my room. Books, I didn't need books, libraries everywhere were full of them. I had no photographs, no clippings, no ticket stubs, no letters. That was the beauty of untainted memory: I'd never needed cues; it had never been necessary, either, for me to study photographs for meaning—a sidelong glance, a bitten lip. It was all in my mind, easily called up, fully understood. I could recite letters, I could recall full conversations. Only people with hazy, distorted minds need sentimentality. When I packed my clothes, I didn't include all the things I'd worn with Maxim. Some appealed to me right then, others didn't, and what I left behind could be fully remembered, his fingers around a delicate button, his mouth pressing through a thin panel of white silk. If I wanted to re-create the sensations, I could close my eyes, touch anything.

I didn't know what to do with the Rolex. It had cost almost four thousand dollars, but I had no special use for the money if I returned it. It had no memory value: every word, every turn of the afternoon Maxim and I'd been together before Christmas was clear in my mind. I didn't want to take the watch with me. I wanted Maxim to have it. I wanted to leave town as soon as the Whitney Bank opened. It was eight minutes to five. Maxim had to have the watch. With no explanations, no details of my plan: he'd get them later, easily, through the Robertsons.

Daylight wasn't due for more than an hour. I tiptoed downstairs, let myself out the back door. It was a cool, wet morning, and the scent of sweet olive was so heady it made me sad to think of leaving it. I associated Nashville with the scent of my own perfume, but I wasn't going to bring along my own sensory cues. I would find new ones. I drove over to the church, trying to choose a place to leave the watch. A Rolex watch, lying around anywhere in New Orleans, would be hot the second anyone saw it. Mary Cook would think she had no limits on her virtue until she saw a four-thousand-dollar watch sticking out of the church mailbox, waiting to be picked up. I could picture her, her round head set on round shoulders, with no neck, like that of a rubber baby doll, swiveling around, eyes frozen forward, checking that she wasn't being seen. I had to get it inside, onto his desk. I tried every door. Locked. The one at the back had a keypad for coding in to disarm the alarm system. I wondered what had happened to churches as sanctuaries. The windows, all the windows had burglar bars. That meant they weren't on the alarm system, but without tools and the knowledge of a criminal, I couldn't get through anyway. It was still dark out, and I could see across to the Walterses' yard. They now had floodlights, and I felt sorry for their plants, bathed in high wattage with unchanging shadows by night, stripped of circadian rhythms. Maybe that was why New Orleans was so full of crazy people, everyone living with security lights and air-conditioning twenty-four hours a day, as if it were always summer at the polar ice cap.

I circled the house, and it was tight against intruders. I stepped back almost into Prytania Street, looking for weak spots, and what I noticed first was the plate-glass window. Huge and fragile, like the fontanel on a complete baby's head: I saw honor in not yielding to the temptation to go through it. I went around to the back again, remembered the ladder in the shed, remembered, too, that the Rolex had two diamonds on it, one at twelve, one at six; I'd go up to the bedroom window, silently cut the glass the way I'd seen in movies, undo the latch, creep in, put the watch on his dresser. He'd find it when he wakened, find the missing pane, too, and by then I'd be on my way to Nashville. He'd understand completely.

Diamonds etch and squeak on glass, but I don't believe they do anything else. I was teetering on the very top of the extension ladder. I closed my ears from the inside to pretend I wasn't making a sound; it's possible to do that if I pull my scalp back with those muscles some people can't use. All I could think about was balance, so it took a while to notice the window wasn't latched. I pushed it up, breaking my index fingernail, and reflexively I pulled back from the movement, hoping to save the nail. I started to fall. I grabbed the outside sill from underneath, but some part of me was still thinking about saving my nails; I didn't hold tight enough, and the ladder pitched backward with me on it. I didn't scream, I watched myself fall in slow motion, inertia leaving my mind behind so I almost enjoyed the rollercoaster thrill in my stomach; I was fearless. I landed in a tender light-dazed young azalea bush, and I could have started over again, but the ladder was aluminum, and all the scalp straining in the world wouldn't make the clatter of aluminum against itself go away.

They both came to the window, jostling each other, brave because they expected to see someone badly and freshly hurt on the ground. Peg Walters saw me, and when I sat up she began screaming, full-throttle, full-throat screams. "Oh, for God's sake, Peg," I heard Maxim say. She kept screaming, and indoor lights began to come on in the upstairs rooms of houses nearby; only the church remained dark. Maxim disappeared from the window, and Peg settled down, not leaving her place, as if she could do something by watching me. I thought Maxim might come running out to the yard, but I also knew that the chances were good he was going to act restrained, and that was all right. I stood up to leave, and Peg began screeching again, "She's getting away, Maxim, go catch her, for Lord's sake." I started to run, and all my muscles worked, carried by intact bones, though I knew the next day I was going to be terribly sore. I made it to the front of the house, remembered my car was parked next to the church, considered cutting back through the yard, began running instead down Prytania Street, then Maxim came loping up easily and grabbed me from behind. His arms were around my chest, strong but not mean, and I stopped running, letting him hold me. The watch box was in my hand, like a runner's baton, the watch itself was looped around my hand. While he held me, I could feel him breathing heavily, then I could feel him getting hard and excited, and I eased my body gently up against his. I put the watch back into its box. "Here," I said, holding the box up to him.

Peg Walters came fast-waddling up from behind. "Oh, no you don't," she said. Maxim let me go, and I considered running, but he was still so close to me that I couldn't move with the thick pull of him. I tried to press the watch into his hand, and she said to me, "The police are on their way. They're going to see that thing on *you*." I told her it was mine to begin with. "You are crazier than I thought," she said.

"Tell her," I said to Maxim.

"I got that watch for Christmas," he said.

TWENTY-THREE

I f anyone asks, I'd be glad to tell why a criminal gets into trouble over and over again. Something starts at the moment of arrest that automatically turns him, in his own mind, into the victim. For me, learning Maxim was not a truth-teller began to transform all my perceptions, so if I'd ever had any notion that breaking into someone's house, even to deposit a gift, had a tinge of wrong, I forgot it quickly. "I have the receipt," I screamed to Peg Walters, to the officers in the car, even to Maxim, and I could see they enjoyed hearing that. I was so full of rage that when I was placed in a cell hours later, I felt I already was a friend of the women who were in there first. I was ready to get even, to struggle for release only so I could go out on the street and expose righteous-looking people for what they were.

Two women already were in the cell. It was late morning; I had no watch now, not mine, certainly not Maxim's. For a second I thought timing was off; this was like a hotel, and I'd arrived before checkout time, before the previous occupants had packed out, before anyone had had a chance to clean up after them. Both women were black, and I figured they were traveling together, but each one sat on a low bench staring into space, not speaking. Neither looked at me until I tried to sit down next to one. "Nuh, uh," she said. I thought I was doing something to make her feel good, being willing to sit next to her without hesitation; most white people would explore every other squirmy option first. I looked at the other, caught her eye; she shook her head no. I considered the floor. I was still wearing the cotton knit Liz Claiborne shirt and skirt I'd worn to Patti Ann's. It now had mint ice cream and pollen and grass stains on it, but it was a floral pattern in pinks and greens and palest yellow, and it still looked like a $182 outfit. I considered the toilet; when I was small I'd sit on the toilet with the lid down and ask my mother questions. The seatless toilet had no water and so much rust in it that Naomi would have refused to come near it, much less try to clean it; it was so foul I expected old excrement would vaporize and seep into all the naked holes under my skirt. I knew eventually I was going to have to pee, if only from boredom, but I was going to put it off as long as possible. "You don't want to sit there, neither. They got mices in there," one woman said.

I sat on the floor, my skirt pulled out from under me, only my bun tips touching the floor through my pantihose. The pantihose were laddered up one leg anyway. My knees pressed my chin, and I was enveloped in the scent of me. It was an after-recess smell, of lunch and playground and immature sweat on once-clean cotton. I'd been in elevators with children from time to time, and the smell of them wafting up had given me this terrific sense of comfort. I breathed in deeply. "I'm Eleanor," I said, still a child, guessing. Neither woman answered. One was wearing black spandex shorts, a T-shirt that said EXERCISE YO' GAME, and bedroom scuffs. Her hair looked as if a lightning storm had just passed through it. The other woman was astonishingly fat, with a belly hanging off the front of her like a geologic shelf, temporarily empty of babies and defying all rules of gravity. She was wearing jeans and a mussed up fuchsia cotton shirt, and I wondered where on earth she found jeans to fit her.

"DWI," the fat one said into the air after a while.

"Definitely," the other one said.

"I beg your pardon?" I said. They were talking into the air, but they were talking to me.

"You DWI, no doubt about it, no matter you *look* stone cold sober," the woman in the T-shirt said. It didn't sound like an insult, the way she said it. I shrugged. "You don't know if you DWI?" She sniffed the air, as if she could smell my offense on me. Without thinking, I sniffed the air, too, and all I could come up with was the close acrid odor of underarms and crotches that hadn't been washed in a day and a half in hot, still weather. I asked her what DWI meant.

"You a kick," the fat one said. "Driving while, what, influence? No, driving *under* the influence."

"Intoxicated," the other said.

"I'm not drunk."

"Nobody like you come in here for nothing *besides* being drunk."

"I was breaking and entering," I said, wanting to be as good as they were at being bad. They looked at each other, and here I was, in school again, the odd one, knowing what the rest were thinking, refusing to talk and clear myself because it probably wasn't possible anyway. "For what?" the fat one said and giggled. "Hey, I got screwed over, all right?" I said.

"Oo-o-o, woo-o-o," the one in the T-shirt said, and both went back to staring into space.

I didn't know why I was locked up. Being in jail is like riding public transportation. It's so simple that dropouts and fools do it all the time, but they learned young, when they had a right to know nothing. The first time I tried to board a streetcar, I tried to get on at the wrong end. I was almost twenty years old. I met with helpful hoots usually reserved for tourists while I banged at the rear door, and I backed away, half into the flow of traffic, letting the street-car go, full of people laughing at me. Downstairs, in the narrow corridor with nothing but pay phones and angry deputies, I'd stood frozen with the knowledge that I had three minutes to learn my way out. "What you think they got bondsmen listed by the phone for?" a man had said to me, and I'd dialed one, hitting the sequence of twenty-five numbers that would put a call on my credit card without my having a quarter. Nothing happened, and the same man came over, dialed a sequence of numbers for me, and said, Tell them you calling collect. "Get me out of here, and I'll have the money for you the minute the Whitney Bank opens," I said, and the voice on the line laughed. I told him I had an American Express Gold Card. "Yeah, and where's it at now?" he said. "You get somebody over to my office, you'll be out for breakfast, eat as much as that gold card can hold," he said, and hung up.

The deputy was a very short man, whose ethnic origins could only be narrowed by the fact that he had stick-straight hair. His skin was brown, his eyes were green, and racially he was the closest thing to me in the place besides the two men and a woman in the holding area who all had pumpkin-orange hair down to the middle of their backs. I looked at him as humbly as I could, and he held up three fingers. It was probably late enough now to call Poppy. I'd read that most heart attacks happen in the predawn hours, and I figured it'd be best if I called after he'd wakened on his own. "Poppy?" I said when he answered, and I heard "Poppy?" and a little whoop of derision behind me. I cupped my hand around the mouthpiece, then thought better of it. "I'm in Central Lockup," I said, as if that were a regular event. The crowded corridor was almost silent behind me. Poppy had no idea what Central Lockup was, and the next thing anyone nearby heard me say was, "Jail," and I heard snickering.

"Christ, Eleanor, now you're going to be the death of *me*," he hollered.

"Shh, shh," I said, though a part of me wanted everyone to hear him through the receiver, wanted me to be able to turn around and say, He thinks I'm going to kill him; I killed my parents, too, you know. "Look, this is just one big misunderstanding. Don't worry about it. All you've got to do is go see this guy, and he'll come get me the hell out of here." I turned, hoping for approving looks, but suddenly everyone was too busy making fast phone calls before the deputy could scream at them and shove them back into the holding cubicle, a place with no phone or toilet or chance to be understood.

Poppy began to cry on the phone. Piteously, the way old men cry when they are lying in bed dying, and the pain between morphine injections is so terrible, and they're all of a sudden realizing that they have amounted to nothing memorable, and they're simply not ready to die.

"Oh, no," I whispered. Poppy was a nowhere man, and I knew my ache created by his hollowness had kept me away from places like the neighborhood drugstore where the pharmacist let his sons work in the summers and knew everyone's name and inevitably failed when K&B and Eckerd Drugs and Walgreen's moved in. There was absolutely no fairness in Poppy having such ease when he was as weak as a wet paper bag, capable of holding almost nothing. He kept sobbing and sniffling and saying, "I'm all right," until I felt it didn't matter to me whether he was all right. "You've got to help me," I said, and I could feel the deputy moving closer to me, measuring out my time in inches. "Oh, this is terrible," Poppy said, moaning in a way that made me know he didn't feel a bit sorry for me. "Poppy!" I said; the noise level in the corridor dropped, and the deputy stepped back a foot, giving me twelve bits of time. My eyes were filling up with tears, but they were angry tears, nothing to be ashamed of, nothing to invite mockery. "I have never asked for help before, and I'll never ask for help again," I said evenly.

"Are you crazy?" Poppy said. I shook my head no. "Are you crazy?" He was screaming. "Do you know what help means?"

Now I was crying, pretending this was my lover on the line, doing me wrong; after all, I was in a corridor full of men who did women wrong, made them cry, said they were sorry, started over again. I couldn't stop crying, and the deputy started toward me again, and I shouted the bondsman's number to Poppy. "Or any bondsman. Or a lawyer.

Ellis Ryan. Anybody," before the deputy gently removed the receiver from my hand and replaced it in the cradle.

A guard took me upstairs when no one had come for me. There was a pay phone in the cell, and I kept trying the house, calling collect, getting no answer. I figured I was waiting fifteen minutes between tries, but I had no way of knowing. I began to take comfort in the pattern of the phone number on the keypad, my fingers at one point following the sign of the cross, up, down, right, left. I'd always wanted to be able to cross myself the way the girls released for catechism did; I saw great drama in that final sweep across their chests. With dial phones, our number had been nothing more than a random sequence. I wondered whose idea the tic-tac-toe pattern had been; why not digits one through eight across, nine and zero beneath them for the thumbs, played like a typewriter keyboard? I punched the numbers again. "You getting on my damn nerves," the fat woman said.

"Sorry," I said. No one answered, and I hung up.

We had bologna sandwiches on French bread with mayonnaise for lunch, and I took mine when it was offered, thinking of World War II soldiers who used chocolate and cigarettes to take advantage wherever they could. I wouldn't eat bologna if it were the last food on earth, if only because I wouldn't want to die with the taste of rubber flesh in my mouth. Jacqueline, the fat woman, ate half my sandwich as if it were a canapé, two bites. "You were born in 1963, I bet," I said to her when she told me her name. "How you know?" "You have eyes like Jackie Kennedy, you probably were born with them," I said, and she gave me a remarkably healthy smile. It was true, too: Jackie Kennedy seen any other way was walleyed and a little hyperthyroid. I could imagine this Jacqueline, a bottle-fed baby with no fat stores in her legs, her mama straightening and bouffanting her hair, set on the track for men to want her for the airs she put on. If she grew up and didn't quite merit the Onassis millions, well then maybe she'd go down to the corner of Iberville and Chartres and turn tricks for ten dollars for men who liked masses of warm flesh and Frenchified names. The other woman, who never would tell her name, left in the late afternoon, slipping Jacqueline two hand-rolled cigarettes from her bra. "Tell you the truth, I'm on vacation," Jacqueline said, by way of explaining why she was still there. "I ain't call nobody when I come in. I got five boys, one girl, and a grandbaby back at my house, I figure I rest a day, let my mama look out for them." Jacqueline stretched out on the bench, supine, Saint-Exupéry's boa, and when she fell asleep I began dialing the phone over and over, just hitting "0" when I tired of all the numerals; Naomi was never there. Or else Poppy had told her not to answer the phone ever again, and he'd given no explanations in case she began to feel sorry for me. I was beginning to get the same operators: even though they were supposed to act like extensions of machines, trained not to think about what they were doing, trying to remember nothing so they could sleep at night, they started to recognize my name and act slightly annoyed. "Why don't you try a different number?" one said after a while, and I gave her the number of Ellis's direct line. Person to person, I told her, to Ellis Ryan. "I can't," I heard him say. I gave her the number of the church, person to person to Maxim Walters. I heard Mary Cook's voice. "I can't accept those charges," Mary said. "She has to ask him, doesn't she have to ask him, this is person to person," I said. Mary put us on hold. "Thanks for the suggestion to call around," I said to the empty air around the operator. "Sure," she said, pleased. Maxim accepted the charges. "Hey, what's your name?" I said to the operator before she got off the line. She'd been the only helpful person I'd met in a long time, and I didn't want to let her go. Operator number one-eleven, she told me. "Thanks a *lot*," I said.

"Eleanor, I can't help you, you know."

"I'm in jail. Isn't there some parable about getting the man who smites you out of jail?" I said. He said he doubted it. "Or maybe there's one about forgiving the righteous man who takes a Rolex watch that he could've owned once, could've even owned right then, but for some reason *didn't*."

"You're making a mockery of all I believe in."

"I'm just joking. Can't you even laugh anymore?" He said nothing, and I felt sorrier for him than I did for myself. "You're not going to make it, Maxim." He was silent. "I don't love you anymore," I said.

"I wish you'd thought of that two days ago."

"Two days ago you hadn't told a greedy, stupid lie."

"You can have the watch back."

"I don't want the watch back. That was the whole point. I was planning to *leave*, if you must know, and I had absolutely no use for it whatsoever, and I figured you could use it, and I was trying to leave it for you, and then look what happens."

"Eleanor, I can't help you."

"Then what'd you accept the charges for?" I said sadly and hung up.

TWENTY-FOUR

The air in the cell still hung with the faded smoke of marijuana cigarettes. Weed, Jacqueline had called it, as she started her barter with me, a match in return for a lungful or two. It was a country scent, what I imagined a mix of hay and pig manure would smell like. Jacqueline had filled the toilet after dinner with a million tiny turds that wouldn't go anywhere. I lay on the bench, directly blaming Poppy for every breath I had to take, every wave of nausea that came over me. All that kept me from vomiting was knowing I'd have to live with it, as if I were in a capsule in weightless space, where every droplet of effluence would break into the air into billions of nasty particles. I'd inhaled some of the smoke, and for a while I had worried that I might become giggly and hungry, but I imagined Jacqueline's lungs were huge bellows, sucking in far more than her share of available air and its pleasures, giving back only toxic carbon dioxide for me.

Hours had passed since lights out, but I had my elbows crossed in front of my eyes, blocking sudden light and jarring sound if morning came. Jacqueline had fallen asleep early, breathing noiselessly for a woman of operatic bulk, but I was restless inside the dark quiet I had made for my-self. I was waiting for the reverberations of footsteps in the corridor, footsteps that would stop at my door. I didn't no-tice when Jacqueline tiptoed over and knelt next to me. "You lonely?" she said, and I nodded, not moving my arms from in front of my eyes. I felt her thick hand moving gen-tly over my breasts, and I was surprised that the touch ex-cited me. I told her to stop. "Shh," she said. I sat up, and she pressed me down gently. I whispered that I was going to scream. "I ain't throwed the roach away yet, you want to be in major trouble, you go hollering for attention," she whispered back. "But truth is, I don't think you want no-body coming."

"I'm not lonely," I said.

"This point it don't make no difference," she said, slip-ping her hand under my skirt and trying to tug off my pantihose. I grabbed her hands, pulled hard, but she was stronger than I was, and not bothered by fingernails dig-ging into her skin. Another nail broke, and I let go. "I thought you were a prostitute." "What that is?" "A hooker." "So?" I pressed my knees together, but she pushed them apart. I was a child being forced to put on clothing I hated, fighting my mother over the wool slacks when I wanted the yellow organza dress. "So you're supposed to like men," I said, breathing hard from the struggle not to scream. She laughed. "What you get paid for, it's hard to like," she said, and I thought I'd like a chance to tell that to Maxim. Then I closed my eyes and let her do what she wanted, I was in the dentist's chair, seeing nothing, think-ing of other things, whimpering when the pain was too much, but not thinking about it, about where it came from. "Give me your hand," she said, and I moved automatically, cooperating with the dentist so he would not cut back the nitrous oxide. It's possible to have no sense of touch whatsoever if you try hard enough, my hand could have been anywhere, doing anything, but it was numb, disembodied. I opened my eyes, and she was right over me, her eyes half out of their sockets; she wasn't seeing me, either. "You wet," she said. I felt a great rip of pain, as if someone had run a meat slicer up inside me. "I want Naomi." I reached for her, sobbing now. "What this is?" she said, recoiling. She held her hand in front of her face, and I saw blood on her fingers. "Aw, baby, don't tell me that," she said. I sat bolt upright. I'd had my period a week ago, and I'd read about women who start getting periods very close together and then the doctor finds that they are flooding estrogen and filling their bodies with cancer, and suddenly I was sick with fear. "How old you is?" Jacqueline said. "Why?" I said. She sat back on her sumo haunches. "Because you too old to be no virgin, that's why." She cocked her head, looking at me. "Your face pretty under all that mess, yeah. No man be put off by that."

I lay on the bench and cried softly into the night. Jacqueline wasn't the sort to feel anything, especially when it came from someone else, but over time, with children who demanded some rituals, she'd learned to hand over something, money, gifts, pleasures, jokes, if someone looked needy enough. She couldn't sleep with my sniffling. "I taken boy cherries, but never no *girl's*," she said, chuckling, thinking she might cheer me up. "You don't understand. I'm in here because my lover's wife called the police." "Yeah," she said, "and your lover got a dick the size of one of them little birthday candles." I began to cry harder. "Hush," she said gently. "No," I said, feeling good with the freedom of crying like a small child. She offered me her other joint. I told her I didn't do that stuff. "Honey, tonight I'm ready to believe just about anything," she said. I rolled over, facing the wall, tugging at my clothes until I was neatly covered. I heard her strike a match. It was that quiet; everyone else up there now had the idea that I was a virgin. I covered my ears. With the motion of her mammoth shadows, I knew she was moving toward me. I didn't turn over, and a cloud of smoke blew softly over my face, filling the little pocket of space by the wall. I told her to stop it. "Take the medicine, baby," she said, laughing softly, inhaling, blowing smoke, a mother bird chewing up the worm. I took in the hempy smell, and she kept feeding it to me. I was enjoying the quiet, the rhythm, and I stopped crying, taken in by the process.

My thoughts began to dance through brilliance. I wanted to say something to Jacqueline, but we knew nothing in common. Except maybe the involuntary processes, breathing, pumping blood, a few spontaneous reactions, blinking. "Minimal experience is universal," I said. She said nothing, kept blowing dry smoke, more lazily now. "I mean, even this baby with no brain could breathe. I wonder if he knew fear. Cockroaches know fear." "Hush, girl," Jacqueline said, and I slipped into a whirring, twirling sleep, of spinning rooms and grand ideas that trailed off to nowhere like banners behind tiny airplanes, flying backward.

When I awakened, Jacqueline was gone, having had enough of her vacation at some moment in the early morning. She hadn't said goodbye, but I didn't expect good manners anymore. Two other women were in the cell with me. They were both skinny and white, the sort who wear jeans so tight you can see a three-inch gap between their thighs. They frightened me. I'd read once about a woman who moved from New Orleans to Baltimore and got herself murdered six weeks later by a white man. "She was so used to being afraid only of blacks uptown, figuring everyone white was bound to be all right," a friend had said to the *Times-Picayune*, and a flurry of senseless letters to the editor had lasted three days after that. I figured anyone white who got thrown in jail had to be innately evil, with nothing to blame behavior on. That was why more white men were executed in the South than black men; they had no earthly excuse, so judges sent them straight to hell.

I stared at the two women, exercising my right of having been there first. "What you looking at?" one said. "Nothing," I said, figuring I didn't look as seasoned as I felt. "You DWI?" I said. "Yeah, right," she said.

I had to wait for almost an hour for the other to give up the pay phone. I lay on the bench as if I didn't care and eavesdropped. I was used to listening in on spoiled, aimless women who had passed forty, had sent at least one child to Dartmouth, and had realized they were going to dedicate the rest of their lives to hiding the lines in their faces. These girls looked as if, having finished with high school one way or the other, they sat around their mamas' living rooms in Arabi watching commercials for beauty college and bartending school, believing they were going to have options whenever they got in the mood. The one on the phone was named Dana, as she sang into the phone after she punched the numbers to call collect—Day-nuh, she said with annoyance after the third call, as if the computer should know her by now. She had stripped white hair with black roots; I could imagine her getting up in the morning, seeing the roots, complaining out loud to no one, Shit, you'd think by now it'd give up and just come out blond. "Jesus, I am so pissed," Dana sang to each person who took her call. She needed to find someone to tape *Days of Our Lives*. So go out and *buy* a tape, she said to one; You don't have to program it, asshole, just do it straight off the set, she said to another. I told her I needed the phone while she had her finger on the hang-up button; the receiver had never left her hand. "This's an emergency, hold on," she said, humping up her hip, annoyed. I was beginning to panic, imagining myself in that cell, for weeks on end, while it filled up with other women's shit.

A deputy came to get me before Dana found someone to tape her television program. "*I'd* have done it for you if you'd only been nice," I said as I left. Never mind that I didn't have a VCR; my philosophy about VCRs was that all television was supposed to be live and ephemeral. With a VCR there was no reason for memory, and I loved the exercise of memory the way some people enjoyed stretching sinew until it popped.

There was no anxiety in leaving, no questions. I expected my grandfather at the release gate, but I'd have gone to anyone; I'd have sworn the Unabomber was my loving brother, that Jeffrey Dahmer was the father of my children, and I'd have walked straight to either with no hitch in my step. I went through locked doors and around hall corners, through a cold arraignment, and I planned what I would say to Poppy. I hope you saw I was packed,

I'd say. You want to be really rid of me, you should've come when I called. He'd say he was having to spend a lot of money for all the trouble I'd caused, and I'd say, So? Maybe he'd shake me and show a scintilla of life.

I looked out, a child at the school gate in a rainstorm, searching for familiarity, for a white face, for a white man's face, for an old white man's face. Quite a number of people were waiting. It was the second weekend of the Jazz Festival, and even though it drew a more sensitive crowd than Mardi Gras, it nevertheless filled the streets with extra thousands of people, so the city pulsed with a sick headache, the way a woman's body might after swallowing too much salt water out in the Gulf of Mexico, bloating as if anticipating death. Even all the hipsters who came to shake their lily-pale backsides slightly out of synch with the music, patronizing in their joy, weren't immune to putting back too much Corona beer, then driving around the crazy Gentilly streets, lost and making U-turns, until a cop pulled them over. "Women don't get *no* special treatment three times a year, Carnival, Jazz Fest, and New Year's," Jacqueline had told me. "Too bad no hotshits get arrested in summer; believe you me they'd air-condition this place inside a *minute*."

I saw a man I knew, but I couldn't place him, except to sense that somewhere he had brushed up against me and excited me. A rich man, clearly a rich man; even from a distance I knew his suit was silk, his white shirt pure cotton, pressed and starched. It drove me nuts when I saw people in public and couldn't identify them except to know that this one had hurt my feelings, that one had cheated me. I liked the fact that most store clerks wore their uni-

forms on their way to and from work: I could see a familiar woman, note her red Winn-Dixie shirt, remember that
she had told me, "I know you're in a hurry, so I'll check you
out this time, but next time don't come through the express line with twenty items, please," as she'd scanned each
of twenty cartons of yogurt. I considered that one item,
but I still liked her fine until I heard her say the exact same
thing to the man behind me with a basket full of packages
of hamburger buns.

The man in the waiting area caught my eye, nodded re-
assuringly, and when I went out the gate I walked straight
toward him. When I saw his hands, fine moon-pale hands
hanging softly out of starched cuffs with platinum links, I
remembered Dr. Farraday. "You're here for me?" I said. He
nodded. I didn't consider the possibility of disaster, I only
thought of his cool hands at the back of my neck, hands
that could probe inside a human brain and shut out all
memory, hands so delicate they cured whatever they
touched. I felt the pressure of his hand at my back as he
directed me across the street, and I smiled with well-being.

TWENTY-FIVE

We didn't exchange a word. Around the Broad Street ramp that circled the K-9 training yard, past the pumping station where construction went on so long it almost destroyed that car dealership and ran out the fish market and Popeye's, all the way up Napoleon Avenue to St. Charles. I could think of a great deal to start up with, because New Orleans has a common language, of floods and foolish mayors and .38-caliber guns; make a pronouncement on any such topic, and agreement will be absolute. That is why New Orleans never burns when all the other cities are on fire.

He pulled up in front of my house, turned off the motor, and said, "He had a stroke." Dr. Farraday's expression was almost apologetic, as if his presence in the neighborhood should have promised that the blood vessels in every head nearby would be as strong as five-eighths-inch rubber bands. I stared at him. Poppy was dead, my terrible luck having pricked a thin sac in his old head, filling it with blood and senselessness, so he'd had a fraction of a lucid second in which he'd known he hated me, and then he'd seen a terrific light, with my grandmother and my father, all in white, calling to him, and he'd said, Well, of course I'll come, all I have left on earth is that dreadful Eleanor. "I didn't know if you wanted to go see him," Dr. Farraday said. I was halfway down the tunnel to God with Poppy, lost in sleepiness and imagination. "See him?" I whispered. He was embarrassed, a city man with country manners that could have accounted for his never having married as far as Naomi and his own housekeeper knew. "I mean, you might want to freshen up." I let out a whistling sigh, realizing now that Poppy wasn't dead. It didn't matter how alive he was, because he'd been walking around as disconnected as a loosed helium balloon for years, stopped only by ceilings in darkened rooms. What mattered was that he still had a chance to get angry with me and get it over with. I looked at Dr. Farraday, and with his black hair and his buttersweet eyes, he was quite beautiful. "Hey," I said, and he looked away. He made it easy to consider saying wild things. I told him I owed him more thanks than I knew, probably than he knew, too. This was a man who could make a thousand dollars a minute, more than a Detroit CEO or a contestant on *Jeopardy* could make. And he could do it forever, at least until his hands began to shake. I reached over and stroked his hand, and he pulled it away slowly enough to be polite and full of regret. He might never have made love to a woman; it was one of those skills that had to be learned early or not at all, like boarding a streetcar. I could picture him with his Mississippi manners, probably in a Tulane dormitory with all the ignorant Long Island boys running around the corridors; he was studious and full of fear among boys who were neither. I asked him if he could come in and wait, figuring I could take a shower and dress in about $20,000 worth of his time. He nodded, took the keys out of the ignition, and I looked at the car clock, measured out how exquisitely valuable time with me must have been to him, and I knew I was going to have to go slowly with this man.

If I'd wanted to, I could have pretended to myself that I'd left the house only an hour ago, gone to Maxim's house, put the watch on his dresser, then returned to find everything exactly as it was. While Dr. Farraday sat in the living room and waited, I scurried through rooms, found a saucer in the kitchen sink where I'd left it at night, Naomi's uniform in the closet where it always hung until midmorning, half-packed clothes strewn about my room for final decisions, Poppy's bed in the disarray of a man who's come awake to an alarm clock, flung covers aside, and stumbled into the bathroom for his shower. I played a game from time to time, where I'd find myself in a room and pretend I was eight years old and knew nothing of anything that had happened since then. I would look at an object, limiting its associations to the time before 1973, pretend I knew nothing of Watergate or puberty or cable television, force out memory. Even in a house where little had changed in as long as I could remember, the game never held for very long, because there were too many intrusions, sleek cars, as streamlined as fish, seen through the window, newsmagazines on a table with so-what nudity on the covers, my own hands with long, slender fingers and nails manicured into sweet ovals.

"Where's Naomi?" I said when I came downstairs seventeen minutes later, smelling of soap instead of sour anger.

"She's with him."

"You don't say very much," I said when we were in the car. I still had the prescription slip where he'd written "Channel 8" when I had my accident. He had uttered only about a dozen words all the time he'd been in my room.

"No," he said and tried out a little laugh.

"I didn't say a word from the time I was ten until I was fourteen."

"I know."

"Poppy told you? My grandfather, I mean." I sat forward, pulling at the seatbelt. It hadn't occurred to me that people bothered to talk about me unless they were plotting, working out unbridled meanness, cruel young boys and envious fat women.

"The man can't talk," he said.

"Sorry," I said. "I guess I just really don't want to know anything about now. I mean, I'm happy he's not dead. I hope you know that. But *you* actually could tell me how he is, and I don't want to hear. If he's lying there, and his skin's all intact, and he's not bleeding and broken, I can pretend anything I want." To me the only kind of people who looked as if they were near death were the ones who were so skinny that their bones were the most of them and the ones whose brains had been spattered on a sidewalk. I'd seen them on television. Anyone else could pass for as healthy as I was.

"I think you're in for a shock," he said quietly.

He left me to Naomi at the ICU. She was in the waiting room in her street clothes, and her eyes were red-rimmed. I ran to her and put my arms around her; she froze, arms at her sides, but I kept on holding on to her.

"You gone way too far this time, girl," she said, pulling away from me.

I asked her to tell me what happened. She looked up at the wall clock. "I ain't saying nothing until you go in there and see what you done. You get five minutes on the hour, I been going in there, like maybe he got to know somebody that knows him, now you take you turn. *Then* you find out what happened."

Poppy had caved in, that is the only way to put it. Where ordinarily muscle makes form, there were sunken troughs, in his chest, in his face, in his belly. His mouth looked as if someone had twisted it with pliers. Poppy still had all his teeth, and I could see all the bottom ones on the right side, kernels of brown corn stripped back almost to the roots. Saliva was dripping off his lip onto his gown, puddling in one place. He had a tube in his nose, thin wires running under his gown to his chest, and an IV in his arm, none of which obstructed my view of him quite enough. He wasn't fractured or split open in any way, but he was a specter of new death for me: the spirit flown out of his loose mouth, an airborne vapor I probably could have seen if I'd been there at the time, leaving him with as little sense as a beaten pup dog. I thought it would be nice to cry, to give him a feeling his death was going to be a terrible loss to me. I thought it would be nice to be sad, too, for my own benefit, but I found myself standing there with only the mildest curiosity, the sort that makes people slow down at traffic accidents or look at pictures of snakes swallowing live baby chicks. "Hey, Poppy," I whispered, wanting to be kind. He didn't react at all. I was the only person on earth who called him Poppy, and I was a relative newcomer in his life. "Mr. Rushing," I said, and he let out a little moan of recognition. His eyes didn't focus or turn. "I'm

Eleanor. Eleanor Rushing. I'm your grandchild." He didn't
respond at all. "I live in your house, I've lived in your house
almost twenty years. You don't know me, right?" No sound
came from him. "You don't love me, right?" I thought I saw
him flinch, hearing a lost woman's voice. I'd never known
my grandmother very well, but I'd figured long ago that
she'd probably actually expired from pure loneliness. "It's
okay, somewhere along the line, I kind of figured out you
weren't going to love me." A droplet of spit fell off his lip.
The wet patch was going to spread until it covered his entire gown, and then someone would come in and change
it, there was no point in wiping his mouth; I could mes-
merize myself, watching the spit stain grow, the way I'd
sometimes watched my bath water rise slowly, only a
trickle coming from the faucet, wondering how long it
would take to drown a saucy little cockroach that was sitting perfectly still on the side of the tub. "You're in there,
right? You can't talk, your brain's probably sending signals,
but you're not saying anything. How's it feel? Hey, Poppy,
hey, Mr. Rushing, I know how it feels. Honest."

"Om," he said, then repeated it, like a mantra, and the
saliva dribbled from his mouth. I pulled a tissue out of the
box on the table nearby and wiped his lip.

"Okay? That better?" He didn't look at me, though I
thought I saw a bit of relief cross his face. "All right! Here,
look, I'm going to tell you everything you need to know.
Let's leave off the past two days." I snapped my fingers.
"There! Gone! See how easy?"

"Om." His eyes flashed toward me a bit.

I patted his hand. He was an animal in a trap, not
knowing where his pain was coming from, knowing only a

vague, constant fear. He had no reason to trust me, unless I came at him slowly, taming him. But then, he'd forget me as soon as I left; all I had to do was make him a little comfortable in the moment. "You're my captive audience, Poppy," I said, smiling. Bared teeth are a menace in nature; maybe he'd forgotten the goodness of smiling, but I thought I'd read that even newborns appreciate a good, broad grin. "And guess what? I'm going to do you a big favor. I'm going to talk. Let me tell you, in case you don't know it already, there is nothing worse than being a captive audience to dead silence. You should've talked to me!"

His head rolled a little to the side, and I lowered my voice. "You should've talked to me. Hey, for maybe the past fifteen years or so, I could've done without it, if you'd just said something at first. Stand over my bed. Holler at me for as long as it takes, tell me the truth. Especially when I'm asleep, just say it over and over. They died in a car crash, and it wasn't your fault, Eleanor, it wasn't your fault." I knelt at the side of the bed, burying my face in the sheets. "I wasn't a house cat, Poppy, people need more doing than that." I was getting louder so he'd hear me and sit up and apologize if my words went deep enough. "Just once, you could've loved me just once. I'd have carried it around for a long time. Tell me you love me. Just one time!" I was too loud, and Naomi came running in, breaking the rules.

"Om. Om, om, om. Omi," Poppy shrilled with recognition at the sight of her. I threw myself on top of him, held on tight, closed my eyes, my ears, did not breathe until I gave myself up to the firm, gentle hands of everyone but Naomi.

Twenty-Six

Naomi was waiting in the corridor. "He all she got," Naomi said, "he all she got."

"That's not true," I said, calmer now that I was out in the hall, away from Poppy. Dr. Farraday came running up. "Sometimes I feel like *I* need to be in a hospital," I said to him, trying to get him to smile. He put his arm around my shoulder, the cool of his million-dollar fingers coming through my dress, and he led me into an empty office. "He's not going to die," he said when the door was closed.

"But he's dying."

He shook his head no, the way knowledgeable people can. "He looks dreadful, but I've never seen anyone his age lying in a hospital who didn't look dreadful. At least no men; a woman'll get a manicurist and a hairdresser into the ICU if she thinks she can get away with it." I pictured Poppy with curlers and a nose tube and a smear of red lipstick, and I giggled with tears in my eyes, the way children do when someone tickles them during a tantrum. He asked me if I wanted a sedative. I nodded. I'd never turned down a prescription in my life, and I had full bottles of antibiotics and painkillers dating back to 1984 in one of my bathroom drawers. Naomi had come across them from time to time, telling me alternately that they were dangerous and useless, and I told her each time, "Well, you can never tell when you're going to need something that no one else thinks is good for you." I didn't plan on packing my collection; I figured in Nashville doctors and everyone else would believe what I told them.

"I got to him on time, really, it's going to be all right," he said as he was writing out the prescription. "He knew something was wrong, and he called me, and I was still home. I mean, he was even joking, said, 'I've got a screaming headache, must be a brain tumor, might as well call in a specialist'; he even opened the door for me. And that was it. Any man who can do that in the time it takes for an aneurysm to blow in his head is not ready to die." So many words. We were getting somewhere.

"Poppy said that?" I had no idea Poppy ever tried jokes, even lame ones. Maybe this was that final burst of energy, like the flash that comes right before the light bulb burns out. Dr. Farraday nodded, handed me the prescription. I automatically looked at the bottom to see whether he'd given me refills. He hadn't, and that was good. I hated filling prescriptions and stashing them away when I knew I could have more. Only once had I gone for the refill a week later, and that had been for Percodan. I'd figured that if ever I wanted to kill myself, Percodan would be a dizzyingly splendid way to do it. Even a phony attempt wouldn't be bad. Valium, the prescription said. I might try Valium. Following a doctor's advice instead of going buck against it might prove to be good for me.

He told me he'd check on me later, and he said it with such directness that I knew he would. I wanted to find out how he'd come to be the one who'd driven over and gotten me out of jail when men of God and law had refused. But I didn't ask him because that was a fast, personal sort of question. I wanted to stay in that room for a long time, for hundreds of thousands of dollars worth of his time, I wanted to move a fraction of an inch closer to him each time he wasn't paying attention, one-two-three-red-light, run up and tag the one who's it, you win. I did not want to go sit in the waiting room with Naomi and listen to a litany of bad things I had done over almost twenty years, ending up with, I sure better stay away from you, you kill everybody come close. "Take her home," he said softly to Naomi when we stepped outside into the corridor, where she was waiting, filling up her mouth with invective, like a kid at the water fountain, swelling his cheek and daring anyone to come near. Naomi swallowed hard. "We going on the streetcar," she said to no one in particular.

I fished in my purse for carfare when we were standing at the stop, brought up two quarters, a dime, and a five-dollar bill. Naomi had not yet said a word to me. "It's a dollar now, just put in the five, three people behind us ride free. You not exactly poor, not that you ever was."

"Poppy's not going to die, Theo said so."

"Who Theo is?"

"Theo Farraday."

"Oh," she said.

"I'm kidding. Dr. Farraday," I said.

"Girl, what I'm going to do with you?"

The streetcar was crowded, running uptown right after Jazz Fest, and Naomi and I were belly to belly, standing at the back. "How about doing nothing? I seem to survive just fine when you do nothing." I'd read about gardens run amok with roses the size of cabbages when left alone.

"Yeah, I do nothing, you still be sitting in jail." She said it as loud as she could, and a dozen people turned around to look, expecting to see a wiry little black mama hollering up at her thick dumb son. I stared blankly at them, then pivoted away, as if I had no earthly idea whom this crazy woman was talking to. I was going to let her get off at our stop, then ride up two blocks, walk back, fool a streetcar full of strangers. "We get off next stop, Eleanor," she said straight at me, then pushed the button at the back door to buzz the conductor. "Damn," I said and avoided the eyes of everyone who was still watching us.

I skipped down the step of the streetcar while Naomi was still holding the door open, and I told her I was going to Eckerd Drugs before she could catch up with me. What for? she wanted to know. A prescription, I said, dangling the slip of paper in front of her. "That stuff dangerous," she said. "What stuff?" "Valium." Val-yum. I looked at her queerly. The handwriting was barely legible, even for a literate person. "How'd you know that?" A Jeep full of girls in Sacred Heart uniforms breezed past, giddy and paying no attention; they came within six inches of us, still on the neutral ground.

"Baby, you keep telling me I can't read. I don't know why you got to think that. Shoot, if I can't read, how come you not in jail? You think about it. I come in the house, and Mr. Rushing ain't there, and that don't mean anything, since he ain't never there, but you ain't there, neither, and that's different. Damn different. I see clothes all over you room, so I go in his room, his bed all messed up, I find this piece of paper, say 'Central Lockup' on it, it don't take no genius figure out who *that* about."

The carload of Sacred Heart girls passed again, this time with two more heads bobbing around, and they looked at us as they came by, as if I were a Sacred Heart girl, the one whose mama sent the housekeeper to walk her home every day, even when she was in high school, because surely a kidnapper was just waiting for an opportunity, and of course he would be completely deterred by a hundred-pound half-toothless woman. "What're you looking at?" I called after them, and the sniggles floated back in the exhaust of the car. "Chill, girl," Naomi said.

I began to walk away from Naomi, testing, and she kept right up with me, as if I expected her to. "I'm nearly thirty years old, I can find the drugstore," I said, speeding up a bit. Naomi was thinking she was getting a little arthritis in her hip, but she kept the pace fine, forgetting; arthritis, as far as I could tell, was more for talking about than it was for anything else; all it ever slowed down was a conversation. "He told me take you home, I'm taking you home, even if this a roundabout way," she said.

"You think he likes me?"

"The man a doctor."

"What's that supposed to mean?"

"Look what he done for you. Without me hardly even asking. Doctors supposed to like everybody."

"Hey, you've got it totally backward. Doctors *hate* everybody. That's their profession. They get paid to put needles in your skin, and they secretly hope you die so they can watch it happen. Everybody secretly wants to watch other people die. Maybe every now and then a doctor loves somebody, but doctors never like anybody."

"Look like you answer you own question."

"Yeh, he loves me," I said, laughing and double-stepping ahead of her as she swatted the air just inches from my backside.

I took a Valium as soon as we returned from the drugstore, and an hour later Maxim Walters rang the doorbell. He had a hat in his hand. He had a hat. Maybe he owned it, maybe he borrowed it: either way, he affected it for looking humble. It's funny how, in an instant, someone can be so transformed. Where once even a patch of him, even the thought of running my finger over a patch of him, could excite me, now what I saw was my childhood image of an old man. He could have been any of a number of safe doorbell-ringers who needed to come in out of the heat to say what they had to say because otherwise they might collapse; I didn't hesitate to ask him in. Naomi came up behind me, not trusting, saw him, recoiled as if he were the navy chaplain come to her door and she were a 1943 mother whose only son was in the Pacific. "Mr. Rushing's doing all right," Maxim said to her. She did her chameleon dance, flouncing and smiling at him, clearly knowing him, then stepping around gracefully so she could hiss into my ear, "For Jesus's sake, behave!" She shuffled out of the room with his hat as if now we'd moved up to 1953, then reappeared seconds later, hatless, to offer him a cup of coffee. Maxim said no, thank you, in the voice of a man who didn't want to give the impression of staying long, and I said I'd like a cup, bring him a cup, just in case, and Naomi backed out of the room, smiling with her bottom teeth showing.

It's possible to be gentle when a man loves you and you don't love him back. Of course, it's tempting to give in to meanness; since he's going to walk away feeling bad, he might as well be given the gift of anger, while you in turn get that unique pleasure only inflicting pain can give. I asked Maxim how I could help him, not protecting him from seeing his loss. For a second he looked perplexed, and then he gave a nothing-matters shrug. "I saw your grandfather's name on the hospital list. Went to the ICU. I'm terribly sorry."

"He's not going to die, you know."

"Still, this must be so difficult for you."

"No."

"I mean, this will be a long, hard process. It's a mighty responsibility."

I hadn't thought of that. I'd figured Poppy was going to lie in bed until he died, slowly getting back just enough of his faculties so he could accept my apologies, drifting away again, losing such small fragments of awareness each day that no one would notice; one morning he'd simply be gone, like a crushed pigeon on the sidewalk, nibbled at by ants and maggots until only the bones and feathers, lighter than air, blew away. "Are you here to make me feel bad?" I said.

He shook his head no, smiling sadly. "I thought I'd make you feel better."

I told him that it does not bring joy into another person's life, telling her she is about to spend months, years even, being responsible for a man who never earned the kind of love that makes drool and crying jags easy to live with. "In case you've forgotten, I was getting ready to leave town when all this trouble started. I mean for good, leave town for good. You can look upstairs, I'm half packed. Matter of fact, I was going through my things when I found the watch, I was *giving* you the watch, remember." At that he reached into his jacket pocket, presented the watch to me. "Isn't that supposed to be evidence or something?" I said, thinking about the trial date in July, another fetter to New Orleans. I'd realized at the time of the arraignment that I'd have to fly back in the sickening wet heat of midsummer, when all the city smelled like an overripe garbage heap, and even the air that leaked between the door of an airplane and the passageway to the gate was enough to take away my breath. I'd given it a second's thought, decided that when the time came I'd fly in, take an air-conditioned limousine to the Westin, take air-conditioned taxis to court, keep myself sealed up in a bubble for all but about thirty seconds of the time I was in New Orleans.

"You're all he has," Maxim said.

"But he's not all I have," I said, in case Naomi was listening. Maxim's face brightened. "Oh, no, that's not what I meant. It's over between us, Maxim. I thought you were a truth-teller, that was what knocked me out when I saw you the very first time. You were the only completely honest person I'd ever seen. With me, you'd have been spectacular, and I was willing to give you time, everything. You could have done anything, and I'd have understood. You know that?" He was staring at me, his eyes so wide, and I noticed for the first time that he had no thin dark line around the pale irises of his eyes; in a certain light he appeared to have two pinpoints of black pupils and no other color in his eyes. Set against a pale wall, he could have disappeared, leaving only two black dots, the way the albino girl in my class had done in the yearbook picture, a rectangle with two small spots peering out; the studio had been lit for children with some pigment. "You could've done anything. Except lie! And lie for such a reason. Tell the man the watch is yours, and he'll carry Eleanor off to prison. A four-thousand-dollar watch: that's a felony. And I can say I have the receipt, and I can look like I'd have a four-thousand-dollar watch ten times before anyone else in the room would have one, and they hear from a minister that it's his, and they believe him." I was standing over him now, enunciating loudly, and I knew Naomi could hear me, and I was sure she was paying attention, and I was glad for once. "I call my old grandfather, and he goes and has a stroke, only I don't know it, I think he's just ignoring me, and then I call you, and for all I know you already've heard that he's in the hospital, and what do you do? You say, 'Eleanor, I can't help you.'"

Naomi came in with two mugs of black coffee, a jar of Coffee-mate, and the kitchen sugar bowl, which was full of tiny brown clumps left by wet spoons. No silver service for Naomi; she slid my coffee in front of me like a bored saloonkeeper. Maxim sipped politely. I had no spoon and, rather than leave or call Naomi, I dumped Coffee-mate and sugar in, sloshed it around, realized the coffee wasn't hot enough to dissolve anything, stirred with my index finger; maybe Maxim would find the gesture erotic and feel worse. "Where are you planning to go?" he said, so circumspectly, as if we were drinking from bone china.

"Nowhere," I said, realizing it was true. "I *was* going to go to Nashville."

"Mmmm," he said, as if the coffee were hot and good.

"It wasn't for starting over or anything, just for getting away. Everyone there was so straightforward. You ought to consider it."

"How many people do you know there?" It wasn't an information-getting question.

"Well, one. Sometimes that's enough, you know." I was getting frazzled. "But I'm not going there, I told you that."

"I've been praying for you since yesterday morning."

"I'm afraid it didn't do much good," I said, thinking of Poppy. If he was wishing on candles for me, he wasn't getting me anything I wanted.

He chuckled, the way pious men do when nonbelievers and unbaptized children cut up a little in front of them. "Maybe this'll be good for you, give you something to concentrate on."

"Please go away," I said. He stood up to leave. "Hey, you can dish it out, but you can't take it," I said.

"Listen, I just came here to help you."

"A good man," I said. His lips were pressed closed tightly. "Do you ever do what you're not supposed to? Wait, that's backward. Well, not backward. Have you ever done something because you *felt* like it?"

"Yes," he said. I smiled triumphantly. "But not what *you're* thinking."

"I'm thinking you're lying."

"Eleanor, I have flaws. But not being human isn't one of them." I nodded. "Good," he said, and he patted my hand. I felt nothing; someone could have been tapping my hand with an inflated surgical glove, and I'd have felt the same. "I'm probably going to try to get the charges dropped," he said.

"Probably." Now the idea of him touching my hand made me squeamy, and I folded both hands into my armpits. "You lied to the police. What you did to try to upset me was also against the law."

"I don't want you bothering me anymore."

I waited a moment. "Don't worry, I hate you just fine," I said. I began laughing. "Just fine."

He left fast. Without the watch. I'll probably give the watch to Theo Farraday for Christmas. He's the sort who'll wear it on weekends with a polo shirt, no big deal. Christmas is almost eight months off. Theo and I are going to take things slowly.

ACKNOWLEDGMENTS

Confetti, balloons, kisses, and other serotonin-soaked expressions of gratitude to:

Jack Shoemaker, Trish Hoard, Julie Kuzneski, Becky Clark, Jessica Kane, Carole McCurdy, Beth Buhot, and Nicole Pagano for being a writer's dream-come-true;

Muriel Nellis, Elizabeth Pokempner, Jennifer Steinbach, and Jessica Tagliafero for unflagging faith and support;

Donice Alverson for her knowledge of Methodists, RaeLynn Waterhouse and Christine Murphey for their knowledge of computers, Madeleine Faust for her knowledge of Dekes, and Carl Walker for his knowledge of jail;

Margie, Lynda, Tommy, and the late Werner Friedmann for never turning out the black sheep;

Rick Blocker for saving us all;

Ed Muchmore for sharing the view; and

Esme and Werner for being, which they do quite well.